Dear Reader,

Here it is! I am so excited to be sharing with you the second novel from my studio. Jessie Weaver's debut is a timely, irreverent, thrilling read that features a murder mystery inspired by our culture's fixation with popular social media figures.

We've all heard of influencers like *Live Your Best Lie*'s Summer Cartwright, whose every post inspires her millions of followers to slurp down green smoothies, wake up each morning doing sun salutations, and perfect that bouncy ponytail. The world follows Summer's every move— because she lovingly documents each one! The reach and influence social media stars have are not to be underestimated. And if you doubt me, my fifteen-year-old daughter just made us order a hummus bowl inspired by a famous YouTuber from CAVA in Culver City for dinner because "they looked good on TikTok." (Dear Reader, they were not.) LOL!

But do we ever really know what's happening behind those perfect posts? Who *is* the girl behind the account? And what is she hiding underneath that filtered façade?

Turns out: Summer's Instagram was more than to die for. Someone's killed for it.

Reminiscent of *One of Us Is Lying* meets Agatha Christie, with a dash of *Gossip Girl* snark, this is one fun beach read teens will devour.

Go ahead. Use that face filter app. Pretend you're partying in Ibiza.

Live YOUR best lie!

xoxo

Melissa de la Cruz

MELISSA de la CRUZ STUDIO

Live Your Best Lie

JESSIE WEAVER

 MELISSA de la CRUZ STUDIO

HYPERION
Los Angeles   New York

All rights reserved. Published by MDLC Studio, an imprint of
Buena Vista Books, Inc. No part of this book may be reproduced or
transmitted in any form or by any means, electronic or mechanical,
including photocopying, recording, or by any information storage and
retrieval system, without written permission from the publisher.
For information address MDLC Studio, 77 West 66th Street,
New York, New York 10023.

First Edition, January 2023
10 9 8 7 6 5 4 3 2 1
FAC-004510-22343
Printed in the United States of America

This book is set in ITC Galliard Pro
Designed by Torborg Davern

Library of Congress Cataloging-in-Publication Data
Names: Weaver, Jessie, author.
Title: Live your best lie / by Jessie Weaver.
Description: First edition. • Los Angeles ; New York : Melissa de la
Cruz Studio/Hyperion, 2023. • Audience: Ages 14–18.
Audience: Grades 10–12.
Summary: "When four teens discover the dead body of influencer
Summer Cartwright, they must piece together the truth behind her
online persona to find out who killed her"—Provided by publisher.
Identifiers: LCCN 2022009419 • ISBN 9781368078368 (hardcover)
ISBN 9781368081122 (paperback) • ISBN 9781368081191 (ebook)
Subjects: CYAC: Social media—Fiction. • Secrets—Fiction.
Identity—Fiction. • Murder—Fiction. • Los Angeles (Calif.)—Fiction.
LCGFT: Thrillers (Fiction) • Novels.
Classification: LCC PZ7.1.W417748 Li 2023 • DDC [Fic]—dc23
LC record available at
https://lccn.loc.gov/2022009419
Reinforced binding

Visit www.HyperionTeens.com

To Ben, who believes in me so much,
I can't help but believe in myself

Live Your Best Lie

PART 1

#TooPrettyToDie

The_Summer_Cartwright

Update post from #SummerLand 🌞 ✨

.

K, first of all, I don't photoshop my lips or my butt, but thanks to so many of you for thinking I do. You're the sweetest everrrr!!! You should see my food baby after the burger I just scarfed. 🍔 Hah!

.

This Wednesday at 10 a.m. PT is the next #SCYogiAdventure. A dozen of my closest friends are coming to my loft to do yoga in my living room with @SierraDitmer of @HomeGYM, and you can, too, via my livestream!! After, we'll make green smoothies with protein powder from @PowerBoost. Link to recipe in bio. #ad #PowerBoost #selfcare

.

Prepare yourself for the most embarrassing moment of my life in this week's posts. It involves my green smoothie and Ryan Gosling's labradoodle. 🐩 Literally dying of shame. Oh, and there's a paparazzi photo to go with it. Cringe!! Also keep an eye out for my next #SummerAlwaysDatesTheWrongGuy reel in which I react to A and me breaking up dramatically in the courtyard at school. Ugh. Someone bring me Rocky Road and a giant spoon?

.

This week in #SummerLoves . . . * Soy lattes from the Beanery * Lying in the grass with daisies in my hair bc

#Cali * Sushi * Reading your DMs!!! * Posting no-makeup makeup secrets for youuuu * Dirty little secrets that I'll take to my grave . . . or will I? *

.

Speaking of graves . . . it's #spookyszn! 🪦 🧟 💀 Stay posted for stories from my Halloween party tonight for all things spooktacular. It's going to be scary fun.

.

You guys are the best. I wish I could give you all the biggest hug ever. ⁺✧squeeze⁺✧
Love,
SumSum 🖤

₪ 💔 ▶

⏻ POSTED 7 HOURS AGO

ONE

Grace Godwin

Saturday, October 31
5:17 p.m.

G race buzzes Summer's loft with one hand and tugs the hem of her dress with the other. If she'd taken a second to think before calling her Lyft, she would have brought her color-blocked watermelon costume to change into instead of wearing it. She's two hours early for Summer's Halloween party, because she promised she'd help set up.

Halloween is about little atmospheric touches, Summer said when she texted her on Thursday. *No one's better at detail stuff than you, Gracie Grace. You know you owe me. Pleaaassseee?* She followed it up with, *With a pineapple on top?* and a picture of her pouting in the pineapple dress she bought as her costume. Ever since Summer met that fruitarian on her trip to Bali in June, she's been almost religiously into fruit and swears she'd be a fruitarian, too, if the scientists of the world would get their act together and create a fruit replacement for cheese.

She also has a spiritual relationship with Gouda.

Summer's pouty face picture was overkill. Grace would have helped her set up without any begging, because she's always been the girl willing to stream streamers or blow up balloons or do calligraphy on envelopes. Feeling needed is a rush. Besides, after her fight with Summer a few days ago, she's been going above and beyond, even measuring on a scale of one to Grace. She's lucky Summer is even talking to her. Tonight has to go smoothly.

So she texted Summer back, saying, *No biggie, I can be there a few hours early,* even though it was kind of a biggie because she had to call out sick from her shift at the taco truck. Grace feels awful about lying to her boss, Sofia, but she's deemed this lie a necessary evil. Though she really, really hopes Sofia doesn't bring get-well tacos to her house. Her mom would murder her for ditching work.

Not to mention that Grace should be using tonight to work on her *A Separate Peace* essay for AP Lit. Her teacher told her it might stand a chance in a scholarship contest hosted by the College Board, and Grace needs all the scholarship money she can get. College isn't cheap.

Still, she and Summer have been friends since middle school. You make sacrifices for long-term relationships.

A gust of wind glues a long strand of Grace's brown hair to her lip gloss. Shivering, she unpeels it, then hugs her arms around her chest. Even in Los Angeles, the October air has enough bite that she wishes she could have worn the polka-dotted tights she picked out to go under her watermelon dress, but apparently, polka-dotted tights aren't sexy. And why be a whimsical fruit if you can be a sexy fruit?

While she waits for Summer to buzz her up to her fifth-floor penthouse loft, Grace glares at the jack-o'-lantern that leers at her from its pedestal on the stoop. *Stop being such a perv, Jack,* she thinks. *My eyes are up here,* then automatically feels bad for being rude. In her head.

To a pumpkin. She blames her dress, which hangs off one shoulder, for being way shorter than is comfortable. It's why she bought tights in the first place. She's pretty sure if she moves the wrong way, everyone will see her butt, or at least the hot-pink underwear that Summer slingshotted at her from across her bedroom yesterday when Grace mentioned her predicament.

"Match your panties and no one will notice," Summer told her.

"I think they might."

"Whatever." Summer rolled her eyes when Grace tried to protest. "If anyone posts photos of your ass online, I'll hunt them down and destroy them."

Grace wasn't sure if she meant the photos or the photographer. With Summer, it could go either way. Summer shimmied so the feathery headband atop her blond hair bobbed. "You like my pineapple top?"

"Gorg."

And it really was. Unsurprising, because Summer makes anything look fabulous. Her closet is packed with Prada and Gucci but also with vintage finds from the secondhand shop, because . . . the environment. One time she wore a boxy skirt from 1991 with the buttons undone halfway up her thigh, and suddenly on TikTok, girls modeled cute-again 90s items from thrift stores for the #Summer-CartwrightChallenge. Her closet fan account reposted her pics with comments like *OMFGGGG this is everything!* and *True beauty inside and out!!*

So if Summer has a fruitarian revelation and says Grace should be a watermelon, she'll be a freaking watermelon. Besides, she can't afford to piss Summer off again.

Just as Grace is beginning to think Summer isn't home—her memory is famously short, which sometimes makes Grace feel like a walking reminder app—Summer's voice echoes tinny through the call box.

"Gracie! You said you'd be here at five."

"Sorry! Traffic."

For a moment, Grace thinks Summer might not let her in, then the door buzzes. Relieved, Grace takes the elevator to the top floor. Summer meets her at the front door to her loft, barefoot and fastening her earrings. In her yellow-and-gold dress, her tanned legs seem longer, and her hair is pure sunshine. She looks much older than sixteen.

"The party is in less than two hours, and the decorations are . . . ugh."

Grace knows her job. When Summer fishes, Grace takes the bait. "I'm sure they look amazing."

"And I've posted so many reminders about this party on Instagram, and I'm going live right at seven, and I look like a banana. I can't look like a banana in front of five million people, one, because I'm supposed to be a pineapple, and two, aren't bananas slutty?"

The word *banana* sounds weird to Grace. If she hears a word too many times over, she either becomes certain that it isn't actually a word, or her brain overloads with fun facts about the word until she goes on a *Jeopardy!*-level rant. For example, bananas are scientifically considered berries, because their seeds are inside. Also, banana peels, when applied daily, can cure warts.

"Bananas aren't slutty, Sum, they're fruit," Grace says. "Anyway, does it matter?"

"You don't have five million people judging your every move. No one cares what you do."

Grace has less than a thousand followers on Instagram, most of whom followed her after Summer tagged her in pictures, and she's logged onto TikTok exactly one time to see what the fuss is about. So no, she doesn't really care what people online think, because no one online cares about her.

"Well, you look like a pineapple to me," she says. Because Summer has told her a thousand times she has to cut it with the fun facts, Grace doesn't tell her that pineapples can be used to tenderize meat.

When Summer motions for Grace to follow her from the foyer into the living room, Grace's jaw drops. The Cartwrights' luxury loft is always impressive with its cathedral ceilings and museum-quality art. But wow. These decorations are not "ugh," especially compared to the Halloween dances Grace went to in her middle school gym, which involved punch bowls shaped like skulls and orange streamers strewn over the basketball hoops.

In the living room, floor-to-ceiling black fabric drapes over the windows, and sheets cover the furniture. Someone's managed to hoist an actual *Phantom of the Opera*–style chandelier above everything. The DJ platform in the corner is the only reminder that it's the twenty-first century. The overall vibe is . . . Grace takes a moment to consider. Sumptuously undead?

It is incongruous with Summer's pineapple costume.

"Sum." Grace widens her eyes. "Your place looks—"

"Like a funeral parlor? I know."

"I was going to say like the Haunted Mansion at Disneyland."

"I guess? The decorator thought we should go more refined, but people are going to be too depressed to, like, dance or anything. And this might be my last party, so it has to be perfect."

Grace is confused. "What? Why do you say that?"

Summer shrugs. "You don't think the decor is too much?"

"No." Grace doesn't miss that Summer ignored her question, and she feels a moment of anxiety that she forces herself to swallow down. Panicking won't help her fix things with Summer. "You got black lights, right?"

"Yeah, and some colored ones."

"Perfect. Lighting will make the room." Grace perches on the edge of a sheet-draped sofa. "Your family coming tonight?"

Summer flops beside her. "Julian and Miranda are in Dubai until next Friday."

"Business trip?"

"For my dad, yeah. He's meeting with some sheikh about using his land for that new movie he's making next spring? *She Falls Hard* or something like that. Mom's going for the spas." She rolls her eyes at the word *spas*, but who knows with Summer's mom. She's probably sleeping in a salt cave for the duration of her trip.

"So you're alone?" Grace asks.

"No. Harrison is staying here while my parents are gone." Summer narrows her eyes. "He's coming to the party, too, if that's what you're asking."

Grace rolls her shoulders and takes a deep breath. She hasn't seen much of Summer's brother this month, what with everything she's had going on, but for the past year Summer has been trying to set her up with him. Grace wants to date him. She really does. Or maybe she wants to want to date him.

Harrison, a film studies major at UCLA, has no problem shoving a camera into Grace's face when she's doing things like eating cereal first thing in the morning or brushing her teeth, because he thinks unguarded moments are the most real. He and Summer argue about that a lot, actually—whether or not what she does is reality. Harrison says her page is too cultivated, too look-at-me-being-perfectly-flawed. Summer says she's putting her best foot forward. Grace refuses to be the tiebreaker, because she thinks both of them are dead wrong. Even though she hasn't always been able to keep her business offline, it hasn't stopped her from trying. With Harrison at the party, she doubts she'll be able to stay off camera.

Summer and Grace spend the next hour applying their makeup (black seed-shaped freckles on pink cheeks for Grace, and glittery gold eyelids and lips for Sum) and sipping smoothies, Summer's current obsession. Green for Summer, strawberry-banana for Grace. Then while Grace sets up the black lights and calls the DJ to make sure he isn't running late, Summer samples the food the caterer prepared.

"Oh my god, Gracie," Summer says. "The lobster crostini are to die for. Don't forget to try some before they're all gone. Laney's coming, and I know how much she eats."

Grace pins her cellphone between her shoulder and face to give Summer a thumbs-up. The DJ needs driving directions. She also tries to ignore Summer's comment about Laney, who probably eats a very normal amount.

Once the DJ arrives and starts the music, the loft buzzes with potential energy—the kinetic will come later once the guests arrive—but Grace's stomach burns like she chugged acid or, like, a gallon of coffee. Maybe she should have eaten something when Sum offered while they were doing their makeup. It probably wouldn't have helped, though, because it's butterflies that are making her feel sick. Adam is coming tonight. Grace hasn't seen him since he and Summer broke up at school last week, and she's not 100 percent certain she can keep it together around him all evening. Summer should have uninvited him. Secretly, though, Grace is glad she didn't. Even though she and Adam have been weird with each other for months, she still likes knowing he's there.

Five minutes before seven o'clock, Grace shuts off the main lights and turns on the black lights. Summer drops dry ice into the punch to make it smoke. They both slide their feet into impossible heels.

They take simultaneous deep breaths.

Then the doorbell rings, and the party begins.

The_Summer_Cartwright

#Bestie appreciation post!!! 👯

.

My best friend G is the actual best. For real, though, I know you guys think your best friend is better than she is, and I'm so happy for you. But you're sadly deluded, because no one is more loyal, more supportive, more awesome than G. She's the girl you call in a pinch, because she's always willing to do what needs to be done.

.

You know how I went live last week from the back of that ambulance because I had a cramp in my side and thought I was dying? Turns out, I kind of was. I had #appendicitis!! Literally, if I hadn't gotten to the hospital when I did, I could have died. 😱

#tooyoung #toopretty #jklswear

.

Anyway, I had promised you guys a tour of my renovated bedroom, and G made it happen. That voice you heard narrating when "I" went live? Obvs not mine. Haha! I just didn't want to let you down while I was slurping Jell-O in a hospital bed. Drop a comment below to tell me what you think of the new room!

#homedecor #renovating #interiordesign

.

So seriously, let's all take a minute for gratitude. Everyone say "Thank you, G!" I'll wait. Good job. Anyway, I'm back now, better than ever, ready to be with you, my other besties, on the Gram.

.

Love you muchly!! SumSum 🤍

₪ 🤍 ▶

TWO

Adam Mahmoud

Saturday, October 31
7:55 p.m.

Adam is late for the party, but he still pauses at the door to Summer's loft. Inside, the music thrums with a bass that resonates like a growl in his chest, and for a moment, he considers turning around and going home, watching reruns of *Family Matters* until he falls asleep. He hates showing up anywhere by himself. Summer told him once that arriving alone to a party makes a statement, and it was up to the person arriving to determine what that statement would be: *Here I am, confident as hell*, or *Here I am, a loser alone*. He wouldn't give Summer the satisfaction of scaring him away.

Besides, Halloween is the perfect time to be someone new. It's not every day that he can shred a white button-down so it shows the dark brown skin on his chest, and coat his eyelids with gold liner. There's something about dressing like a pirate that makes him feel reckless,

less worried about being the guy Summer expects him to be. He's not her boyfriend anymore.

Bouncing on the balls of his feet, he takes a breath and knocks, three hard raps. When Grace Godwin opens the door, the volume of the music doubles.

"Adam." She blinks twice, then looks down at her clipboard. "You came."

"Is that a bad thing?"

"No. Um . . . sorry. You were late, so I wasn't sure that . . ." Grace tucks a strand of hair behind her ear and makes a mark on her clipboard. "You're good to go in."

"I got caught up playing *Mythos*. My team had set up a raid . . . Anyway. Lost track of time."

Grace smiles. "Did you kill all the bad guys and save all the good guys and get all the loot?"

She's teasing him, but gently, which is one of the things Adam loves about her. He can nerd out about *Mythos* and other video games, and even though Grace isn't into them herself, she'll listen. Adam never told Summer about *Mythos* or his Twitch channel, because he knew she'd think it was stupid.

"Nah," he says. "Some noob blew up the bridge."

"Bummer."

"Whatever. I logged off after that."

Adam wants to tell Grace a million things, like the only reason he knocked instead of going home to finish the raid with his team was her. But he doesn't. Instead, he tries to make her laugh. "You the bouncer?"

She doesn't even smile. "Summer's worried about uninvited guests."

"Because everyone wants to hang out with Summer?"

"She's been getting DMs from private accounts ever since she announced her book deal. Mostly just people telling her that no one cares about her personal life, or threats to sue if she writes anything that makes them look bad. You know how it goes. Probably just other influencers who know she could trash them, and it would totally be true. But a few got creepy."

"How so?"

"One guy said he knows where she lives. He included pics of her bedroom, which freaked her out."

Adam is sure that whoever is DMing Summer got the pics off her own Instagram. If she doesn't want people knowing what her bedroom looks like, she shouldn't post about it to five million people. But he wants to agree with Grace, to get her on his side again, to talk like they used to a year ago when it was effortless. Tonight, he's so full of wants and fears that he might explode. He hasn't talked to Grace since breaking up with Summer last week, and for the first time in months, he feels hopeful that maybe the time could be right for the two of them.

So he only says, "Pics of her bedroom? She should probably tell someone about that. Police or whatever."

"What could they do? You can't get a restraining order on someone whose only name you know is TrollKing6969."

For a millisecond, Grace looks Adam in the eyes, and she's Gracie again. An instant later, she's not. Even though he's gone to school with her since sixth grade, tonight she looks new, her hazel eyes more luminous, the round apples of her cheeks more pronounced. What if she's outgrown him?

If someone were to ask Adam who Grace would be in the movie of his life, he'd say the girl next door. What he'd try to explain is how complex that cliché is—how it means knowing someone for years, wanting to be near them, taking them completely for granted until it's too late. But what if it isn't too late?

He leans in to give her a hug, but Grace sidesteps, gesturing for him to come fully into the foyer. She locks the door behind him. "Make sure you use the hall bathroom, because the front one is clogged. You're the last to arrive, so I'm going to check on Sum. See you around?"

And before Adam can stop her, Grace disappears into the living room.

He wanders after her, not sure what to do or who to talk to, his arms tingling with the sensation of absence. So she didn't hug him. It's not a big deal, is it? She's busy. Because he's so lost in his own head, he collides with Laney Miyamoto at the entrance to the living room.

"Ouch." She rubs her elbow. "Watch where you're going!"

Adam's head is too full of Grace to fully process how random it is that his chem lab partner got an invite to Summer's party. Laney isn't Summer's usual. Adam doesn't even know her that well, since she's new to Westwood Preparatory Academy this year, but what he does know about her he's not sure he likes. She's . . . prickly.

Tonight, she's pulled her shiny, dark hair into a high ponytail, and her oversize T-shirt, one of the ones that makes him wonder if she's wearing shorts underneath or not, is splattered with fake blood. Cardboard cutouts of different breakfast cereals—Lucky Charms, Cheerios, Cap'n Crunch—are pinned all over it. She's clutching an alarmingly huge knife. Adam hopes it's rubber.

"What are you supposed to be?" he asks.

Laney gapes at him like he's stupid. "A cereal killer?" The *obviously* is implied. Before Adam has time to let that sink in, she charges back into the living room where most of Summer's guests are hanging out. He follows her.

Adam is immediately overwhelmed by the crush of bodies, the smell of beer and sweat and perfume, the flashing lights and black lights that make his white shirt glow purple. As he follows Laney across the dance floor Summer created by pushing her living room furniture back against the wall, skin brushes his skin with every step. He starts to sweat. Above it all, Summer's set up a camera to livestream the party. Adam tracks the camera's gaze. If he sticks to the edges of the room, he won't be on display for Sum's followers like she'd want him to be. She loves drama, even in her own breakups, and would be more than happy to spin him as a party-crashing ex. No thanks.

Leaning close to Laney so she can hear him over the music, Adam shouts, "Where's Summer?"

"Why?" Laney tosses over her shoulder. "You guys getting back together?"

"Definitely not. I just figured I should say hello."

"She was talking to some blond guy by the food table a second ago. He was setting up a tripod to video."

Adam curses under his breath. Summer's brother, Harrison, is here. Harrison's a good guy, but he's the last person Adam wants to see tonight. Not only will he be filming everything, but he also has a thing for Grace, something about her "unspoiled essence." Adam hadn't thought Grace was into Harrison, but according to Summer, they've been texting more. Harrison took her out to coffee. To a concert. In front of Sum, Adam tried to keep his cool, but every one of his cells rebelled at the idea.

Adam can't hate Harrison, not when he's the guy who took him under his wing when Adam was a full-scholarship freshman with bad acne and worse sneakers. It was in Harrison's car sophomore year that Summer first talked to him. They joked about their geometry teacher's pleated khaki pants, Summer put her number in his phone, and minus a few weeks of will-they/won't-they uncertainty, that was that. Adam didn't have to choose to date her, he just did, and even though he'd always been decisive in every other area of his life—lacrosse, his Twitch channel—the ability to sit back and let Summer make the decisions was kind of nice. For a while, anyway.

Laney snaps her gum. "Find Summer if you need to, then come hang out with me. I don't know anyone here."

He nods to a guy on the sheet-draped sectional. "You know Oscar."

"Stepbrothers don't count."

"No one else from film society is here?"

"Does Summer strike you as the type to hang out with the film society? Seriously, come sit with me. I'm feeling weird as hell. This is the wrong venue for a punny costume. I should have just been a sexy gumball machine or something."

"Maybe in a bit, okay?"

"Fine." Laney waves dismissively, then threads her way through the crowd to join Oscar on the couch.

Adam is scanning the room for Summer's blond hair when he feels a tap on his shoulder. He turns to find her glittering beneath the lights—gold lips, gold eyelids, gold bangles. She is beautiful. Her lips quirk like she knows what he's thinking, like she's daring him to do something about it. Every moment with Summer is a dare.

"Hey." He's acutely aware of how sweaty he's gotten in the crowded loft. Why didn't he take two minutes to think out what to say to Summer? But he pauses long enough that she fills the gap.

"Hey, yourself. I was worried you weren't going to come." She leans in conspiratorially. "You know, because of everything."

"Well, just because we aren't—"

"Exactly. We can still be friends, can't we?" There is a challenge in her voice, and her eyes are flinty. "Even after everything?"

Adam can feel people watching them. He swallows hard, hating that he's still attracted to her. That's the weird thing about love. It gets so mixed up with lust that he can simultaneously hate Summer and want to kiss her, and her ability to make him want her melts his hate so it's lava instead of rock. Hotter. More volatile.

"Not feeling guilty, are you, Adam?" Summer asks, sending a surge of adrenaline through his core.

"You mean about—"

"Make me a plate of food, will you? Grab me some of the lobster crostini." Summer catches one finger in the collar of his shredded shirt, then smiles again. "Nice costume."

Adam can't tell if she means it or not, but it's easier to take Summer at face value. And it's easier to get her food than to argue that she should get her own. Because yes, he does feel guilty about so many things.

A few moments later, when Adam looks up from scooping salsa onto a plate, he sees Grace watching him from across the room. She looks away, but not before Adam feels the punch to his gut.

The_Summer_Cartwright

Allow me to introduce the man of the hour! 🔥🔥🔥

.

Meet A, my hot ass boyfriend with curls for dayssssssss and a pair of brown eyes that could launch ships. Don't be jealous, sweet followers. Or do, your call. But no touchy. That's just for me.

.

A has been friends with my bestie G forever, and in a classic #FriendstoLovers move, I convinced my brother to give him a ride home a few weeks ago. Snuck my number in his phone and called myself. And that's how it's done. No more waiting around for the guy to make the first move. #feminism 💪 👩

.

Why A, you ask? Clearly you haven't seen him all sweaty on the lacrosse field. But it's more than that with us. We have this super intense connection that you can't fabricate, and here's the biggest thing. He's seriously the sweetest guy ever. So respectful. Almost too respectful, if you know what I'm saying! LOL! #KissMeAlreadyDammit

.

Anyway, cheers to new love and old friends.

.

Mwah!!
SumSum 🖤

₪ 🖤 ▶

⊙ NOVEMBER 15, LAST YEAR

THREE

Elaine Miyamoto

Saturday, October 31
8:30 p.m.

L aney rolls her eyes when Adam brings Summer a plate of food.
Even though he isn't dating her anymore, he hasn't escaped her
orbit. But that's Summer. It's like she's got more social mass than
anyone else. Even if you don't want to hang out with her, even if she
scares you a little, if she wants you to go somewhere you don't want
to go, you go anyway, helpless against her gravitational pull. And nine
times out of ten, the stuff you do for Summer is filmed for posterity.
That pisses Laney off.

She winces when she sips her punch. It's spiked with something
that has a sharp bite.

Not for the first time, Laney wishes she didn't have to be here.
She's not antisocial—though sometimes she thinks if she were the last
human alive, she'd be cool with that—but she's way more comfortable
at kickbacks around a fire pit with friends from her old school. God,

she never thought she'd be that girl thinking nostalgically about her "old school." It wasn't perfect, far from it. The lack of AP classes was appalling, the cafeteria food was worse, and after freshman year when Melanie Ito transferred, Laney was the only Japanese American student. But even though her old school had its issues, they were familiar issues.

Setting her cup and plastic butcher knife on a side table, Laney plops on the couch beside Oscar, who's humming to himself and massaging his knees just above the braces. Because he has spina bifida and uses ankle/foot orthoses to walk, his legs get sore if he stands for too long.

"What are you humming?" Laney asks.

Oscar pushes his floppy brown hair away from his face and warbles to the tune of "Yankee Doodle": "Oscar is awesome, so awesome and amazing!"

"Oh my god." Laney glances around the room to see if anyone is listening. She already regrets asking. "Can you not?"

"Join me on the chorus!"

He sings the Oscar song in the bathroom at home while he does his hair, which mysteriously involves a blow dryer and mousse and ends up looking like he did nothing. The worst part is that his songs are freaking earworms, and some mornings, she'll find herself singing about him while she toasts her waffles. He loves it way too much. Deep down, though, Laney wonders if Oscar needs to fill the air so the room doesn't feel so empty and quiet. As much as she hates to admit it, she'd get that.

But singing the Oscar song in public is new. He must be nervous for once, and Laney doesn't blame him. Not tonight. The people in this room are famous on social media, hot in a tall-blond-tan way like Summer, and/or hot in an I-don't-even-try way like Adam. And the crowd . . . it's overwhelming. If Oscar didn't have a massive, unrequited crush on Summer, whom he's talked to a total of three times ever, they'd be home avoiding this whole evening, watching crap TV in their pajamas. It's a new Saturday night tradition they've created in the two months since Laney and her dad moved in with Oscar and his mom, Rebekah Stern.

Her dad proposed to Rebekah while Laney was in England attending Cambridge University's month-long international summer school. She took film classes and fencing at ISSOS. Meanwhile, her dad picked out a ring and got down on one knee. When Laney got home, she had a new stepmom, and not the stereotypical wicked kind who favored her own kid and made life hell. Rebekah tried so hard. She did things like hiring a carpenter to soundproof Laney's new room so she could work on her YouTube stuff, and creating a shared spreadsheet with Laney and Oscar to rate all the movies they watched based on ten distinct categories.

Laney wanted to hate Rebekah, but she couldn't. That was worse.

ISSOS is how Oscar convinced Laney to come to the party tonight. She'd been in her room working on a new YouTube video she was doing on ways to create horror sound effects. Foley artists were the unsung heroes of the movie industry, and Laney was determined to get her name out there now while she was still young. She already had five thousand subscribers.

"You and Summer spent a month rooming together. Wouldn't it look weird if you didn't show up to her party?" Oscar asked when he barged into her room without knocking and saw she still hadn't changed out of her polar-bear-print pajamas. He gestured to the line of Mason jars on her desk. "What's the deal with all these?"

Laney blew over the top of one to create the sound of tunneling wind.

"Cool, cool, cool," Oscar said. "But tonight is my chance to meet interesting people, maybe even talk to Summer, and I can't go without you. Besides, didn't you want to talk to Summer about something? Costume on." He yanked her headphones from around her neck, hid them on top of her wardrobe where she couldn't reach them, and ordered their Lyft to the party.

Now, with her ears ringing from the music and her head pounding from dehydration because Summer is parked with Adam beside the drink cooler, Laney shifts to find a comfortable spot on the stiff couch. She hates the way her stomach drops at the thought of being in a room with Summer, the way she still goes out of her way to avoid any unnecessary interactions. She's got to get over it.

"This party blows," she says.

"It could be worse." Oscar grins. "That girl over there gave me her number."

"What, did you hand her a petition against global warming and ask for her contact info?"

"Ha-ha."

"I thought you love Summer."

"I also love zebras. Doesn't mean I'll get one of my very own. Malia, on the other hand . . ." He shows Laney a napkin with a ten-digit number doodled inside a heart.

The girl he points at waves and smiles, the bell sleeves of her Renaissance dress flapping under her arms. Only Oscar could get a girl's number fifteen minutes into a party that he wasn't even invited to. His incessant good cheer gets under her skin, which, according to her dad, says more about her than about Oscar. But come on. He's already talking about putting up a Christmas tree tomorrow—November 1!—and he's Jewish. Rebekah and her dad compromised and decided they'd celebrate Chrismukkah this year. It makes no sense, but she's afraid if she complains, she won't get presents, and she really needs a new laptop.

"You're perfect for each other," Laney says when Oscar waves back at the girl. "How nice for you."

"You could cut your bitter with a knife, Elaine."

Laney picks up her plastic knife off the side table. "I could cut you instead."

"So violent. Too many horror movies lately?"

"I'm not violent. I'm just finished with this party."

"Socialization is important to the teenage experience."

Shouldn't Laney be able to determine her own teenage experience? Maybe she wants to experience sleep and snacks instead of parties. What's so wrong with that? "Are you sixteen or ninety?"

"Irrelevant."

"So what's your point?"

"You know we can't leave yet. Besides, I look awesome."

With his chest puffed out, Oscar gestures to his Robin Hood costume, the same one he wore to Comic Con, bow and arrows and all. His hair is covered by a hood, and his vest is either leather or a good imitation. Laney hopes no cows were harmed in the transformation of Oscar into Robin. She's a vegan.

Her dad likes to point out the irony of her being a vegan with aggression issues, but Laney doesn't think it's ironic. Maybe if people weren't assholes, she'd feel protective of them, too.

Laney is about to say something about how Oscar's hood is what makes him look awesome—it blocks his face—when Summer climbs onto the DJ platform and grabs the mic. When she steps into the light, her skin looks Photoshopped, it's so perfect. Funny how someone can be so beautiful but so ugly inside. Then again, Satan was a fallen angel. Grace Godwin is there, too, right beside Summer, ready to jump if she needs anything.

"Thank you so much for coming," Summer says, her voice saccharine if a little breathless. Everyone cheers. She presses a hand to her belly, and her smile strains. "You all look fabulous. And shout-out to my fellow influencers here tonight. Together we can change the world! Also, hey to all my besties watching the livestream! Love you! In my darkest hours, you were always there for me, even when my real-life friends weren't." Her gaze sweeps the room. Does it land on someone in particular? "I'm the luckiest girl ever. Keep an eye out for an appreciation giveaway soon on my account!"

She blows a kiss toward the camera mounted in the corner of the room, then hops off the platform as the DJ plays "Bohemian Rhapsody." Everyone in the room laughs and starts to sing about the poor boy, but Laney jumps up from the couch to follow Summer. She catches her between the kitchen and the food table. It's now or never.

"Wait." Laney grabs Summer's arm. "We need to talk about the letter."

Summer looks around to make sure no one is watching. "Are you for real right now?"

"If you just give it to me, I'll—"

"Why would I?"

"Because it's the right thing to do."

"We're way past worrying about the right thing, Laney, don't you think?" Summer smiles before disappearing in the crush of music and shouting and bodies and lights. Laney's heart skips a beat, then palpitates in her chest, stealing her air. It's too much like that night this past July at Cambridge. Like the party she and Summer snuck off campus to attend, that moment when Laney, fueled by party endorphins and warm beer, made the deal with Summer she's regretted ever since.

When Laney gets back to the couch, her seat beside Oscar has been taken by the girl who gave him her number. Laney jabs Oscar in the shoulder.

"Ouch! Back so soon, Elaine?"

"Move over."

She shoves herself beside him so that he and Renaissance girl are basically on top of each other. He should thank her. Four entire songs play while the two of them blabber on about items people juggle at Ren Faires—knives, balls, fire, axes—and Laney slowly dies inside. She's about to pry Oscar off the couch with a crowbar, when someone on the dance floor shrieks.

Laney scans the crowd. Cora Pruitt, her eyes so wide they could be silver dollars, holds out her phone to a tall Black girl with box braids so she can read the post on her screen. The light of Cora's cellphone on her face reflects off the obscene amount of glitter she's used on her cheeks and pale hair to make herself into Glinda the Good Witch. Her frothy dress screams money, but Laney, like everyone else at WW Prep, knows that Cora is just the knockoff version of Summer.

The music cuts off, and a mic squeaks. "Everyone okay out there?" the DJ asks.

The girl with Cora waves at the DJ. "Fine. My friend here is just a drama queen."

The DJ restarts the music, but Cora says something to the people around her that makes them take out their phones. Texting so fast that she's got to have thumb cramps, Cora darts past Laney and Oscar toward the back hallway, where the working bathroom is.

Oscar turns around on the couch. "Cora, wait! What's going on?"

She backtracks a few steps. "Have you seen Summer?" Her voice squeaks.

"Sure, like fifteen minutes ago when she welcomed everyone. Why?"

"OMG, you didn't see it?"

"See what?" Laney asks, hating herself for engaging the drama.

"There's a new post on Summer's account."

"And it's worth screaming about?" Oscar grabs Cora's outstretched phone, using the opportunity to put an arm around Renaissance girl.

"It's . . . kind of creepy?"

"So? It's Halloween." Laney opens Instagram and goes to Summer's page. Above the newsy post she saw earlier, the one she double-tapped to like only because there's not a button on Instagram for I-know-you're-fake-you-reviled-worm-of-a-human, there's a new pic. Sort of. It's the same selfie of Summer from earlier, but this one, timestamped 8:57 pm, has a red X drawn over her face.

At the bottom of the post, it says:

> Okay, but for real. You know you love me. Everyone does. Except maybe they don't, because in five minutes, I'll be dead. #byebyesummer

Laney rolls her eyes. "Nothing says pay attention to me like faking death threats."

"She's probably setting us up for a joke or something," Oscar says. Renaissance girl giggles like Oscar made the joke, then stops when Laney glares at her. If she could ban one thing, like one thing in the whole world, it would be giggling. Maybe the fur coat industry, but probably giggling. This whole thing is annoying, more so because now it'll be impossible to drag Oscar from the party.

"Yeah, maybe you're right," Cora says. "Except . . . where is Summer?"

The_Summer_Cartwright

Sometimes it's hard to reach out to someone new.

.

As you all know from my stories, I'm currently at #ISSOS in jolly old #England for the next few weeks! 👑 I've been keeping a close eye out for William since I already met Harry in LA last year. Every girl needs a matching set of prince photos.

.

Anywayyyy, I've got a roomie here at #Cambridge, and she's so sweet, but . . . she's a hard nut to crack 🫣. I've invited her to so many things, and she always says no, she's too busy, even though I'm a million percent sure she's not busy at all. She's, like, really into sound effects, so maybe I should show her the epic cricket noise I used to do in Frau Sabine's German class?? Idk! Lol!

.

So what do I do? My mom always says: "Summer, you can't force friendship, but you can be a relentless force for good in someone's life. They'll either appreciate you for who you are, or they won't. But never stop trying." So should I be #relentless? Should I give my roomie her space? Drop your advice in the comments!! 🔽

.

Oh, important to note—roomie's actually moving to LA in a few weeks! Her future stepmom knows my mom, and they arranged for us to room together, so added pressure! Ugh, I wish #friendship was easy.

.

Squishy hugs for everyone!!

SumSum

₪ 💜 ▶

FOUR

Grace Godwin

Saturday, October 31
9:02 p.m.

Grace wobbles in her heels, and her friend Blossom Vasquez catches her arm to steady her. Someone—not her, obviously—dumped vodka in the punch, and even though she tasted it in her first glass, she poured herself another a few minutes ago. Almost everyone has been on their phones all evening, taking pics to post with the tag **#SumSumDoesHalloween**, and watching Summer's livestream. Her new post is hard to miss, and with Summer currently MIA, people will start to wonder what it's about.

"You should sit." Blossom nods toward the already-crowded couch where Laney, Oscar, and Cora lean together to look at Cora's phone.

"I'm fine."

"Sure you are."

"Seriously."

"Obviously."

"Really."

"Too many adverbs for me to believe you, girl."

Grace met Blossom in AP Language and Comp last year, and they ended up in the same AP Lit class this year. With her middle-parted dark hair hanging in her face, Blossom is the spitting image of the girl from that old movie *The Ring*, the one who crawls out of TVs to eat your face. But Blossom still has in her nose ring and eyebrow stud, and even though it doesn't go with her costume, her eyes are lined in purple. She's not Summer's type at all, but Grace finagled her an invite because she's an incredible photographer. Summer knows the value of free pics. Usually she'd be glued in front of the cameras, so where is she?

"What is Summer trying to do?" Grace asks.

"Who the hell knows?" Blossom says. "It's Summer. She'd shave her head live if she thought it would go viral."

"It probably would."

"Valid. Maybe next week she'll do that and donate it to a children's cancer ward. Hashtag helping babies."

"Babies are usually bald."

"You're missing the point, Grace."

Grace is about to ask Blossom to read Summer's post aloud so they can overanalyze it, like on a line level, but she's interrupted by the arrival of Harrison Cartwright.

"Babygirl!" Harrison pulls Grace to his chest to give her one of his too-long hugs. His camera digs into her ribs, making her squirm.

"Where's your costume?" Blossom brushes her hair out of her face and smiles. She doesn't understand why Grace isn't super into Harrison. Like, is hot, older, and rich not enough? Grace can't explain what exactly holds her back, especially when Harrison likes her so much. Or maybe she could explain it, but no need to get the rumor mill churning.

"Not a fan of masking my true self, you know?" Harrison's blond hair is cropped short on the sides and combed over on the top. He hasn't bothered putting on shoes. Grace wants to like him, because it would make Summer happy, but he's just so . . . *Harrison*. His conversations usually start with something like, "This one time, when I was hiking Kilimanjaro . . ." and end with something pseudo-deep about life or the universe. "Did you see Sum's post?"

"Of course we did," Blossom says.

Harrison pops a spinach puff in his mouth. "Wild, right? Even I have to admit this might be her best idea yet."

"What idea?" Grace shouts over the music. Two months ago, Summer would have brainstormed the entire party with her, so just the fact that Harrison knows about plans for tonight that Grace hasn't heard about is concerning. She has to repeat herself twice before Harrison hears her.

"A murder mystery party, you know? What better opportunity to document visceral humanity? Look at everyone's faces! Half these people hate Sum. The other half love her and the drama equally." Harrison shoulders his camera, then kisses Grace on the cheek before he heads off to film. His face is scratchy with stubble.

Grace and Blossom exchange a look. A murder mystery? Harrison should know Summer would never miss a moment of her own party, especially when she is livestreaming. Grace tries to stay calm, but her palms are sweaty. The post was added at 8:53. It's 9:08 now. If Summer doesn't show up soon, people will start talking.

"Relax." Blossom sits on the drink cooler and crosses one Doc Marten over the other. "I'm sure everything is going according to plan."

"Whose plan?" Grace's laughter has an edge, but she takes a deep breath and straightens her shoulders. "You're right. I'm sure Summer knows what she's doing."

"Let people talk. You find Summer and figure out what the deal is. Maybe let people know the game has started? On a scale of one to AP exams, this is nothing."

But something is wrong, Grace is sure of it. She wobbles again. Whoever spiked the punch didn't hold back.

Before she can talk herself out of covering for Summer, Grace taps the DJ on the shoulder. He ignores her and starts playing a new song. She taps his shoulder again.

"Yeah?" He pulls his headphones down around his neck.

"I . . . Sorry, but I just need to . . . make an announcement?"

"What sort?" He looks suspicious. If Grace had to guess, she'd say this happens a lot and ends with some guy declaring his love for a girl named Skylar or a drunken tirade about how life isn't fair.

"Summer needs me to?"

The DJ rolls his eyes. "Go for it." When he fades the music out and hands Grace the mic, she takes a deep breath and counts to five before letting it go.

"Hey!" She jumps when she hears her own amplified voice. The lights blind her until all she can see are bodies, bodies, bodies in the dark room, all waiting for her. "Um. Hey, everyone. So I'm guessing you've all seen the post on Summer's Instagram." Grace clears her throat. "She has a surprise for you tonight. Um. It's . . ." She falters.

"It's a murder mystery party!" Harrison shouts from somewhere in the crowd. A few people cheer, then everyone starts talking at once. Everyone loves a good whodunit.

Grace looks across the anonymous crowd until her eyes land on someone standing right in front of the platform. Adam. His gaze is inscrutable. Before he started dating Summer, Grace was able to tell every thought that went through his head, but a year can change a lot.

"Summer doesn't do anything halfway," Grace says. "So, I guess . . . let the game begin."

The_Summer_Cartwright
#FOMO vs. #JOMO

.

Today I cancelled plans with people for something important, and they decided to keep the plans without me. Old Summer, less actualized Summer, would have had major FOMO and tried to do all the things even though there's no way one person can do EVERYTHING.

.

Example: A few months ago, I committed to judging a young talent fashion competition on a Saturday afternoon, and the night before, G (bestie) called me and was all like, Let's go to the beach tomorrow evening to watch the sunset and talk! And I said yes, of course. Because I'm a good friend. Then A (boyfraaaaaand) texted and was all, Let's do brunch. I miss you a million! And I said yes, of course, because #AlltheHeartEyes, and I want to be a good girlfriend.

.

What happened you ask? #Exhaustion 😵 and what I like to call #fractioning—everyone got a little of me, but no one got the best!! So I decided that day to cultivate JOMO or the Joy of Missing Out. New Summer still felt a pang knowing that my crew was hanging out in Griffith Park today when I couldn't be there, but just a little one. The fact is, I know it wasn't the same without me, so why worry about missing out? Besides, how cool that they all got to know each other! 😇😇😇

.

Yours philosophically,
SumSum 🖤

₪ ❤ ▶

───────────────────────────────

🕐 OCTOBER 16, TWO WEEKS AGO

FIVE

Cora Pruitt

Saturday, October 31
9:11 p.m.

Cora feels like her ears might pop from curiosity. Even the DJ playing "Rain on Me" doesn't distract her, and it's her favorite song. Smoothing her frothy Glinda dress beneath her, she snatches her phone back from Oscar and Laney and sits on the arm of the couch beside a girl she's never met who's dressed as Queen Elizabeth I. Cora doesn't know Oscar or Laney, not really. They do not need to be going through her phone.

Queen Elizabeth hoists herself from the low couch. "I'm going to go check in with my friends. You want to come, Oscar? Maybe we could solve the mystery together?"

"I will be right with you. Promise." He smiles and waves her off, then pulls out his own phone to scroll through Instagram. "It's only been fifteen minutes since Summer's post, and her hashtag is already trending top ten. Smart girl."

"We're never leaving this party, are we?" Laney flops her head on the back of the couch. "I live here now."

Murder mystery party? It's genius. Cora wishes she'd thought of it first. Not that even half of these people would have come to a party at her place. Though she doesn't want to have a party at her house anyway, because her parents would both be there, just, like, watching from the corner and setting out plates of lame things like those little sweet pickles and carrots with hummus.

Part of Cora isn't sure Summer would set up a party that required her to disappear for most of it. Not that Summer told her anything about it. Of course Summer would confide in Grace, though Cora cannot for the life of her figure out why Summer and Grace are even friends. They have nothing in common, not like Summer and Cora do. And like Cora, Summer is not the type to ditch out on parties. She's not. Cora's been to a lot of the same parties that Summer has—people at school, mutual friends of their parents—and Summer likes to be at the very center of things. She's the girl who shows off her jewelry and laughs loudly and widens her eyes to show how closely she's listening. Granted, this is the first of Summer's parties that Cora has been invited to, but still. Why should that change anything?

Ignoring Laney's sour face the best she can, Cora goes to the Summer Cartwright fan page she follows on Instagram and finds a post about the murder mystery party already there with over two hundred likes and thirty comments, even though it's, like, five minutes old.

SummerCFandom16 OMGGGGGG murder mystery party!!!
💀 🔎 It's a dark and stormy night here in Summer's loft, and she's gone missing! Who do you think the *killer* might be?

Rumor has it that the winner of the game gets an amazing
prize, so don't be shy! **#murder #LikeClueButBetter**

See all 31 responses

Fashionista2004 Ummm . . . I vote plot twist! Summer
is actually the killer!

Sunshine.and.lemonade Is she dating anyone? It's
always the SO, right?

Kylalalala Is it too much to ask that she's actually dead?
🙁

Marley_Mae Helloooooo, isn't Avalon James at that
party? If Summer's fake dead, Avalon's somewhere
holding the fake bloody knife.

Sunshine.and.lemonade @Kylalalala ummmm why the
hate? If you don't like Summer, unfollow. It's that easy.

Kylalalala @Sunshine.and.lemonade 💀 💀 💀 god take
a joke

If Cora were to solve the mystery first, Summer would have to
acknowledge her on her account, right? Any mention is a good mention. Still . . .

"What if something is actually wrong with Summer?" she asked.

Oscar has his own phone out now. "Then according to the folks of
the internet, Avalon James is the killer."

"Avalon is so nice! And like, really talented. People don't know what they're talking about." Cora can hear her own voice getting higher pitched than it already is. When she was in elementary school, people used to tease her about always sounding like she sucked helium from a balloon. Now that she's a sophomore, people think it's put on, but it isn't. It's just what her voice sounds like.

"Summer isn't dead." Laney rolls her eyes. "And people are only saying Avalon because Summer screwed her over. Like a fake death would even the score. Do you think Summer will come back as a zombie before the clock tolls midnight?"

"I'd caution you to be less flippant, Elaine. You're the one actually holding the fake, bloody knife."

"Hilarious." Laney stands. "If I say I'm the murderer, can we leave?"

"Absolutely."

"Then call me Laney the Ripper." She grabs her butcher knife, curtsies by holding out the edges of her baggy T-shirt, and pushes through the crowd.

"Sorry about her," Oscar says. "She's pointy tonight."

"Do you think Summer is okay? Should we—"

"It's a game," Oscar says. "Relax."

That word is like a needle straight into Cora's brain. She hates it when people tell her to relax. How do they know she isn't relaxed? But she can't say anything, because people already don't like her. People think she's dramatic, that her Summer Cartwright closet account on Instagram is dumb. But the joke's on them. She makes a decent amount of money through commissioned links, enough to keep her in the season's latest looks, which isn't cheap. The clothes her mom picks out for her make her look like an old lady on her way to a fundraiser tea, so she has to change after leaving home. She doesn't know a single other person over the age of ten whose mom picks out their clothes.

The platform lights catch on the glitter beside her eyes, making them water. She rubs them.

"You just smeared your mascara below your eyes," Oscar says. "Right one, outside corner."

"Oh my god, this is the most stressful night of my life!"

Oscar laughs. "You've had an easy life, huh?"

"Yes, I have," Cora snaps. "That's not something to be ashamed of."

"I never said it was."

But Cora can tell from the tone of Oscar's voice that he'd respect her a little more if she'd suffered or had a hideous childhood. Why were people like that? It's not her fault that she had a nice childhood, that her family has plenty of money. Being well-off isn't a sin. Besides, she knows for a fact that Oscar lives in Malibu so it's not like he's struggling either.

"I'm going to go look for Summer," Cora says.

Oscar returns his focus to his phone and waves absently.

If she were Summer, where would she go? Cora chews her lip, then licks her teeth to make sure no lipstick got on them. Maybe she should check the bedrooms? That made sense. If she were going to hide, that's where she'd go.

When she reaches the back hallway, she stops short. Adam and Grace are just outside the kitchen, and his hand is on her waist. Grace steps away from Adam and swallows hard. She clutches her shoes— Louboutins she must have borrowed from Summer—in her hand. Adam runs a hand through his curls to get them out of his face. Both look guilty, like Cora caught them making out. *Oh my god*, Cora thinks. *That would be a plot twist.* Adam and Summer broke up last week, everyone knows that, but if Adam hooked up with someone else at Summer's party . . .

Cora blinks. It's probably nothing. Adam and Grace have been friends for literally years, like since middle school. Summer posted about it a few months ago.

"What are you doing back here?" Grace asks. "The bathroom is—"

"I'm looking for Summer. Or . . . clues, I guess? I was going to check Summer's room."

"Oh. Okay, yeah. I could"—Grace exchanges a glance with Adam—"look back there with you?"

"I'll come, too," Adam says.

Cora wants to say no, because she doesn't want to share the credit for winning the game with anyone else, but maybe Grace and Adam know more about where Summer would hide clues than she does. They could give her an advantage. She follows them farther down the hall.

The hallway is stark white with a single abstract painting in a silver frame, way more chic than Cora's place, where her mom has glutted the hallways with family portraits in which Cora and her sister, Amanda, wear matching Christmas dresses or white polos with jeans.

Summer's room blows Cora away even though she's already seen it. On the bed, metallic throw pillows accent a fuzzy white comforter. She takes in the framed vintage art prints from the 60s, the fiddle leaf fig in the copper pot in the corner, the wicker chandelier. Cute, cute, cute. The Instagram live tour and pictures did not do the new room justice. Cora hangs back from Grace and Adam to snap a few pics for her closet account. She doubts her followers will mind a small departure from wardrobe to decor, especially if she can find the affiliate links.

"Summer? You in here?" Grace wanders to the french doors that lead to Summer's balcony, then jumps backward. "Oh my god, Laney, you scared me. What are you doing?"

In the small alcove where Summer's tucked her dresser, Laney slams a drawer shut, then straightens. "Same thing you're doing.

Looking for 'clues.'" She uses air quotes for the word *clues*. "Any idea what we're supposed to be finding? Don't these things usually have character cards or a starting point? A riddle?"

"It's Summer. Who knows?" Adam says. "But once again, everyone is talking about her, so wherever she is, I'm sure she's thrilled."

Before Cora can protest—she really wants to find Summer, both to win the game and to make sure she's okay—she feels someone standing behind her. Summer? She turns and smiles, hoping to make a good impression. She's done her best to be *on* all night, no mistakes. No awkwardness.

But it's Harrison.

"What're you guys doing in Sum's room?" He eyes Adam suspiciously. "The only reason guests should be in this hallway is for the bathroom, and I already don't love that."

"Yeah. Sorry." Grace puts a hand on Adam's arm when it looks like he's about to say something. "But we can't find Summer."

"That's the fun of the mystery." Harrison flops on Summer's bed, knocking one of her throw pillows to the floor. "She's around here somewhere."

Cora can tell her chance to look at more of Summer's stuff is quickly fleeting, so before Harrison can kick them all back into the living room, she asks, "Should we check her bathroom? Just to make sure she's all right?"

"Would that make you feel better, Grace?" Adam asks.

"This isn't about me."

"But perhaps there's a clue," Laney says drily.

"Fine." Harrison bounces himself off the bed again and hops toward Summer's bathroom door. He opens it with a flourish. "After you."

Cora wanders after the others, her phone camera still open to document, when she notices the stillness in the bathroom, like the air has been sucked out, leaving a vacuum behind. She smells the sharp odor of vomit.

And then Cora sees what the others are looking at. Her phone clatters to the tile, shattering the screen.

Summer is collapsed by the toilet like an abandoned marionette, her legs splayed to the side. Vomit leaks from the corner of her mouth, as if she fell just after rushing to the toilet to puke. One gold stiletto has fallen from her foot. Her mascara is smeared and she's eerily still. Cora barely resists the urge to shake her.

Grace is the first to speak. "Summer?"

Her voice breaks the spell, and she rushes to push long strands of corn silk hair from Summer's face, like that'll do anything. Adam picks up Summer's hand, which seems romantic at first, but he's taking her pulse. One second. Two.

"Can you hear me, Sum?" Harrison's voice is tense with fear.

"I don't feel anything." Adam swallows hard like he's about to throw up, too.

"Call nine-one-one," Harrison says. "Hurry."

Vaguely, Cora is aware of Adam dialing, of Grace sobbing, of Laney choking out a laugh that's sharp and out of place and wrong. Of Harrison smoothing and ruffling, smoothing and ruffling his hair.

But Cora can't stop staring at Summer's face. Against the backdrop of her gold lips and eyelids, #TOXIC is written over and over again in red lipstick. On her forehead. On her cheeks. On her throat. #TOXIC #TOXIC #TOXIC

Again and again and again and again.

Cora can't breathe. She can't think. Because through her brain fog, she is certain of one thing.

Summer Cartwright is dead.

The_Summer_Cartwright

#repost 😊

I basically NEVER do this, but OMG loving these pics @SumSums_Closet posted this week! I think the one of me at the @DaniellaMazanaroDesigns show is my fave pic of me everrrr aside from the one the paparazzi scored when I had dinner that time with Hailee Steinfeld. Also, you guys should def take advantage of that deal on the necklace I'm wearing bc it's 50% off!

_ _ _ _

SumSums_Closet Spotted 👀 at LA Fashion Week yesterday at @DaniellaMazanaroDesigns show! Daniella herself styled Summer for the occasion. Swipe for close-ups of each piece and use my code SUMSUM for 20% off your first order online or at any #DaniellaMazanaro brick and mortar.

.

Also, keep your eyes peeled—I'm going live at 4 p.m. PT to show you how to recreate Summer's adorable braid crown that she wore to school last week. Not only is it super adorbs and effortless (just like Summer!!), it's also practical for keeping your hair out of your face for your fitness electives. Summer takes #PiYo if any of you wondered!

.

Links to Summer's black off-the-shoulder romper, chunky gold necklace, and camel-colored sandals in my bio! 🐍 ✨

.

#commissionedlinks #SummerCartwright
#SummerCartwrightCloset #fashionweek #fashiongoals
#fashioninfluencer #inspo #goals

See all 1,890 responses

SumSums_Closet
@The_Summer_Cartwright thank youuuuu so
much for the boost! 😈 😈 😈 #girlbosses

KyrenMMM Lol that Cora chick is in my class
shes the worst.

VintageVal OMG
@the_Summer_Cartwright your style is serious
goalsssss! Love all your upcycled pieces!
Check out my #ootd in my stories and let me
know what you think! 😌

A.Man.Duh @KyrenMMM and you're something
special? I've been to almost every lacrosse
game, and I've never seen your ass leave the
bench.

SuzieQBoutique 🔥 🔥 Have you thought about modeling? Check your DMs for an opportunity!

Avalon.James Cora is a sweetheart! @KyrenMMM

KyrenMMM @A.Man.Duh you're in like 5th grade so learn to respect your elders. @Avalon.James isnt sweetheart what people call people too ugly to call hot?

A.Man.Duh Good one @KyrenMMM. 💬 Good luck on your college apps.

Kylalalala lolololol the only thing more pathetic than being an "influencer" is obsessing over one.

The_Summer_Cartwright And yet here you are, still commenting @Kylalalala? All the love to you. 🙄 🖤

PART 2

#GoneButNotForgotten

SIX

Grace Godwin

Monday, November 2
6:22 a.m.

Monday morning, Grace wakes up heavy, her limbs sore from tensing her muscles even in her sleep. After finding Summer on her bathroom floor Saturday night, Adam called 911. Paramedics confirmed Summer was dead. Grace has never experienced anything more surreal than the LAPD swarming the loft and taking their statements, or the cold numbness she felt seeping through her limbs as she and Adam bolted to his car while random people shouted after them to ask what happened. Was it true? Suicide? An accident? Her heart?

Summer is really gone. Grace knows that for sure.

The rising sun through her window stripes her yellow quilt with shadows, wrong, all wrong. How can the sun still rise? How can she? It's been two nights and a day since Summer died, time that Grace has still lived.

She silences the alarm on her phone. Even though she'd rather spend at least another week buried in her pillows with Pippi, the stuffed hippo she's had since birth, it's time to get up for swim practice before school. If she misses practice, she can't swim in the meet Friday, and if she misses school, she ruins the perfect attendance she's been keeping up since freshman year. Still caring about this stuff feels so pointless, but she does. She needs scholarships to go away to college, and escape has never been more tantalizing.

When she checks the time on her phone, she groans into her pillow. She has thirty-two unread texts and three missed calls, most from Adam. She deletes his messages unread because she can't handle anyone's feelings but her own. Maybe not even those. Seven of the texts are from Blossom, who's probably at the end of her sensitivity limits after a full thirty-six hours of pretending to respect Grace's privacy.

BV:

You okay, boo? I'm hella worried!

BV:

I looked for you after the police came, but you were nowhere.

BV:

K, text me back so I can stop assuming you're dead.

BV:

Not to be that person, but like . . . if you miss Lit, I can't give you the notes. It's not fair to people who come to class. Just saying, boo. 😔

BV:

Call me before I DIE!

BV:

K, I see how flippant remarks about death are ill-advised right now. My bad. 😩 But call me!!!!!

The last text is a pic with the message THIS IS MY WORRIED FACE!!!

In the photo, Blossom's brown eyes are wide, and her mouth is pressed into the wiggly line that she knows makes Grace laugh. Her nose ring looks infected again.

Grace texts Blossom back to let her know she'll be in class, no notes needed, then lies back onto her pillow with Pippi. How is she going to get through swim practice and school and work? How does she move past "My best friend died on Halloween," past "I should have saved her," past "Summer's gone forever"? Past the empty space where Summer used to be and will never be again? Grace can still feel Adam's hand in her own as they sat on Summer's bed while CSI taped off the bathroom. In the back of her mind, that guilty voice still whispers, despite everything, that holding hands with him felt right. What is wrong with her?

When Grace finally drags herself into the kitchen of the two-bedroom apartment she shares with her mom, Gina, she isn't hungry at all. Her stomach twists into knots and swells like the Auntie Anne's pretzel she dropped into the fountain at the Grove when she was eleven. Soggy. Puffy. Coming apart at the edges. Grace almost dove into the fountain that day to retrieve her pretzel so she could eat it even though it was falling apart in oozy clumps. She'd do anything for her mom, and she hadn't wanted her to feel bad about the wasted pretzel.

She'll do the same today and choke down her mom's questionable bacon and eggs with a smile. After spending the entire day in bed yesterday, if Grace wants any semblance of privacy, she'll have to prove to her mom that she's both physically and mentally bursting with health and will avoid undue attention at school from counselors, etc. She has to prove she can lie low and carry on.

"Horrible, just horrible, all of this," Gina says. This morning, her brown hair is scraped into a low ponytail, and with the heat from the stove flushing her round cheeks, she looks even more like an older version of Grace. Grace has always loved being her mom's twin. It's a connection. They moved a lot when Grace was a kid, and her mom, rather than any building, is her roots.

Gina salts the bacon, two swift shakes that she mirrors with her wide hips. Grace gave up telling her not to salt the bacon months ago when she caught her dumping salt into her potato chip bag. "Coffee's on the table. We only have that raspberry-flavored creamer you hate, but I'll run to the store today."

Grace sits in the least wobbly chair. "Black is fine, Mom. Thanks."

"You deserve pumpkin spice."

"Well, so do you."

"I deserve two percent milk at best. I'm under no illusions."

Despite herself, Grace laughs, then aches because she can still laugh, and Summer never will again. It's not something her mom's LIFE ISN'T ABOUT WAITING FOR THE STORM TO PASS. IT'S ABOUT LEARNING TO DANCE IN THE RAIN Etsy sign can fix. She props her feet on the chair across from her and takes a sip of coffee so her hands are busy. It tastes like old crackers soaked in battery acid.

Compared to the kitchen at Summer's place, with its stainless-steel appliances and Carrara marble countertops, Grace's kitchen is a dump. She likes it better, though, because it feels like her mom, a little worn down but comfortable and cheery. Magnets from road trip destinations all over the US litter the refrigerator. Old coffee stains the pot. Burned-on bits of cheese and crumbs are glued forever to the bottom of the oven. A filing cabinet filled with Grace's life—honor roll certificates and vaccination records—is the only thing remotely near organized, but it's home, and home is Grace and Gina, and the pressure to be neat at Summer's loft is oppressive anyway.

Was.

Grace probably won't go back to Sum's loft again. Why would she? It will be a small death, just like every memory of her and Summer will be. When she goes to the beach, Grace will die a little when Summer doesn't bury her feet in the sand and take hot dog leg pics. When she rides the Pacific Park Ferris wheel, she'll die a little when she can't share a pack of Twizzlers with Summer. At school, she'll die a little more when Summer doesn't steal Grace's favorite purple pen. How many small deaths can someone die before her body is a shell going through the motions, controlled by a functional brain but not fueled by a heart?

"Are you sure you want to go to school today?" Grease from the bacon leaps from the pan to splatter Gina's wrist. "Ouch! We could . . . go shopping!"

"Even one missed day ruins my chances at the Excellence Grant."

"You'd think considering the circumstances—"

"And I have swim practice this morning."

"You're so responsible." Gina sits at the table with Grace, setting the plate of bacon and eggs between them. "Can you make it all day without crying your face off?"

"Mom."

"We could swing by Target for waterproof mascara."

"Mom!"

"I'm just saying."

Grace takes one piece of bacon and a spoonful of eggs. Her mom is worried about her, she gets that, but she doesn't have the energy to comfort her mom all day long. At least at school, there's an element of anonymity if Grace chooses to take advantage of it. And if all else fails, there's always the back parking lot, where the stoners hide out.

When Grace's phone rings while she's got egg in her mouth, she almost silences it without looking. It's either Adam or Blossom. But on the third ring, she checks the screen. It's Harrison Cartwright. Her hands rebel and hit the answer button before her brain registers what's happening. When she hears his deep voice, her mom nudges her foot under the table to check to see if she's all right. Is it possible to feel pale?

"Harrison. Hey."

"Hey, babygirl."

Grace has told him a hundred times not to call her that, both because she isn't a baby and the nickname is super belittling to someone who is taking five AP classes when he didn't take a single one in his four years of high school. And also because she's not *his* girl anyway. Coffee and a concert don't add up to dating.

"What's up?" Grace asks.

There's a long silence on Harrison's end, then he sighs. "I just needed to hear your voice. I'm . . . God, I don't know what to do." It's the sincerest he's ever sounded.

"Me either. You okay?"

"I don't even know. I was alone in the loft all weekend once the police left. I thought about going back to campus, but . . . There was a forensics team and everything, and the police are all up in my business right now. They called me to say I had to go in for an interview yesterday afternoon if I wanted to avoid them showing up on campus."

"They just want to find out what happened to Summer."

When the police arrived at the party Saturday night, a middle-aged detective pulled Grace, Laney, and Adam aside to get their statements. Cora had been way too emotional, so they asked her to come to the station the next day. Harrison was busy ushering other guests out of the loft as another detective took down all of their names and contact info at the door, no small feat when half the room was trying to go live with their reactions to Summer's death.

"What did you tell the detective?" Harrison asks. Even through the phone, his voice sounds choked, which makes Grace nervous. What did *he* tell them?

"The truth," Grace says. "How the night went, what we saw."

"Did you mention you have Summer's Instagram password?"

"It didn't come up. Does she even have the same password now? It's been months." Grace wonders why he's asking. Did he tell the detectives? And if he did, does it look bad that she didn't mention it?

He pauses. "My parents got home from Dubai yesterday, and they asked me to help with some of the arrangements."

"Arrangements? You mean the funeral?"

"Nah, Dad's hired someone to take care of that. But Mom thinks we need something for the students at WW Prep. To let everyone show how much they'll miss Sum."

"Like . . . a candlelight vigil?" Grace has no experience with death or its trappings.

"Yeah," Harrison says. "Exactly. Could you figure out a way to tell all the students that we're going to have it tomorrow night? At the park right behind school."

"Sure."

"You need a ride to school today?"

Grace hates riding the city bus, but showing up with Summer's brother the first school day after her death isn't going to help with anonymity, so she says no thanks, promises to get the word out for the vigil, hangs up, and relays the conversation so her mom doesn't melt from curiosity.

"Why do people think that lighting candles does anything for a dead person?" Gina asks. "Don't you think Summer would rather you lived a full life, went shopping with your mom, ate your damn eggs?"

Grace shrugs and heads to the front door for her backpack.

"Wait! You need caffeine!" There's a pouring sound and the click of a lid as Gina transfers the battery acid into a tumbler.

When Grace grabs her backpack from the hook by the front door, it seems to leap onto her shoulders. Surprised, she turns to find her mom lifting it to make it easier for her to slide on. Gina hands Grace the tumbler.

"Thanks," Grace says.

"I almost added some whiskey, but the mommy blogs frown on that."

Grace laughs and her pretzel stomach unknots a little. Funny how someone you love can do that for you, can make you laugh when the world is at its darkest and life seems way too long.

She'll survive school today. Probably.

Saturday, July 4, four months ago, 9:00 p.m.
Santa Monica Pier

The Pacific Park Ferris wheel ground to a halt when Grace, Summer, Adam, and Harrison were all the way at the top. The tinny theme park music muted, the lights of Santa Monica Pier dimmed, and the national anthem blared from an invisible speaker as the first fireworks burst over the dark ocean. The red paint of the Ferris wheel bucket they rode in washed their skin rosy.

Below them, a man cursed. "C'mon, man, start the ride again. I can't see."

The Ferris wheel operator ignored him.

"How'd you get the guy to stop us at the top for the fireworks?" Adam asked.

Summer tossed her Dutch braids over her shoulders and adjusted the strap of her flag-printed tank top. Her white shorts, frayed at the bottom, showed off the tanned legs she pressed against Adam's, and aside from a swipe of glittery highlight on her cheeks, her face looked bare. Grace knew better. Summer had spent at least thirty minutes on her makeup back at the loft.

"Easy." Summer snuggled into Adam's shoulder. "My dad knows the guy who runs the pier."

"Isn't he losing money from new riders not getting on?" Grace asked.

"It's taken care of," Harrison said. "Enjoy the show."

Adam and Grace exchanged a surreptitious glance above Summer's head. Even though Grace and Summer had been friends for years and

Adam had been dating Sum ten months, neither of them was used to a world where extravagant favors were no big deal and money was never an issue. But when Adam tried to mouth something to her, Grace looked away. He was dating Summer, and because of that, things were different with them. They had to be.

"Take a pic of Adam and me!" Summer handed her phone to Grace, who tried not to think too hard about how perfect Summer looked with Adam, even making a silly face with her tongue sticking out.

"You guys want one?" Summer asked.

"No thanks," Grace said.

"Aw, come on. Just one?" Harrison took out his phone and snapped a selfie of him kissing her hair. Grace tried to paste a smile on her face.

As the fireworks rained gold dust over the Pacific and burst in sprays of red and green and blue, Harrison stretched an arm around Grace's shoulder. They weren't really dating, but they weren't not dating, and Grace hadn't been able to sort out her feelings. On one hand, it was super flattering, and as Sum liked to remind her, How fun would it be if one day we were sisters? *On the other hand, every time Harrison touched her, she cringed a little. He wasn't a bad guy, but she was sure he wasn't her guy. Also, Grace had a strange sense that Harrison and Summer were always locked in a sort of sibling competition for . . . well, everything, including who-had-the-cutest-relationship.*

Not to mention that July Fourth had been a fraught time in Grace's life since she was little, fireworks always tied to her mom packing up her car to move the two of them across the country away from all of Grace's friends. Move in July, new school in August. It had left a bad taste in her mouth. She and her mom had been in LA for almost five years, which was far longer than Grace had lived anywhere. She never wanted to leave.

Just when Grace was starting to pray for the fireworks finale,

Summer shoved Harrison to the side so she could sit by her. The Ferris wheel bucket rocked gently.

"Bestie time," Summer said, and as though she could sense Grace's discomfort, offered her a Twizzler from the pack she'd bought on the pier. Summer and Grace had used Twizzlers as soda straws at their middle school sleepovers. To Grace, they still sort of tasted like Sprite and prank calls and the way it felt to have every kid in their eighth-grade class call them Summerandgrace, all one word.

"God, aren't you glad we aren't on that? Hurl." Summer nodded at the Sea Dragon ride below them that had rocked itself almost upright. The next rock would flip it all the way upside down.

"For sure." Grace ripped off a piece of Twizzler with her teeth.

And in that isolated moment, as they watched the smoky, sparkling explosion of the finale set in time to "Stars and Stripes Forever," Grace wouldn't have changed a thing. Not the smell of gunpowder. Not the too-hot night air on her neck or the way her sweaty, bare legs stuck to the seat of the bucket. Not the mumbled curses of the man in the yellow bucket below who was pissed to be missing the best views.

That was the thing about Summer. She could read people, tell when they were feeling crappy, and know exactly how to make them feel good again. More than that, she knew how to create magic moments in an otherwise mundane world. Taste magic once, and you had to have more. For better or worse, they were still Summerandgrace. So even though Grace always felt a little like she was on the Sea Dragon, inches away from her life flipping upside down, she was an addict.

SEVEN

Adam Mahmoud

Monday, November 2
8:02 a.m.

When he gets to school Monday morning, Adam swipes his key card to let himself into the back building that houses the indoor pool. Its massive windows fog whenever it's chilly outside. The air has a chemical bite, and the sound of water shoved aside by bodies is hypnotic. From the gym through the double doors, he can hear the rhythmic squeak of sneakers paired with hollow pops. The volleyball team has the court before school.

"Stay focused!" Coach Pezzulo shouts, her voice echoing off the cement walls. "Your competition isn't in the other lanes. It's in your own mind."

Adam recognizes a few of the swimmers, even with their caps and goggles. Oscar is in lane one. He's pretty sure that's Ellie Carmichael in lane two, because she's the only Black student on the swim team, really one of the only other Black students at school, so they can't help but notice each other. Ellie crushes at the butterfly stroke. She has a full-ride swim scholarship to Howard University next year.

In the pool's third lane, Grace's strong arms cut through the water. This past weekend, she ignored all his texts. He thought that things would be different after the breakup, or at least back to how they were before Summer. Apparently not. Grace doesn't want to talk to him, and even though he knows he should probably leave her alone, he needs to show her the *LA Times* article posted yesterday.

Adam settles onto the bleachers to wait. He breathes in the humidity and lets the air loosen his lungs. This momentary stillness feels dangerous. He hasn't stopped moving since the moment he saw Summer's body. He called 911, comforted Grace, talked to the police, then late that night, held his mom while she sobbed with relief that he was okay. Sunday, he wrote a US History essay two weeks early, took his little sisters to Build-a-Bear, and played *Mythos* long enough into the night that by the time he collapsed into bed, he was asleep in seconds. Maybe it's fear that he'll be mobbed at school by people asking questions, but this morning, he's not tired despite his lack of sleep.

Or maybe, the conflict is in his own mind. Adrenaline.

Oscar finishes his lap and surfaces by Adam's feet, making him jump enough to feel embarrassed.

"Adam! What're you doing here?"

"Just waiting for Grace."

"I think she has another lap at least."

"I thought you weren't supposed to be clocking people in the other lanes?"

Oscar pulls himself out of the water to sit beside Adam. A puddle forms around him and soaks the side of Adam's uniform pants. "Well, ya know. Only so many scholarships to go around. Want me to pass a message along so you don't have to wait?"

"Nah, it's okay."

"It's just that you kind of look like a huge perv sitting by the side of the pool watching people in their bathing suits."

"Hey!"

"Just saying." Oscar flexes his feet. "Nothing like that feeling of no calf cramps after a good swim. You ready to face the chaos today?"

"You mean after . . ."

"Obviously."

"Yeah. I guess, yeah."

Oscar tilts his head to observe Adam's face. "I'm not sure if you are. Everyone is talking about Summer's death. Even the teachers. Some people are saying it wasn't an accident."

"Everyone can mind their own business."

"Oooo, but that's the problem, my friend. According to the world at large, Summer *is* their business. That's what happens when you let five million people follow every aspect of your life online. People get possessive, and those possessive people know about the breakup."

Adam snorts. "She didn't share every aspect. Just the things that made her look good."

"I'd watch that attitude at school. Makes you sound . . . bitter, maybe? Not ideal." Oscar stands slowly and stretches his back. "Well, I'll leave you to your perving. Gotta shower or I'll smell like pool all day."

When Oscar leaves, Adam pinches the bridge of his nose until it hurts. Oscar's right. He can't seem like the bitter ex, not after what he read in the *LA Times* this morning. So he'll focus on proving that even though he and Summer broke up, he misses her. He'll be the grieving boyfriend, the justice seeker, because what if it turns out that it wasn't an accident, that Sum didn't kill herself? Everyone knows that murder is usually committed by the significant other. The husband, the partner, the boyfriend. The ex.

It won't be too hard to play the grieving boyfriend, because he does miss Summer. The good stuff anyway. The Summer he fell for was sharp and funny and ambitious, yes, but she was also a girl who wondered if people loved her for who she was or for what she could give them. One lazy afternoon, when the two of them were curled up on a bench at the Santa Monica Pier drinking boba tea, she confessed to him that she wished her family was more like his. She wanted warm conversations around the dinner table instead of strategy sessions for getting her into Stanford. She wanted to really live now, not just exist until she accomplished all that she needed to be as successful as her parents wanted her to be.

But when all their dates morphed into photoshoots, Adam started to feel more like a prop than her boyfriend. She didn't understand why it bothered him, and they'd drifted apart. Then Adam messed up big time, and Summer found out.

When Grace surfaces a few minutes later, Coach Pezzulo crouches beside the pool, clicking her pen while she double-checks stats on her clipboard. "Slower than usual today. You tired?"

"I guess." Grace climbs the ladder and grabs her towel from the floor. She doesn't seem to see Adam.

"Get some rest before the meet Friday. College scouts will be there."

"Are you serious?"

"They just confirmed over the weekend." She tucks the clipboard under her arm. "I need you to be present, and not just in body." Her eyes soften just a fraction. "Unless you think you need some time? We could talk to your mom about—"

"I'll be fine. Thanks, Coach." Adam can feel Grace's discomfort from the other side of the pool.

Coach Pezzulo claps Grace on the shoulder with an I'm-rooting-for-you smile, then disappears through a door that leads to her office.

The other swimmers are drying off, stretching, gathering in little clumps to talk. Judging by their unsubtle glances at him, he knows what they're gossiping about. He clenches his fists and swallows hard, forcing himself not to barge into their conversation to defend himself. His head pounds from tension, and school hasn't even started.

When Grace has wrapped her towel around herself and removed her swim cap so her hair falls around her shoulders and her damp baby hairs form a halo around her face, her eyes meet his across the pool. As though by some unspoken agreement, they meet halfway. Grace smells like chlorine and strawberry shampoo, and without any makeup on, she looks like the girl who twisted the chains of their playground swings tight, then held her legs out straight while she spun. He misses that girl. He misses the way he was with her.

"What are you doing here?" she asks.

"Why didn't you respond to my texts?"

"You know why not."

He does. Grace doesn't process trauma by talking about it. She needs time and space and usually her stuffed hippo, though he doubts she'd admit that anymore. "I have something to show you."

"Can it wait until lunch? I need to shower."

The rumors will be bad enough without the two of them hanging out—two days after Sum's death, and they're already moving on?—but won't it look worse if they stop sitting together now that Summer won't be in the seat between them? Either way, he wants to show Grace the article before someone else does. Because someone else will.

"It'll only take a second," Adam says.

"Okay. I guess."

Her reluctance to be near him twinges even though it's been this way ever since he and Summer got together.

He takes his phone from his back pocket and opens the *LA Times* article he saved this morning after reading it so many times he basically has it memorized. It's short and to the point with a photo of Summer smiling, her eyes soft above her off-the-shoulder sweater. It was the perfect choice if the goal was to make Summer look as fragile and innocent as possible.

Famous Influencer's Body Found in Century City Loft

By Amy Littleton
Nov. 1 UPDATED 2:37 PM PT

Amid one of the bloodiest weeks in LA history, one face stands out from the rest. Sixteen-year-old Summer Cartwright, a junior at the prestigious Westwood Preparatory Academy and daughter of Golden Gate studio head Julian Cartwright, was found dead in her bathroom on Saturday evening. Authorities have not ruled out foul play. The city coroner's initial findings place time of death between 8:45 p.m. and 9:15 p.m. Despite pressure from Mayor Alton and Mr. Cartwright, whose new movie *She Falls Hard* is expected to dominate box offices this year, no arrests have been made at this time. According to Cecilia Gomez, press secretary for the LAPD, investigations into a narrowed pool of suspects are under way, pending a full autopsy report.

Summer scored top honors at WW Prep and hoped to attend Stanford University after graduation. Always free with her sweet smile, Summer was a popular influencer known for her fashion tips, frank sense of humor, and stunning beauty. Her debut memoir *All Your Likes Can't Buy Me Love*, based on Instagram posts about her life, sold at auction to Swift Eagle Press for nearly seven figures and was set to publish this spring.

Swift Eagle declined to comment on its future.

If you have information regarding Summer Cartwright's death, please call the LAPD major crimes tip line at (213) 555-7803.

Grace looks up sharply after reading the article. "Foul play? So they're thinking murder?"

"I don't know, but that's why I wanted to show this to you. We should be careful. Lie low."

"Why would we be suspects?"

"I'm her ex. And after your fight . . . I don't know."

"You're right." Grace massages her forehead where her swim cap left a red line. "What do we do? Ellie already asked me this morning what Summer's body looked like when we found her."

"None of the articles I saw mentioned any details, and no one's talking about the word *toxic* written on her face. Maybe that won't come out."

"That's exactly why people are going to bombard us with questions. They want the gory details."

"We could ditch school."

"You know I can't. My scholarship."

Adam nods. "We'll have to face all the questions at some point." He doesn't bother adding that them skipping school might look bad anyway, like they have something to hide. The last thing either of them needs is to end up as the next article on the school blog.

"I've got to go shower before homeroom," Grace says. "I'll see you around?"

He wants to hold her back, to talk for longer, but he nods. "Yeah. Okay."

Even though Adam has places to be, too, he sits on the edge of the pool, alone in the flickering blue light. He wants to plunge in, to let the water fill his ears and block out the screaming in the back of his mind. He can't get the image of Summer's body out of his head—the trail of vomit, the word #*TOXIC* written again and again—because no matter how fast he moves, no matter how much he tries to not think, there she is. Cold and empty where she used to be full of life.

He's almost convinced himself to stay on dry land when his phone dings. It's a message from one of his followers on Twitch.

> **FemFatale15:** Man of Mythos where you been? You going live tonight or what?

Adam hesitates, then responds. Try and stop me.

Friday, January 11, ten months ago, 6:16 p.m.
Adam's Apartment

Adam shoved his hands deep into his pockets as he opened his apartment door for Summer. He had warned her that it wasn't much—a sort of crappy three-bedroom with white walls and everything hung with Command Strips to not leave nail holes. He'd never minded it before. It had seemed cozy, all his family needed, but seeing the homes of his classmates had burrowed doubt like a worm into his mind. What if she judged him? They'd been dating a little over two months, but he still hadn't gotten used to the fact that Summer Cartwright was his girlfriend.

She squeezed his arm. "Relax, Adam."

He took a deep breath. "Yeah."

As Adam closed the door behind them, it occurred to him that he should be the one reassuring Summer—she was meeting his family, after all—but she seemed completely at ease. That was one of the things that drew him to Summer. She had an uncanny ability to listen to his silences that made him feel important.

His mom was waiting for them in the kitchen. She had an apron tied over her nurse's scrubs and a fresh coat of her favorite lipstick. "Summer! Lovely to meet you."

"This is for you." Summer handed her a tiny potted Monstera plant. "I grew it myself from a cutting."

"How thoughtful!" His mom hugged her, and Adam's shoulders relaxed.

Then his five-year-old twin sisters bounced into the kitchen and grabbed Summer's arms to drag her away.

"Are you wearing eyeliner?" Lea asked. "I love it."

"I love it more!" Samia said.

"No, you don't."

"Are you Adam's girlfriend?"

Summer let the twins drag her out of the kitchen. "Sure am."

Lea giggled. "Yuck!"

"Come see our room!"

With Summer in it, the hallway looked dingy and narrow. Adam cringed at the thought of her seeing the framed first-grade picture of him missing his two front teeth, the family photo from five years ago when he'd had braces and a palate expander and a green polo shirt, but Summer brushed her finger along the frame of the family photo.

"Your family seems great," she said.

"They're a lot. A little overwhelming."

She chewed the inside of her cheek. "A lot is great. They really love you."

"Yeah, for sure."

"Are you coming or what?" Samia yelled from her room.

The entire evening, Adam was on edge, waiting for his family to say something that would freak Summer out, waiting for Summer's nose to wrinkle at the shawarma his mother served, but that didn't happen. Lea tried to steal Samia's last bite, so Samia hit her with a spoon. Adam's dad ranted about how every new movie was a sequel or a remake and asked what Summer's dad thought about it. Adam's mom heaped seconds onto Summer's plate with abandon and talked to her about leaf cuttings. And through it all, Summer was gracious and warm, the perfect guest. He could tell his parents were impressed with her.

So what was bothering him?

Maybe he just didn't know how to behave. Maybe having Summer *over wasn't the same as having Grace to dinner, because his family had accepted Grace as one of their own so long ago that her coming to dinner didn't feel like having a guest anymore. But that just meant his family needed more time with Summer to get to know her. Didn't it?*

Two hours later, as he walked Summer to his Jeep to drive her home, she stopped in the middle of the road that separated Adam's building from Grace's and looked up at the sky. There weren't any stars tonight, or at least none visible against the electric glow of the corner gas station, but Summer seemed to search for something above her. She was so beautiful, and when he wrapped an arm around her as they leaned against the hood of his Jeep, she laid her head on his shoulder. He couldn't believe he was lucky enough to be dating her.

"I wish my family ate dinner together like that," she said.

"You don't?" Adam had never known anything different.

"We do sometimes, but . . . it's not the same. No one listens. We all just . . . talk at each other until someone gets a phone call."

Adam didn't know what to say. Summer had never invited him over when her family was home, and until that moment, he'd assumed she was embarrassed by him, that they didn't make sense together and deep down she knew it. He hadn't considered that he wasn't the one who embarrassed her.

"You're welcome to come have dinner with us whenever you want," he said.

"I don't want to impose."

"Not at all! Grace eats with us all the time, and my mom never minds."

Summer lifted her head from his shoulder to look him in the eyes. "Oh yeah?"

"She likes hanging out with my mom."

"Gotcha."

"Hers works late." Adam stuck his keys in the driver-side door. *"You ready to go?"*

"You know what?" Summer smiled again, but this smile was the one she used with the people at school who approached her to talk about her Instagram account. It was bright but didn't reach her eyes. *"I'll call an Uber. You're already home. No point in driving me all the way across the city."*

"I don't mind."

"I'll call you tonight." She kissed him on the cheek.

And because Adam wasn't sure if she wanted him to argue with her about it or let her go, she rode away a few minutes later in a random red Honda. A horrible thought occurred to him then. Did it bother her that he spent so much time with Grace? Was that why she didn't want him to drive her home?

What if he was forced to choose between them, his best friend and his girlfriend? Was he capable of doing that? And if he had to, what decision would he make?

EIGHT

Elaine Miyamoto

Monday, November 2
10:21 a.m.

Laney pours glue, cornstarch, and borax into a glass dish while Adam stirs. They're making polymer bouncy balls, and despite her hatred of WW Prep and high school in general—she's beyond ready for college—Laney has to admit that chemistry class is awesome sometimes.

Although the lab is mostly sterile white—the walls, the cabinets beneath the lab counters, the linoleum floors—the walls are slathered with bright, sarcastic posters (*Chemistry! It's like cooking . . . just don't lick the spoon!*), and floor-to-ceiling windows cover the back wall so the room is washed in natural light. The chem teacher, Mr. Miller, a tall man with a bushy beard that's somehow un-singed despite the number of fires he lights, circulates the room to look in each bowl.

"Stir faster," Laney tells Adam. The cornstarch isn't dissolving, probably because Adam is staring at Grace on the other side of the

U-shaped desk setup instead of putting his back into it. "I swear, if these balls don't bounce—"

"Chill." Adam gives her an exasperated look. "My arm will fly out of its socket if I stir any harder."

"Will you just talk to Grace instead of gazing at her like you're some kind of eighteenth-century book hero?"

"What? I'm not—"

"Spare me. You love her, Mr. Darcy."

"Laney, she's like my sister. We grew up together."

"Just saying, I have a new stepbrother, and I don't look at him like that."

As they talk, the cornstarch, glue, and borax slowly morph into a sticky ball at the bottom of their bowl. Adam wipes his hands on a towel while Laney documents the bouncy ball's appearance in their lab notes beneath their hypothesis and materials.

"Your notes could be more thorough," Adam says over her shoulder.

She drops her pen. "You could do them yourself."

He laughs. "Aw, man, sorry. My arm is way too tired from stirring."

Laney doesn't miss the way Grace looks at Adam from under her eyelashes when he laughs, so shy, so sweet. Bull. Shit. Grace was friends with Summer, so there's no way she's as innocent as she acts. With Summer dead, she might be the only one who knows what Laney did, the only one who could still drop sparks into the gasoline can of Laney's secrets, set fire to Laney's life and plans. Laney was forced to grow a hard shell around the roiling shame inside her until no oxygen could reach it. It's chemistry. Deprive the secrets of air, and they can't catch fire. And now that Summer is dead, no one needs to know what she did. Grace has to get that, right?

Adam jabs Laney with his pencil and nods at Mr. Miller, who leans across the counter to check their polymer compound.

"Consistency looks good. Label your bowl and set it on the back counter, and let's try to keep the conversation chemistry-related, right?"

Before Laney and Adam can respond to Mr. Miller's eyebrow waggle request, the principal's voice crackles over the intercom. After the boring daily announcements that play every afternoon— lunch menu for the next day, sporting events, theater troupe wins at competition—he adds, "In light of this weekend's events, a professional grief counselor will be on site for the week. Appointments may be scheduled at the front office or via the school's website. In addition, tomorrow evening at seven, the Cartwright family will host a candlelight vigil in Summer's memory at the park behind the football field."

Despite Mr. Miller's best efforts to get the class under control, for the last five minutes of the period students buzz with interest over the news. Most of them tell their lab partners that they will for sure be at the vigil that night, even if it means they have to skip dance or SAT prep or whatever.

"Got to love how all of a sudden, Summer is a glowing star, plucked too soon from the galaxy," Laney says, forgetting for a second that Adam probably feels that way about Summer himself, breakup or no. She scrapes spilled corn starch into her hand to throw it in the trash can at the back of the room so she can avoid a sappy defense from him.

But instead, Adam surprises her by asking, "What's your explanation, then? For all of the people who will be at her vigil?"

"Trauma porn. People love using other people's pain to make themselves feel better."

Trauma porn is nothing new to Laney, not after her mom died three years ago. Her friends were, like, *So sorry, oh my god, that's so awful, but . . . at least you still have your dad. At least we're here for you.*

At least you had thirteen years with her. At least, at least, at least until Laney wanted to strangle the next person who said those words.

So no, she's not surprised. People rubberneck at car accidents all the time. They enjoy the drama when a fellow student gets diagnosed with cancer, and they basically make popcorn when someone gets pregnant. There'll be hundreds of people at the candlelight vigil tonight, not because they care about Summer, but because they want other people to see them grieving and being a good person.

"Look," Laney says. "I know you were in Summer's love bubble or whatever? But she wasn't a nice person."

"Did you guys even know each other? Aside from that one month at ISSOS?"

"That one month was plenty. Look at what she did to Avalon James in less time."

He shakes his head. "Even when we were dating, I thought it was messed up what Summer did to Avalon. Black influencers don't get second chances the way Summer always does, you know? She should have understood that."

Summer's feud with Avalon is infamous online. BuzzFeed did a whole series of articles on it, and for a solid two weeks on TikTok, people stitched their reactions to Summer's video post about Avalon's makeup line drop. After that, it didn't matter that Avalon got the idea for her makeup line because she was studying theater at UCLA and could never find a base that matched her skin tone. It didn't matter that the play she wrote was selected as one of only three for the student theater festival. Avalon was known for being a failure.

"Think Avalon will show up at the vigil tomorrow night?"

"Probably," Adam says. "Or risk being seen as bitter, or worse, guilty if the LAPD decides Summer's death was murder. Avalon was at the Halloween party."

"Please, it wasn't murder. Summer just got too wasted and died of alcohol poisoning or something. Maybe she OD'd."

Adam shakes his head. "Summer wasn't like that."

"I beg to differ."

Adam's probably right about Avalon feeling compelled to show up tomorrow. Dread gathers in the pit of Laney's stomach. When she saw Avalon across the room when she first arrived at Summer's party, Laney almost turned around and left. She would have if Oscar hadn't already swerved through the crowd to say hello to Summer. Seeing Avalon in person made one of her little favors for Summer seem a lot more real.

Laney squares her shoulders and goes back to her lab report. When she's in film school at USC, she won't care or even remember all this junior year crap. Everything she's done will be worth it. The problem is, she isn't sure how many stares and questions about Summer she can weather before the door in the back of her mind cracks open and the truth spills out—Laney is glad Summer is dead.

Monday, July 13, three and a half months ago, 12:27 a.m.
Cambridge University ISSOS

Dew from the grass soaked through Laney's jacket, making her skin cold.
Beside her, Summer lay on her cardigan staring up at the stars above the
quad at Cambridge. The orange castellated buildings towered over them,
a shade darker than the navy sky. It was beautiful here, slower, older.
Laney felt like she could breathe without the world flying past her.

She and Summer had been roommates for just under a week. Instead
of going to the campus party they'd been invited to, after pregaming with
a few White Claws, they crashed on the quad. Summer wasn't the type of
person Laney usually hung out with, but her buzz made her feel looser,
more open to giving Summer a chance. More willing to talk. She'd never
had alcohol before. Was this what college would be like?

As they talked about nothing in particular, Laney puzzled at how
real and nice Summer seemed to be. Maybe she shouldn't have judged
her so quickly. But between Summer's huge following online, which she
showed Laney on day one, and the cutesy dorm decorations Summer put
up for a three-week session, Summer had seemed like one of those girls
who was more focused on her hair than the brain beneath it.

She said as much—the nice part anyway—to Summer.

Summer laughed. "I'm actually a huge bitch, like ninety percent of
the time."

"So you're not as disgustingly sweet as you come across?"

"Being sweet makes people like you, but being a bitch gets you what
you want."

"I can get on board with brutal honesty. But for my own edification, I'm going to need an example."

"Hmmm." Summer pursed her lips. "Okay, how about this. One time, my best friend, Grace, made me mad by keeping secrets from me, so I got her back."

Laney sat up onto her elbows. "What did you do?"

"She wants to be valedictorian, right?" Summer flopped her arm above her head. She wasn't drunk, but her words slurred just enough for Laney to wonder if she'd be so willing to share if she hadn't had the White Claws. "Vale-dick-torian. Anyway, she had a huge pre-calc test, and her teacher didn't allow makeups without a doctor's note. So I convinced one of the student tech guys to disable her school key card so she was locked out of the building."

"For real? That's evil."

Summer smiled. "Aren't we all sometimes?"

"No remorse?"

"Oh, I feel remorse. I just don't let myself think about it. It works. You should try it."

"That's messed up." Laney stood and brushed grass off her jeans.

"Do you want to get doughnuts?"

Laney paused, but only for a second. "Okay."

"I'll buy! Because while we eat, there's a little favor I want to ask you."

The two of them gorged themselves on the entire dozen in their room that night and laughed like old friends. But when Laney woke up the next day having agreed to her first little favor—nothing big, just covering for Summer with the RA that night so she could stay out late—Summer had already gone to breakfast without her. Laney didn't know then how Summer's little favors snowballed. How if you said no, Summer would ruin you.

The_Summer_Cartwright

Update post from #SummerLand 🌞 ✨

.

Seriously, does it feel to anyone else like this school year will never end?? All my teachers are like, PILE IT ON!! 🙄 Just saying, if they aren't doing a good enough job teaching it in school, what makes them think homework will make me learn it any better? But if I want #Stanford to even look at me, I have to care. Ugh!

.

Keep an eye out for this week's #SumAndGraceReview livestream on Tuesday at 5 p.m. PT in which G and I will check out the new makeup line by #AvalonJames. Not going to lie, guys, it was a huge disappointment. I wanted to like it so, so bad, but swiiiipe for pics of the HAIRS I found in the lipstick. 🙀 🔒 #notkidding @Real.Avalon.James, sweetie, this sucks, because I was cheering for you, like so hard! But . . . did anyone else think it was weird that the PR packs arrived the same week as the product went live online? 💬 Did Avalon know there were issues and want to make as many sales as she could before people realized? A little #sus, right?

.

Also, stay tuned for my next post in which I tell yet another story of me embarrassing myself. This one involves a spray tan, a lack of exfoliation, and a very tiny bikini. 🍑 #helpme

.

This week in #SummerLoves . . . * Mac lipstick in the shade Cream in Your Coffee * Gazing into the far distance wishing for #summertime * Street tacossss * Poetry by #RupiKaur * Wicker lamps * Monstera plants!! * Pursuing my #goals without hesitation or guilt 😎 *

.

Love you all, love you most!
SumSum 🖤

₪ 🖤 ▶

🕐 AUGUST 8, THREE MONTHS AGO

View all 3,898 comments

SumSum's_Closet So gross! 🤮 I just got my lipstick in the mail, and it had a hair in it, too! Reached out to get a new lipstick, and @Real.Avalon.James won't give me my money back. Wtf?!? #cancelled #CancelAvalonJames #theft

ClassyLadyyy @Real.Avalon.James come on girl, get your poop in a group!

The_Summer_Cartwright Let's #KeepItKind here, guys! Influencers gotta influence, but it doesn't mean we need to be rude! 😌

Oliviathegreat OMGGG I love Monstera plants, too!

L.Miy2006 @SumSum's_Closet I'm with you. **#CancelAvalonJames** @The_Summer_Cartwright **ur being too nice girl**

NINE

Cora Pruitt

Monday, November 2
2:35 p.m.

Cora sits on her bed massaging her aching wrist after scribbling in her diary for an hour. She is surrounded by twenty-three items, including: a folded note, a few pens, a fuzzy sweater, a pair of flip-flops, a lip gloss, a sparkly binder clip, a PR box of PowerBoost granola bars that she almost didn't open, and a pair of glow-in-the-dark sunglasses from a beach bonfire in June hosted by the lacrosse team. She keeps all the items in a chest at the bottom of her bed, but she has to throw them away. She doesn't want to. It's necessary.

She skipped school today. Even though her parents are big proponents of the whole "if you're not dead, you don't stay in bed" mentality, apparently in the case of a friend's death, they're willing to make an exception. At first, lying in bed beneath her fluffy blanket blasting her Billie Eilish/Olivia Rodrigo/Taylor Swift angsty-lady-vibe mix was nice, but as the day crawled by, Cora wished she had forced herself to go to school. At home, she doesn't know what people are saying: about Summer, about that night, maybe even about her if word got out that she was one of the ones who found Summer's body. Cora isn't a gossip, but she loves news so much that without it she almost has a caffeine-withdrawal headache. Social media is weirdly silent aside from #RIPSummer posts and tributes. All the articles are the same—Summer was amazing, now she's dead, it might not have been an accident, the complete autopsy report hasn't come back.

"Are you still in your pajamas?" Cora's thirteen-year-old sister, Amanda, pokes her head into Cora's bedroom. Her light brown hair is the same color as Cora's roots, and her leggings are faux leather, Amanda's favorite combo—comfort and bad-assery. "Mom never lets me do that."

"My friend just died." Cora shoves her diary beneath her covers. Amanda knows it exists in theory, but no need to give her any ideas about reading it while Cora is out. "I think I can spend one day home in my pajamas."

Because Amanda has epilepsy, she's homeschooled, though according to Amanda, that will change for high school, because she wants the full experience. Cora isn't so certain. Since Amanda had a grand mal seizure last year, their mom rarely goes anywhere without her. She hardly talks about anything but Amanda.

"I didn't realize you and Summer were actually friends," Amanda says. "I thought it was more . . . I don't know . . . like she was your obsession."

"You make me sound like a total stalker!"

"I'm just stating facts."

"Get out of my room, butt face."

"Wow, good one. Hey, maybe I should start a true crime podcast about the Summer Cartwright case. I'm so close to the story, I bet

I could get tons of clicks! Suicide? Murder? What's the dark truth behind the rising star?"

"If you do that, I'll kill you. Like actually murder you."

"I'd be careful saying that these days." Amanda plops onto the end of Cora's bed and picks up a pen. "What is all this stuff?"

"Put that down."

She clicks it open and closed instead. "Your bed looks like a thrift store with that crap all over it. Better clean it up before Mom sees."

Their mom is famously tidy to the point that she tucked dividers inside their dresser drawers so that each pair of socks has its own little slot. If she saw the mishmash of random stuff on Cora's bed, she'd melt. Cora has always imagined her mom as a snowwoman. She can only keep her shape when she's cold.

"It's not crap," Cora says.

"Then what?"

For a moment, Cora considers telling Amanda the truth—that the connection between the items is that they all once belonged to Summer Cartwright. Cora didn't steal them all. Some things, like the note folded into a tiny triangle, Summer gave her. Summer left the sunglasses behind on a log by the bonfire. Cora borrowed the pen and never gave it back. But the sweater, the flip-flops, the lipstick . . . She shoved those in her bag the night of the party. After all, there was a good chance she'd never get invited back to Summer's place, so why not? It felt good to own them . . . at least until the police arrived and Cora realized if she went to the station that night, she wouldn't be able to explain the contents of her purse.

But Amanda already called her a stalker today. No need to add to the judgment list.

"Go away, Amanda," Cora says, resisting the urge to gather her twenty-three things into her arms. If she could explain her obsession with them, she would, but all she knows is that the things make her feel connected to Summer. They make her feel like she could be like Summer one day. They remind her that the most popular girl in school knew who Cora was before she died, and even took the time to write her a note. A handwritten note, folded like a triangle, delivered to her locker through the slats.

"Fine, I'll go," Amanda says, gripping Cora's doorknob. "But just so you know, Dad came home on his lunch break to take work calls in private, so if I were you, I'd turn your music down before he freaks out."

Cora makes a face and cranks her music louder, a small act of rebellion.

After Amanda goes back to her own room, Cora goes downstairs to grab a trash bag from beneath the kitchen sink, shoves Summer's things inside, then covers it all with coffee grounds and crumpled up pieces of newspaper in case anyone cuts into the bag.

On her way to take the trash out, Cora passes the french doors that separate her father's cluttery home office—aka the bane of her mother's existence and worthy of mention if divorce papers are ever filed—from the hallway. She peers in. Her father, in suit pants with his tie loosened and his jacket tossed over his chair, presses his phone to his ear. His expression reminds Cora of the one time he folded laundry and found out she owned a thong.

"I don't know, Julian," he says, just loud enough for Cora to hear. "You gotta give me a few days to figure this out. It's a complex situation."

Cora knows most things about Summer Cartwright, so of course she knows her father's name is Julian. She could list most of her cousins, too, if anyone ever asked. So before her father sees her lurking on the other side of his french doors, she presses herself against the wall to listen.

"You can't blame Swift Eagle Press for . . . No, it's not sensitive, but they're a business . . . Fine. I'll reach out again today."

Because her dad is totally old school, he always handles business calls on a landline. Even the fact that they have a landline is ridiculous, but it does work in her favor today. There's another phone in the kitchen. Cora creeps back and lifts it from its cradle.

"I blame that boyfriend of hers, honestly, for getting Summer in with the wrong crowd. And her friend Grace Godwin. Nice kid, broken family and all. She needed stability, and we were happy to provide it," Julian Cartwright was saying, his tenor voice too loud against Cora's ear. "Not that I think any of her friends killed her, nah. They probably just got her in with the wrong crowd, maybe there was a drug situation. Who knows?"

"I understand," Cora's dad says. "Those two aren't the type of kids I'd want Cora spending time with either."

"Exactly. I've been kicking myself ever since—"

As quietly as possible, Cora sets the phone back in the cradle. Is it possible that her dad is really that judgy? And does Mr. Cartwright really think that Adam and Grace got Summer involved with drug dealers? It's laughable, actually. Adam will be the lacrosse team captain next year. There's no way he's into drugs. And Grace has never done anything wrong in her life. Cora would probably like her even more if she'd talk about someone behind their back or shoplift. Just once.

Silence follows, then the scrape of her father's desk chair as he stands, the same low groan he makes whenever he's pissed about work stuff. Before he can leave his office, Cora rushes outside with the trash bag of Summer's things to the narrow alley that separates her house from the Altamontes' next door. Obviously, she knows Summer had a book deal with Swift Eagle Press. Everyone knows. But what could the publishing company possibly be asking Mr. Cartwright for even before Summer's funeral? The book? The money back?

Cora shoves the trash bag deep into the Altamontes' can. Trash day is tomorrow. By noon, all of Summer's things will be in a dump far away from Cora.

All except the note. That's in Cora's pocket as proof that once upon a time, Cora was worth noticing.

Monday, September 28, last year, 3:07 p.m.
Westwood Preparatory Academy

*A warm breeze gusted under the overhang where students waited for
their parents in car circle. It was mostly freshmen and a few losers who
didn't have a friend with a car or a car of their own. Ugh. Cora was a
freshman, too, but she hated the car circle with every fiber of her being.*

*While she waited at the curb for her mom, Cora tried her best to
be inconspicuous so none of the upperclassmen hanging out with their
friends across the courtyard would notice her. She twisted the hem of her
burgundy school blazer between her fingers. She'd already unrolled the
hem of her plaid skirt so it was back down to no-more-than-three-inches-
above-the-knee as stated in the WW Prep handbook, which her mom
had totally checked and double-checked before school started, because
apparently, she was the type of mom who wanted her child to die a social
death before Christmas.*

*Across the courtyard, Summer Cartwright sat atop one of the picnic
tables, blazer slung over the leather bag beside her, shirt untucked
and tie loosened. Grace Godwin slouched beside her reading a copy of*
Wuthering Heights, *somehow making it look cool, and two guys from
the lacrosse team had a faux sword fight with their sticks, trying to get
Summer's attention. Cora would give anything to trade places with
Summer, or really, with Grace. To just . . . be a part of them.*

*"Hey! Cora, right?" A tall redheaded girl joined her on the curb,
breaking her concentration. "Do you remember if we had to do all of the
problems from lesson three point eight or just the evens?"*

Cora blinked at the girl, trying to place her. She must be in her algebra class. "Evens."

"Sweet." The girl held out a hand. "I'm Madison. I've been meaning to introduce myself to you."

Cora took a moment to clock Madison, to form her first impression, which was always the most important one. At least, that's what they taught in Cotillion, which Cora's dad forced her to go to even though no one really cared about that kind of thing on the West Coast, especially not in the twenty-first century. Madison's skirt was appropriate handbook length. Her blazer pressed. Shirt totally buttoned. Tie knotted at her throat. She was probably studious and respectful of authority. She seemed like everything Cora wasn't but her mom wanted her to be. Like the kind of friend her parents would be thrilled to have her bring home. That made Cora nervous. If other people saw Cora talking to Madison, they might assume that she was like Madison, even though inside, Cora was totally different or at least was planning to be soon. Next year, she'd be at those picnic tables, not here in car circle.

Across the courtyard, Summer slung her bag over her shoulder. Her brother's car, a blue Range Rover with the shiniest rims Cora had ever seen, was parked in the south lot right behind the car circle. Summer had to walk right past Cora.

She debated if she should say something back to Madison, if it would be worth the risk of Summer thinking that Cora and Madison were friends. Cora vaguely responded to Madison's rambles about algebra, but her brain scrambled for conversation starters. A compliment was always welcome, right? Everyone liked compliments.

As Summer passed a few feet away, Cora blurted, "Cute tote bag, Summer."

Summer stopped and smiled. "Thanks . . ."

"Cora."

"*Pretty necklace, Cora.*"

Summer moved on and Madison resumed the conversation where Cora had interrupted her, but Cora clutched the silver eternity necklace with the little diamonds in the middle she'd gotten for Christmas from her aunt.

Cora was relieved when her mom pulled up in the car circle in her cashmere cardigan twinset and pearls, all the style of Ann Taylor at designer prices, which Cora would never understand. But at least she could end the conversation with Madison.

"*Gotta go,*" *she said.*

"*See you tomorrow?*" *Madison asked.*

Cora nodded, but even though she'd see Madison at school tomorrow, she'd make sure they didn't become friends. She couldn't afford a friendship with her. She wasn't a Madison. She was a Summer, or she would be if she had anything to do with it. The problem was, she didn't know where to start.

Maybe she'd get highlights. Or a boyfriend. Or a whole new attitude.

TEN

Adam Mahmoud

Tuesday, November 3
6:15 p.m.

Adam drops his controller onto his bedroom floor and presses his head into his hands. Even though he knows he needs to keep streaming on Twitch to avoid losing followers and sponsorships, he isn't up for it. He's ready to explode from the pressure of the thoughts that roil inside his head. What if his breakup with Summer was the final straw that made her snap? Or what if the autopsy shows that Summer was murdered? What then? He's an easy suspect.

When his little sister bashes through his door hard enough her pigtail braids swing, he yanks his gold Zeus mask off his face. Samia thinks the mask's stiff expression and chunky curls make him look creepy. Maybe. But the mask also lends him a sense of mystery he doesn't naturally have. It makes him feel like more than he really is.

Adam picks up his controller from the carpet. "Samia! You know you have to knock!"

"Sorry." Samia knocks on his open door. The movement makes the sparkly butterfly wings she's wearing wave like she's about to take flight. "But did you die yet?"

When Adam got home from school, he promised Lea and Samia he'd play Unicorn Detectives with them as soon as he died in his game. He is always the villain, hiding somewhere in their apartment, and his sisters are magical unicorns named Sparkle Nose and Glitter Hoof who use their horns to solve crimes. Adam loves playing Unicorn Detectives with them, chasing them until they fall into a giggle pile on the floor.

So even though he's a mess, after the blood finishes trickling down the kill screen, Adam hits exit instead of respawning. He probably won't log onto his Man of Mythos Twitch account again tonight. Blasting mythical creatures to bits hasn't given him any relief or distraction since Summer died.

"Fine. Go count to thirty, Glitter Hoof," he says.

"Yay!" Samia bounces back out of his room. "Lea, Adam's ready to play with us now!"

After shutting off his Xbox, Adam crawls into the hall linen closet to hide and tucks his long legs up to his chest so he can close the door. He buries his head in his hands. No one at school said a word to him about Summer, which is worse than if they had. He knows they're talking about him behind his back. How could they not be?

The linen closet smells like the cinnamon candle his mom lights for her book club. If Adam had his way, he'd stay in here all night, fling open the tiny window that overlooks the highway. He'd let sirens and car horns and squealing brakes fill his head with their soothing cacophony.

"Adam!" Lea yells. "Your girlfriend is here!"

For a second, Adam freezes. His mind manufactures the image of

Summer back from the dead and waiting for him in his doorway. He takes a deep breath.

He opens the closet door to yell, "I don't have a girlfriend."

"Told you, Lea!" Samia says. "Adam is all alone."

"He's not alone. He has us."

"Have you even watched TV? He can't live in a house with us forever."

"Why not? My house is going to have lots of rooms."

"Yeah, but you said those were for your red macaw and pet cats you're going to get."

"That's true. Sorry, Adam, you have to get your own house!" Lea yells.

Adam groans. Yesterday morning after the party, his parents sat him down and asked him not to mention Summer's death to his sisters. *We will talk to them. We'll tell them eventually, but we want it to come from us.*

"Girls! That's enough." Adam's mom's voice carries down the hall. "Hello, Grace. It's been too long."

"Hi, Mrs. Mahmoud. It smells amazing in here. Are you making baba ghanoush?"

"I am! You're staying for dinner." It's not a question.

"I wish I could, but . . . I'm just here to ask Adam if he can drive me to the vigil? It starts in thirty minutes, and the buses are too slow." There's a muffled grunt. "Hey, girls. Hug too tight. Can't breathe."

Lea and Samia's giggles grow louder as they run back to their room.

"I'm sure he would be happy to," Adam's mom says. "But you come to dinner soon, okay? Bring your mother."

"I will."

Adam doesn't miss the fact that Grace had checked the bus schedule before asking him for a ride, even though she knows he's going anyway. Not that he wants to go. The police will probably be there. He hasn't talked to them since Saturday night when he walked them through his version of the night's events, but it's only a matter of time, isn't it? He just broke up with Summer last week. He has to be at the vigil to publicly mourn her death, to look just the right amount of sad, or the LAPD might start digging into his life. The last thing he needs is to get pulled down to the station, especially when his whole life, his dad's taught him to avoid police if possible, to be respectful if it's not. Hands up if he gets pulled over, hood down at night. But what would that mean in a murder investigation?

He meets Grace by the front door. She's wearing black jeans and a maroon sweater with her gold bar initial necklace. "Do you mind driving me tonight?" she asks.

"Of course not." Adam grabs his keys from the hook his mom command-stripped to the wall by the door. "Bye!"

"Bye, Mrs. Mahmoud."

Adam's mom hugs them both for a little too long, knocking the scarf she's tied in her dark hair askew. She's still in her scrubs from her job as an elementary school nurse. After years of study dates and street soccer and popsicles on the balcony, Grace is a part of their family. At least she was until Adam started dating Summer and fractured their relationship somehow.

Samia runs back down the hall. She's smeared her eyelids so heavily with blue shadow that particles dust her long eyelashes. "Hey, Gracie, will you be Adam's new girlfriend so he doesn't have to live in a house by himself when he's a grown-up?"

"Nope." Grace tickles Samia's belly until she folds in half with laughter.

"Hey!"

"Punishment for silliness. Sorry not sorry." Grace winks when Lea pouts. "Do I need to tickle you, too?" Lea runs screaming down the hallway.

A dull ache fills Adam's throat. He's missed this, missed Grace. For so many years, he told himself that she was like his sister, but seeing her with his actual sisters proves to him that he hasn't felt that way about her for a long time.

"Ready?" she asks.

"Yeah, let me just grab my jacket." He pauses on his way to the door to whisper in Samia's ear. "It's a good thing you're cute. Otherwise, I'd keep Lea and return you to the sister store."

"Nuh-uh. You love me too much." She pinches his arm, then runs away.

A few minutes later, when he and Grace are buckled into his battered Jeep and wedged in traffic, he turns down the radio. "Sorry about Samia. She's going through . . . a phase or something."

"Long phase."

"Just ignore everything she said."

"It's just me, Adam." Grace looks out her window. "I know where we stand."

He doesn't, but he doesn't know how to ask. Instead, he rolls down their windows to let in the evening air—hibiscus and car exhaust—and cranks the radio so loud he can't hear his own thoughts.

When they arrive at WW Prep, it's almost dark. The sun sinks behind the school so the sprawling jacaranda trees are dark silhouettes against the park. They leave Adam's car in the lot behind the football field and walk to the gazebo in the park's center, where Harrison has arranged for a sound system, a huge portrait of Summer on an easel, and a projector screen for a slideshow. Already, the area hums with activity. Cellphones blink on and off like fireflies where their classmates gather in uncomfortable groups, clutching their arms across their chests and shifting their weight from foot to foot. How many selfies will be posted tonight with #RIPSummer? How many tribute posts will be written? The area in front of the stage is half-buried under flowers and lit candles, teddy bears with angel wings and FOR-EVER IN OUR HEARTS posters.

"This is so weird." Grace rubs her right palm with her left thumb. "What now?"

"Wait, I guess," Adam says. "I'm sure it'll be starting soon."

"Grace!" Blossom jogs around a park bench to join them. Her eyes are lined in black instead of purple tonight, and her hair is braided to the side. "Didn't you see my texts? I sent, like, a million and one offering to give you a ride."

"Oh." Grace glances at her phone. "No, sorry. I was—"

"Busy?" Blossom raises her eyebrows at Adam. "I brought a blanket for us to sit on."

Before Adam can decide if Blossom is inviting him to hang out with her and Grace or if he'd be safer with the other lacrosse guys over by the trees, Grace grabs his elbow. "There's a news van here from KTLA."

"Where?"

Grace points to the left of the stage.

"Is the reporter interviewing Cora Pruitt? Gross." Blossom shades her eyes against the stage lights to better see the reporter who's holding a microphone out to a blond girl. "Ugh, she is. Cora must be living her dream right now. All the attention."

"Maybe," Grace says. "Summer—"

"Was the actual worst and made more than one person's life hell, including Cora's. Some of us just had enough self-respect to leave her alone." Blossom crosses her arms. "Blanket's over there, Grace. You coming or what?"

"In a minute." She rolls her eyes at Adam when Blossom leaves. "Blossom's just bitter because Summer always called her Wednesday Addams. I actually feel a little bad for Cora. I've gotten pulled along by Summer, too, you know?"

"Who hasn't?" Adam knows all about Summer's sweet smile paired with the sentence, *Will you do me a little favor?*

On the other side of the stage, Harrison Cartwright, his face drawn and tense, speaks to a woman in a pantsuit. Adam doesn't recognize her, but there's something about her upright posture that's off-putting.

"Do you know who that is?" Adam asks.

"I don't think so. Another reporter?"

But as the park fills and Harrison waves the woman away so he can mount the stage, a man joins her. Dark brown skin, close-cropped graying hair, a tailored suit, hands in his pockets. The sight of him makes Adam sweaty. He expected this, but expecting something doesn't always make it easier. "Is that . . ."

"Detective Mwanthi. The detective who talked to us Saturday night. Yeah." Grace wraps her arms around herself, one of the first signs that she's about to start spiraling. "Why is he here? This is for family and friends, not a . . . a police investigation. What does he think he'll find out?"

Adam grabs her hand to reassure her but drops it again when the detective's eyes flick in their direction. Adam looks away before they make eye contact. What if the police start to suspect his feelings for Grace? He knows how that could look.

The more Adam avoids Detective Mwanthi's gaze, the more people he recognizes in the previously anonymous clusters hidden by the twilight. Oscar and Laney to his left, both holding lit candles. Avalon James with a tall guy Adam hasn't met. Mr. Cartwright on his cellphone. Mrs. Cartwright in a lawn chair at the front, fanning herself with a program, her brave smile pasted on. Summer hated that smile, the one that said, *Life is terribly hard, but we do our best.* Mrs. Cartwright wore that smile when Summer scuffed her leather sofa, when people asked about Harrison's impractical major, when she fought with her husband over politics or money or whether salt should go in a shaker or a grinder.

Harrison clears his throat to begin his presentation, but just as he's thanking everyone for coming, the dull murmur of voices in the crowd crescendos to a roar as people look at their phones. Grace's forehead creases.

"What is it?" Adam asks.

She holds out her phone, open to Instagram. "I don't understand . . . Summer's account. There's a new post."

The_Summer_Cartwright
#RIPMe 💀 🫥

.

Word's out, I guess. I'm dead! Lol #awkward! Will someone please make sure they don't mess up my contouring for the funeral? The number of people who can pull off a good natural makeup look seems to be dropping by the day. Also none of those too-cute kid pics in the slideshow at the vigil. I want to be remembered as I was—a girl who got what she wanted when she wanted it, even if it hurt someone else. I wonder if that's why I'm dead? 💬 #FoodForThought

.

BTW, there's a huge candlelight vigil for me tonight in the park behind WW Prep, and I know you're all dying to be there. A little bird told me I'm not the only guest of honor— my killer will be in attendance, too, holding a candle and pretending to care. 👀 Sweet, no?

.

Swiiiiipe to see pics of the people who might have wanted me dead. Incidentally they're the exact same people who found my body. Hmmmm. They don't know this, but I'm not the only one who knows their secrets. 💀 Take note and take care, frenemies. Just because I'm dead doesn't mean your secrets are. #oops

.

#RIPSummer #YouKnowYouLoveMe
#OrIsThatFeelingHate?

.

Hugs and kisses from beyond the grave,
SumSum 🖤

₪ 🖤 ▸

⏲ 1 MINUTE AGO

PART 3

#PerfectlyImperfect

ELEVEN

Grace Godwin

Tuesday, November 3
7:17 p.m.

Killer? Summer's killer?

In the moments after Grace reads the new post on Summer's page, the park fades in her vision until the jacaranda trees and benches look like crayon drawings. Her brain can't process this. For a millisecond, Grace believes that Summer wrote the new post herself. Of course death hasn't stopped her. Nothing could.

Beside her, Adam tenses, his own breathing ragged as he curses under his breath. Grace also forces herself to breathe, to focus. No, it wasn't Summer who wrote the post. Of course not. Someone—some horrible, cruel person—is screwing with them. That has to be it. But who?

There are five pictures in Summer's post, starting with one of Summer smiling angelically, her skin dewy, her eyes shiny, her tan glowy.

Grace might puke.

Stop, stop, stop, stop, stop. She cannot panic, at least not outwardly. The detectives are here, they're watching everyone's reactions to the post, and Grace can't afford to lose it. And why is she freaking out now? Summer's been dead for three days. Shouldn't this freak-out have happened Saturday night? Granted, Saturday night, everyone assumed Summer killed herself or OD'd or had an accident. No one jumped to the extreme of murder, even after seeing the writing on Summer's face. Yeah, that was weird, but it didn't mean someone killed her.

Across the faces in the next photos, their names are emblazoned in red font—Adam, Laney, Cora, and . . . Grace. There are no motives listed in the post, but that doesn't matter. Summer did know her secret, the Big One, which is why Grace worked so hard after their fight to win back Summer's trust. How could she afford to let Summer go when she knew everything?

A warm hand touches her elbow. "Who could have written that post?" Adam asks.

"I have no idea. Oh my god . . . what do we do?"

"I don't know."

The murmurs of the crowd dull the sappy music Harrison chose. Grace doesn't want to listen to the gossip that's already spreading, but the voices are all around her. She squeezes her eyes shut.

"Oh my god, murder? Are we safe? What if it's a serial killer?"

"Do you think one of them actually murdered her?"

"Her brother's kind of weird, don't you think?"

"She was so beautiful. I bet it was Adam Mahmoud. She dumped him, right? Maybe he couldn't handle it."

"Did you hear she had this huge book deal? They paid her like a bajillion dollars."

"Maybe Grace did it, like as a jealousy thing? Did you hear they had a massive—"

When Grace opens her eyes again, Adam isn't the only one in her field of vision. The detective she talked to Saturday night and the poised woman with the slicked-back bun wait a few feet away. Their expressions are grave.

Grace knew it was possible that if the police determined Summer's death was murder, they could suspect her, because she was there, she found the body, she was Summer's best friend. And now, her name is on a list on Summer's Instagram page. So yeah, she's freaking out, like a lot. She's not okay.

"Grace, I'm Detective Lombardo," the poised woman says. She gestures to the male detective beside her. "You remember Detective Mwanthi?"

Grace nods, her throat too tight to speak.

"We'd like to speak with you again regarding Summer Cartwright's death. Does tomorrow morning work for you? Say, nine o'clock?" Her tone is polite, but Grace isn't foolish enough to think she has a choice.

"Why me?"

Detective Mwanthi smiles. "In every murder investigation, we have to start somewhere."

Murder? Grace closes her eyes so hard little dots of light float behind her eyelids. It's her nightmare, getting pulled into a murder investigation like this, all the attention. Around Grace, her class-mates clump together in even tighter groups. She hears them whisper *murder* more than once. People know Summer was murdered, and whether she likes it or not, they know that the police think Grace could be connected.

"What about school?" Grace asks. "I have perfect attendance, and there's an AP Lit test tomorrow, and—"

"We'll write you a note. I'm sure your teachers will understand."

Beside Grace, Adam is frozen, like the detectives are T. rexes and they can't see him if he doesn't move, though actually, that's a misconception purely based on *Jurassic Park*'s use of frog DNA in T. rex genetic makeup. And like real life T. rexes, Grace is sure the detectives see Adam, too. After all, Summer's post says he has reason to want her dead. News straight from the (un)dead source.

Grace nods. "Okay. I'll be there."

"Great. See you then."

The detectives meander back through the crowd, him with hands in his pockets, her with confident strides, as though they are in their own little worlds. But they're listening to the gossip. How could they not be?

Grace tugs Adam toward his car, desperate to be home with her mom, to cry in the privacy of her own bed, but it takes them almost ten minutes to weave through the crowd. Their classmates are too curious, even their friends. A few guys from the lacrosse team block Adam's exit to teasingly ask him if he knocked Summer up and had to kill her, but behind their joking expressions, Grace can tell they're partially serious. Even Blossom seems uncertain when she grabs Grace's arm to stop her.

"You okay, boo?" she asks.

Grace shakes her head and tries to push past to the parking lot. She feels like she's choking on her own air.

"I know you didn't kill Summer. But it does look bad, you know?"

"Leave her alone, Blossom." Adam takes Grace's elbow. "We're leaving."

"Maybe it's better if you guys stayed home for a while," Blossom says. "Until this blows over?"

"It's not your business."

Grace can't speak. As she and Adam push through the last of the crowd to his car, she can't help but think that none-of-your-business was Summer's main business. Summer could be toxic, but she wasn't the only one, was she?

RIP.Summer.Cartwright

.

We lost a beautiful person this weekend. 🪦 Since Summer's account was disabled (we hope temporarily!) after that new post showed up during the vigil, we've decided to turn our fan page into a memorial page. So if you're seeing our username and wondering who we are, we used to be @SummerCFandom16.

.

We will always remember Summer for her gorgeous long hair, for her bold fashion sense, and for the way she could laugh at herself and be so real in a world where everyone wants to look perfect online. As you may know, the LAPD has confirmed that Summer's death is an active murder investigation. And like many of you, we want to know who killed Summer. She deserves justice!! Earlier today, we found out that the police have opened up an anonymous tip line for anyone who has real information. If you know anything, call, call, call!!!

.

Swipe for our favorite pics of Summer, a true down-to-earth Cali girl and our forever hero, and don't forget to take the polls linked in our bio!! Who really killed Summer in your opinion? Adam or Cora? Laney or Grace? Or is it someone else? So far, there's a CLEAR lean toward Adam Mahmoud, but we're curious to see what happens when we put him in a bracket against Grace. It's always the ones closest to the victim, right?

#RIPSummer #JusticeforSummer #TooYoungtoDie
#16Forever

₪ ♥ ▶

🕐 NOVEMBER 3

See all 68 responses.

L.Miy2006 This is twisted. I hope you're happy.

RIP.Summer.Cartwright lol @L.Miy2006 you
would say that bc you don't want anyone
looking at you. 🙄 🙄

Sunshine.and.lemonade
@L.Miy2006 @RIP.Summer.Cartwright
innocent until proven guilty, right? Summer
wouldn't want us to turn on each other!!

A.man.duh Idk I don't think it's Adam. Too
obvious. If he was planning to kill her, why
dump her?

RIP.Summer.Cartwright So who @A.man.duh?
Didn't see your response in the poll. 😶

A.man.duh I don't think it's any of the 4. My money's on the brother. @RIP.Summer.Cartwright

JennaK14 @A.man.duh literally what would be his motive? People don't just kill people for no reason.

L.Miy2006 💀 💀 💀 Just wait until you hear about serial killers @JennaK14.

A.man.duh @JennaK14 Money. Jealousy. All I'm saying is that this is probably way more complex than most people think.

TWELVE

Cora Pruitt

Tuesday, November 3
11:31 p.m.

Cora and Amanda sit curled up on the microfiber sofa in their living room. They've got pints of ice cream. They've got fuzzy blankets. Their faces are slathered in green rejuvenating masks. It should be the ultimate sisters' night in, except it isn't, because Cora can't stop thinking about her face appearing in the new post on Summer's Instagram at the candlelight vigil along with the worst accusation she's ever faced. Murder. The LAPD believes that someone took Summer's life on purpose. What if they take the accusation against her seriously? What if people at school think she's a killer? Cora has never felt so helpless.

And if the lack of information isn't bad enough, all Amanda wants to do is talk about Summer's murder. Why does she have to be so into murdery podcasts? Why couldn't she like smutty fan fiction or nail art?

Around a huge bite of her Pistachio Pistachio ice cream, Amanda asks, "Do you think whoever posted on Summer's account is right?"

"Are you asking me if I killed Summer?" Cora digs her spoon into her Netflix and Chilll'd as hard as she can and glares at Amanda. "Because as my sister, I would think that you would at least—"

"I'm not! Calm down. I just mean, do you think one of the others might have done it if this person seems to think you all have motives?"

"I have no idea."

"What is your alleged motive anyway? Jealousy? Obsession?"

"Oh my god, Amanda. I hate you so much sometimes."

"Just asking."

"Well, don't. I don't have a motive."

"Okay." Amanda licks her spoon. "But if you did, you could tell me, and I'd still believe you're innocent."

"So nice of you."

"You need some serious therapy and probably meds of some sort, but I don't think you'd snap and kill someone."

Cora punches Amanda's arm so she drops a bite of ice cream into her lap. "I missed the day you got your BS degree in being the worst sister ever."

"It was an online thing."

"Ha-ha."

Despite the looks on everyone's faces as she left the vigil—the whispers and the stares—Cora's not ready to believe she's a real suspect. When she gave her statement to the detectives Sunday morning, they hadn't seemed to think she or anyone else murdered Summer. They said they were just getting the facts straight. Now, Cora's a little nervous, because if she gets arrested, won't she go to the main jail with, like, murderers and stuff? She can't go there. Also, her parents would be *so* mad at her.

That said, she has to admit that the attention felt kind of good.

No one has ever believed her to be capable of much, and even though murder is totally horrible, it's a little nice to think that people believe her to be capable of the planning needed to kill someone.

But it's still horrible.

"I just think you should be careful, is all. I wasn't going to say anything about this, but . . ." Amanda pulls her blanket closer around her shoulders. "I know you were hanging out with Adam, Grace, and Laney in Griffith Park a couple weeks before Summer was killed."

"What? How do you know?"

"I heard you talking to someone about it. One of your friends or something."

Cora doesn't remember telling anyone that she hung out with that group, but it is something she'd do. They were friends with Summer. It was worth telling, even after how poorly everything had gone that day. "Just because I hung out with them, it doesn't mean that— "

"No, but the police might think you guys planned something together, you know? It's too much of a coincidence that the four of you were together, then all four of you were named as people with motive to kill Summer. It's not like you usually hang out, right?"

Cora shrugs herself out of her blanket and stands, her ice cream forgotten in one hand. "You can't tell anyone."

"I won't. I haven't yet, have I?"

"No. But why bring it up?"

"I know you didn't hurt Summer, and the police should know that, too. But maybe they don't. So just be careful, okay?"

"How can I be more careful than I already am?"

Amanda rolls her eyes, and not for the first time Cora wonders why Amanda always seems like the older sister even though she's two years younger. "You and I both know how you are. You talk. You say things without thinking, and there's a tip line that anyone can call."

Amanda is right. Anyone could call with information. Summer pissed off tons of people to get to where she was, and the police should know that. Insider scoops are valuable.

"Maybe I should call the tip line," Cora says.

"And say what?"

"I don't know. That . . . we aren't the only four with motive. Avalon James could have killed Summer."

"What makes you say that?"

"They had that whole feud."

"I thought you and Avalon got along?"

"We do. She offered to let me do a closet account for her, but . . ." Cora bites the inside of her cheek. "I decided to focus on Summer."

"Do you know Avalon James killed Summer? Do you have any indication that that could be true?"

"No, but—"

"Someone is for real going to jail for this. You can't just throw accusations around like that." Amanda puts the lid on her ice cream and folds up her blanket. "I'm going to bed. Don't be stupid, okay?"

Before Cora can even begin to process her conversation with Amanda, she's alone in the living room.

Amanda knows she hung out with Adam, Grace, and Laney shortly before Summer's death. So what? She doesn't know about the rest of it because Cora's never told anyone, not a single person. She's fine. Everything is fine.

But as Cora brushes her teeth before bed, she can't help but think about what her dad always says. *The first person to come forward always gets the best treatment.* Maybe she should tell the detectives about what happened that day a few weeks ago in Griffith Park before one of the others cracks and tells. Would that hurt her worse, or would it prove to the police that she's willing to work with them, that she has nothing to hide?

She doesn't know what to do, not at all. She has no one to ask for advice, no one to talk to, and scribbling in her diary just lathers her emotions into a foamy mess. Even mindlessly scrolling through Instagram doesn't help, because how is it possible that girls her age are so perfect? They know how to pose, how to highlight their best angles, and how to laugh so they look cute and candid instead of like they just huffed a bag of sugar. And the clothes. God. Cora would kill to own a fraction of Avalon James's wardrobe, not to mention Summer's. The Prada. The Tom Ford. The Marc Jacobs, and not his line for Target. If only her dad understood that money was meant to be spent on beautiful things, not locked away in a hedge fund.

She clicks on an old picture on Summer's Instagram from the Books for Botswana charity gala last Christmas. Summer wore the most gorgeous silver slip dress with these chunky heels that shouldn't have worked but totally did. That gala was the first time Summer said more than a passing comment to Cora. If they hadn't talked at the gala, would Cora still be in this mess? Or would she be besties with Madison and passing algebra?

She rubs her forehead to ease her headache.

If the police think Summer was murdered, Cora has to give them other suspects as options. Amanda was just telling her the other day about one of her creepy crime podcasts. The police focused so hard on the husband of the murdered woman that they didn't open their eyes to see that her neighbor had hated her for years. What if the police don't search for other suspects?

Cora looks up Laney's and Adam's phone numbers in the school directory—thankfully she has Grace's from one time when she texted her about a post for her closet account, because Grace's number is unlisted—then grabs her phone and types out a text.

> If not us, then who? 🙄 If you're innocent like I think you are, the best way to prove it is to find out who did it. Should we meet?

In a weird way, like a really dark, weird way, she feels like she's in a movie, one with a band of unlikely friends who have to beat the clock to track the killer. Except wait! They're the suspects! Suspects in movies never get ignored, because they're either wounded souls, wrongly suspected, or else they're the killers.

While she waits for a response, Cora opens her jewelry box and takes out Summer's note.

Hey, C!!

Just wanted to say THANKS AGAIN for everything and sorry about the other night. Don't worry about the others at school. They're small-minded people who will never understand what it feels like to go after what they want, not like we do.

Anyway, come to my Halloween party next week. You're the only sophomore invited. That's how grateful I am to you for what you did, and for keeping our secret.

You're the best everrrrr!

XOXO,
SumSum ♡

Will it look worse for Cora if she tells the police about Summer's note or if they find out about it later? Then again, how could they ever find out? The note isn't online. There are no other copies. Cora folds it back up and slides it beneath the necklaces in her jewelry box. It's safe to keep it.

Summer thought that Cora knew what it was like to go after what she wanted, but does she? Not really, not like Summer did. What if what Summer wanted was dangerous? Is it possible that's what got her killed?

Maybe it's time for Cora to go after what she wants, and if that's dangerous, well, maybe a little danger would make her life more interesting. That can't be a bad thing.

Friday, December 13, eleven months ago, 9:18 p.m.
Museum of Contemporary Art

*Cora's self-loathing was at an all-time high. Only her mother would make
her go to a black-tie gala in this stiff, stupid dress. The lace around her
neck was going to give her a rash. At least it was black like everyone else's,
but god. How was it possible for such an ugly dress to cost so much? All
around her, women dressed in the most beautiful designer gowns flitted
between tables that required a minimum $5,000 donation per seat. Men
in tuxes sipped from crystal champagne flutes. Between the crisp black
tablecloths and white anemone centerpieces, it was almost like the room
was leeched of color except for the greenery wall surrounding them.*

*Supposedly, the gala tonight was all about education for children in
Botswana, but Cora knew better. It was about seeing and being seen,
about middle-aged women proving they could pull off backless gowns still
because they'd spent every morning in hot yoga and barre classes. It was
about the young and the rich flirting and making valuable connections
for down the road.*

*And Cora was in a dress that looked like it should be worn by a
creepy porcelain doll. No wonder she seemed to attract the Madisons of
the freshman class, even after she'd dyed her hair blond, started loosening
her uniform tie, and regularly didn't turn in her algebra homework.
Sometimes, she hated her mother.*

*So when her mother wasn't looking, Cora escaped the main ballroom
to wander one of the museum galleries. It was dark aside from the
emergency lighting on the floors, but the stark walls made it seem lighter.*

She paused in front of a long painting—black with flecks of neon—when she heard footsteps and turned to find Summer Cartwright.

In her silver slip dress, Summer looked way more mature than Cora, even though she was only a year older. She carried an entire bottle of champagne with her. "You too?"

"Me too . . . what?" Cora asked, then immediately wanted to punch her own face for sounding so dumb in front of Summer Cartwright. The Summer Cartwright.

"Bored. I might die if I have to smile at some old guy my dad works with and say 'Oh yes, thank you so much, I have grown up since you last saw me' one more freaking time." She sat on the waxed floor and tucked her legs beneath her. When she saw Cora staring at the champagne bottle, she held it out. "Want some?"

"How did you get it?"

"I asked the waiter."

"And he said yes?"

Summer shrugged. "Yeah."

Cora sat beside Summer and took a swig from the bottle. It burned a little in her nose. "I asked two different waiters for a glass and none of them would give it to me."

"It's because you're too nice. Only kids are nice at things like this. All of the adults know that nice gets you screwed over."

"That's so depressing."

"It is what it is." Summer drank deeply from the bottle. It was far from full. "You've got to put yourself first because no one else will." Her voice echoed off the gallery walls.

"But—"

"So what if you had a thing for a guy who was single but then you found out he was into another girl? Would you just watch him fall for her, or would you do something about it?"

"What if . . . I don't know . . . they were meant to be together?"

Summer's mouth turned down. For a long moment, she stared at the neon painting across from her. "You're sweet, Cora."

It didn't feel like a compliment, so Cora didn't say anything. Instead, she looked at the artwork on the walls and wondered for the hundredth time who decided which art was good. Cora had always liked this museum. It was simple and mostly empty, which made each piece of artwork feel more expensive even though it would have been worth the same amount in a storage closet. Maybe that was the point—to make the paintings look more expensive than they were. Did the way things seemed to be matter more than the way things were? Is that what Summer was saying?

Still . . . "You can't always think about yourself," Cora said.

"Why not? How do you think my dad's gotten as far as he has?" For a fraction of a second, Summer looked so heartbreakingly sad that Cora wanted to give her a hug. Then Summer shrugged. "Hollywood isn't for the weak."

"But you could hurt someone."

"Believe me, Cora. No one has ever cared about what I wanted but me." Summer drained the rest of the champagne. "I should get back. My dad wants to introduce me to some businesswoman he thinks I'll find inspirational or whatever. Can't wait to see my boring future."

Summer left, but Cora couldn't move. Summer was right. When had anyone ever bothered with Cora at all? Her dad was so busy with work, he didn't even talk to her outside of family dinners, and that was just the expected how-was-school-don't-do-drugs type stuff. Her mom only cared about Amanda.

It felt like a revelation.

When Cora rejoined her family in the ballroom a few minutes later, she wasn't quite the same sweet Cora whom Summer had left behind.

THIRTEEN

Grace Godwin

Wednesday, November 4
8:56 a.m.

Grace squirms in the police station's waiting area, hating the way the skin between her uniform skirt and knee highs sticks to the pleather chair. She's by herself. After driving Grace to school yesterday morning, her mom got stuck in traffic and was late to work. If she's late again, she'll get a written warning. They can't afford for her to lose her job. Honestly, Grace can't afford to miss school, even if she does get an excused absence, because she's missing a test today in AP Lit. She can feel potential scholarships slipping through her fingers.

When Gina dropped Grace off at the station fifteen minutes early for her interview, she signed a release form stating that Detectives Mwanthi and Lombardo were allowed to speak with her minor child, but not before instilling the fear of God in Grace in the parking lot.

"You don't tell them anything personal, got it?"

"I know, Mom."

"And if it feels like they're trying to manipulate you into saying something specific, you shut up and leave."

"I know."

"You have nothing to hide. So be helpful. It's about balance."

"What if a reporter—"

"You don't talk to them," Gina said. "And if they try to take a picture of you, you remind them you're a minor. They aren't allowed to run any photos with your face in them. This will all blow over."

But when the precinct secretary tells Grace she can go to room two, she feels anything but balanced. What if she says something that makes her look bad? What if she forgets to mention something and the detectives think she's hiding information?

She pokes her head into room two and is surprised at how normal the room feels. Crime TV shows always make it look like the interview rooms are sterile and poorly lit, surrounded with one-way glass so other cops can watch suspects' reactions. This room is painted light blue, and on the folding table in the center of the room, there's a small vase of wilting flowers. In the back, there's a coffee maker and a basket of dusty-looking tea bags. Detective Lombardo stirs sugar into her cup. Her hair, loose around her face, is center-parted and slick, effortlessly professional.

Detective Mwanthi, dressed today in navy pants and a white button-down, gestures for Grace to sit at the table. "Thanks for coming, Grace. Coffee? Water?"

"No thanks." She sits in the metal folding chair. It's cold against her back, but she can feel her muscles relax, just a fraction.

Detective Lombardo joins them. "Before I forget to tell you, we called your school this morning to let them know where you are. The secretary said she'd get a message to your teachers, and it wouldn't count against your attendance record."

"Oh. Thanks."

"Sounded like it will be no problem for you to make up your test at lunch today."

"Great." Relief washes over her, and she's so grateful to Detective Lombardo that she wants to make it up to her by giving her something worthwhile. She stiffens. Is that how it works? Make the interviewee owe you? Because if so, Summer would have made a fabulous detective.

"We record all of our interviews." Detective Mwanthi crosses one leg over his opposite knee and rests a finger on a recorder. "That okay?"

It's so not. What if she says something dumb? But she squares her shoulders. "Yeah, of course."

"You're probably wondering why we wanted to talk to you again today."

"Does it have to do with the new post on Summer's account last night?"

"It does, in fact. You may know we spoke with Summer's brother, Harrison Cartwright, a few days ago?"

Grace hesitates. This isn't the direction she expected the conversation to go. "He told me."

"You've been holding out on us, Grace."

"What . . . do you mean?"

"Harrison mentioned you have access to Summer's Instagram account. She shared her passwords with you. Is that so?" Detective Lombardo asks.

Grace swallows hard. "Um. Yeah, that's true. I just didn't think about it because I haven't logged in as Sum in forever. She gave it to me a few months ago. She had appendicitis, so she asked me to keep up with it for her while she was in the hospital. But that doesn't—" She strains forward as subtly as she can to see what Detective Mwanthi is writing in his notebook. He tilts it away from her. "It doesn't mean

I posted anything new on Summer's account. I mean, is it even the same password still?"

"We aren't accusing you, Grace," he says. "Just getting our ducks in a row. Mind sharing the password you have with us?"

"Summer with a three instead of an *E*, then heart all lowercase. Like Summer love." Grace pauses. "But can't you trace the location of the person who posted?"

Detective Lombardo slurps her coffee, then winces. "Worse every day. And no. Not if they're using a VPN to hide their location. The info on the post shows that the person posting was in . . . Where was it?"

"Dubuque, Iowa," Detective Mwanthi says.

"Right. Not likely that anyone there cares about Summer."

"She has five million followers!" Grace hears her own voice get louder and forces herself to calm down. "Some of them have to be in Iowa."

"Do you really think the person posting was in Iowa, Grace? Really?"

"No."

"Neither do we," Detective Lombardo says. "So it's up to us to find out who had access to her account. We'll disable it for now while we do some digging. Can you think of anyone else who might have her password?"

Grace wraps her arms around herself. How is she supposed to know when the right time to stop talking is? When it's best to be helpful? "I don't know of anyone else. But there must have been someone, because I didn't post anything."

There's a long pause, then Detective Mwanthi flips a page in his notebook and smiles again. Does he know Grace feels uncomfortable? Is that a bad thing?

"Let's talk about something else for a minute," he says.

"Okay." Grace forces herself to sit up straight with her hands in her lap. "Whatever helps."

"Great. You mentioned the other night that you checked off names at the door at the beginning of Summer's party, correct?"

"Yeah."

"How long were you at the door?"

"From about seven oh five until maybe . . . eight fifteen-ish?"

"And you didn't leave?"

Grace considers. If she tells them that she left her post to go to the bathroom, that's not a big deal, right? Everyone has to pee. They can't read anything into that, can they? She looks up from her hands to find Detective Mwanthi poised with his pencil over his notebook and Detective Lombardo appraising her with dark eyes.

She's paused too long to say no. "Just to go to the bathroom. I was nervous, and whenever I'm nervous, I drink tons of water." She cringes. Way TMI.

"How long were you gone?" Detective Lombardo asks.

"Why does it matter?"

Lombardo shrugs. "The devil's in the details."

"Maybe five minutes? The front hall toilet overflowed, so I had to use the one in the back hallway."

"Why were you nervous?" Mwanthi leans forward so his elbows rest on his knees.

Grace licks her lips. It feels like she's getting into dangerous territory, stuff that her mom would tell her to shut up about. But . . . isn't it true that lying to detectives or leaving out important info always comes back to bite suspects in the ass?

"Am I a suspect?" she blurts before she can stop herself. "I saw in the *LA Times* that—"

Lombardo smiles. "No suspects at this point, Grace. We're just trying to figure out the order of events, who was where, who may have
had motive . . ."

"Being nervous about the party doesn't mean I had motive to want
Summer dead." Oh god. She's steering herself closer and closer to personal, to volunteering information, to all the things her mom warned
her against.

"Of course not," Mwanthi says. "But a few people we talked to
at the party—kids from your class, I believe—did mention to us that
you and Summer had a fight a few weeks ago? You didn't sit together
at lunch for a few days, which was unusual. Did that play into your
nerves?"

Grace swallows. "I mean . . . yeah. We were fine again, but I wanted
everything to go exactly right. It felt a little like . . . like she was testing
me, like my loyalty or something?"

"Sounds complicated," Mwanthi says.

"You don't know teenaged girls, Mwanthi. Just wait until your
daughters get to be this age." Lombardo laughs. "I bet it was hard
being friends with someone like Summer."

Grace leans back in her chair. It *was* hard being friends with
Summer, and it was also intoxicating. Summer could make her feel
like she was the most important person in the world with a flick
of her eyebrows, or she could destroy Grace's entire day with two
words. Grace is on track to be valedictorian of her class, she has
more volunteer hours than almost anyone, she holds down a job at
the taco truck, and she is one of the top swimmers on the WW Prep
team. But somehow, her friendship with Summer became the most
important thing in her life, or at least, second only to her relationship with her mom.

Grace nods. "Summer never messed up."

"Really?" Lombardo asks. "Because on her Instagram, she's fairly candid about making lots of mistakes."

"She thought about every word. Self-deprecating gets more likes than perfect."

"You seem rather put together yourself," Mwanthi says. "Your résumé is impressive."

"It's decent."

"Did that bother Summer? Were you competitive?"

"No." Grace chewed the inside of her cheek. "Summer didn't need to compete with me. She had everything she wanted."

Almost everything. Grace was a nobody, the girl who did everything and still wasn't anything special. She was like every other applicant that the good colleges would get. Well-rounded, sure. Good grades. But statistically, Ivy League schools rejected more students with 4.5 GPAs and 1500 SAT scores than they allowed in. Besides, she wasn't interesting like Summer, and she never would be. That fact kept their relationship in a fragile homeostasis until the day Summer lost something she wanted to Grace.

"That should be all for today," Lombardo says. "Unless there's anything about your relationship with Summer you think we should know? Or your relationship with the others mentioned in the new post?"

For a moment, Grace is torn. Should she tell them about that day in Griffith Park when the four of them were all together, about their conversation that turned dark without warning? About how Summer set them up? No. It would only make them look bad. Besides, maybe Cora is right. Her text said she thought they should all work together to give the police new suspects. That makes sense.

"I don't think so?" Grace says.

The three of them stand as though choreographed, but when Detective Lombardo holds out a hand toward the door, Grace can't help but ask the question that's been weighing on her mind all week. "How did she die?"

"Excuse me?" Lombardo asks.

"I've been wondering . . . how exactly did Summer die?"

Detective Mwanthi tilts his head appraisingly. "What's your best guess?"

Grace can hear her mom in her head. *You shut up and leave. Shut up and leave.* Still, she wants answers. "It's just a guess . . . but there wasn't any blood, so if it wasn't an accident or suicide . . . poison, maybe?"

Lombardo nods. "You're right."

"Well . . . I thought . . . she puked, so what else could it have been?"

Mwanthi and Lombardo exchange a glance. Did she make a huge mistake guessing correctly? Should she have been more clueless?

"Summer did die of poisoning," Mwanthi says. "Though not like in detective novels. It was nicotine."

"From cigarettes?"

"Likely the liquid contents of an e-cigarette. Someone probably added it to something she was eating or drinking. Did you notice Summer consuming anything unusual at the party or while you were getting ready?"

"I don't think so? Nothing unusual. She was in and out of her room. She tasted all of the catered food, the lobster crostini for sure."

"We tested samples of the catered items. No nicotine."

"Did you . . . find it somewhere else?" Grace's heart is racing. She knows how suspicious it looks that she was the one there at the loft while Summer was getting ready.

"Not yet. But we will," Mwanthi says as he puts a hand on the doorknob. "What we do know is that someone dosed Summer with enough nicotine to knock out a horse."

As the detectives usher Grace from the station, offering her a ride to school that she declines in favor of the city bus, she stays calm, pleasant even. But she can't stop her brain from functioning on overdrive, listing all the information she knows about nicotine. Like nicotine causes dopamine release in the human brain. And it's as hard to quit as heroin. It's a stimulant, not a downer, so what was Summer feeling in the moments leading to her death? Did her heart beat like it was about to explode the way Grace's heart feels right now?

The_Summer_Cartwright

Life is a balancing act.

.

If you sweet followers are anything like me (and I have a sneaking suspicion we have tons in common 🙃), then you're struggling to find balance in your lives! Today in chemistry class, we talked about something called #homeostasis. I didn't listen to the entire lesson, because, bleh, but this is what I did take away—even in nature, balance is crucial for survival.

.

So how's a girl to balance school and extracurriculars and friends and a boyfriend? What girl has time for it all?

.

The answer? No one does have time for it all!! Here's the key, or at least what I've decided to focus on—#selflove first, and everything else after. Friends and boyfriends have to mesh in order for there to be time for everyone. So if I'm doing the beach with my girlfriends, I need them to be cool with my BF tagging along, and vice versa! There you have it. ✨Balance!!✨

.

So to recap, if you wanna be my lover, you gotta get with my friends. Just don't let your lovers get with your friends. Amiright? LOL! Thank goodness my bestie G and boyfriend A are sooooo good at this balancing act.
#SpiceGirls #wisdom #throwback #ButItsStillTrue

Love, SumSum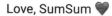

₪ ♥ ▶

🕐 OCTOBER 10, THREE WEEKS AGO

FOURTEEN

Elaine Miyamoto

Wednesday, November 4
4:22 p.m.

Laney cranks the volume on her computer until her headphones vibrate against her ears. She's at her desk in her new room, the desk that's stocked with anything she could ever want or need for recording, thanks to Rebekah. New software for her old laptop. Top-of-the-line microphone and headphones. A small mixing board. In the box at her feet, she keeps a conglomeration of her commonly used sound effect items—a staple gun for distant gunshots, a pouch of flour for snow crunching, gloves to flap for birds' wings. One day, she'll win that Emmy she and her mom dreamed about.

After school, she dragged Oscar home before he had a chance to even stop by his locker—she promised to let him borrow her textbooks—and ran straight to her room to record. She needed the silence of her sound effects. The aloneness that had nothing to do with loneliness. It's in the alone with her sound gear that she's closest to her mom, and she needs her mom today. Even though Laney hated Summer, she's the first person in her life to die since her mom and the first dead body she's ever seen. Her mom's funeral was closed casket.

Laney snaps a stick of celery to simulate bones breaking. In her mind, she hears metal crunching, the squeal of tires, a truck horn.

She shouldn't be so worked up by Cora's text asking her to help figure out who really killed Summer. It's not that weird that Cora reached out, even though they didn't really know each other and only spent time together once. That day was supposed to be a fluke. Laney didn't know the others would be there in Griffith Park. She was only there in the first place because Summer made her go, supposedly to take pictures of her hiking with her Hydro Flask and lululemons and PowerBoost bars for sponsored posts. Not that Laney was even a good photographer. She hiked all the way to the top of the trail to meet Summer, and Summer hadn't bothered to show up.

She set them up.

There's a light rap on Laney's door, then Rebekah cracks it open. Her brown hair is perfectly blown out around the shoulders of her work blazer, but she's replaced her heels with the slippers she calls house shoes. "Knock, knock! Can I come in?"

Laney considers pretending she can't hear her but instead takes off her headphones. If she hurts Rebekah's feelings, Rebekah might mention it to Laney's dad. "I guess."

Rebekah sits on the edge of the bed and smooths her hand over the gray quilt she and Laney picked out at Urban Outfitters a few weeks ago. She'd love it if Laney would share what she's working on. Share anything, probably.

"I just wanted to . . . check in, I guess?" She twists her wedding ring absentmindedly. "Make sure you're hanging in there after Saturday?"

Laney swivels her chair to face Rebekah. "Summer and I weren't friends."

"Oh, I know. Oscar told me. But—"

"I have a therapist, Rebekah." The thought of her and Oscar talking about her, discussing her, makes her blood boil. It's invasive.

"What happened . . . it's a lot. It's okay if it feels heavy."

When Laney doesn't respond, Rebekah's smile strains. "If you ever want to talk—about anything, not just Summer—I'm here. You could think of me like an aunt or something? Maybe as a friend?"

Laney doesn't know what to say, so she nods. "Yeah, maybe."

"Great." Rebekah goes to the door. "I was thinking I could pick up burgers for dinner? That new place has a vegan bean burger I hear is to die for. I mean . . . well. You know what I mean."

"Sure."

"All right, then." Rebekah tries to laugh away her discomfort. "And Laney? I know you and your mom—"

"If I wanted to chitchat with you about my mom, I would." Laney smiles woodenly until Rebekah leaves, then tears her headphones from around her neck. Rebekah has no idea what she's talking about.

When Laney is certain Rebekah has left to get the burgers, she pads in her socked feet into the kitchen, which Rebekah—of course—keeps stocked with every vegan snack Laney likes, even though Laney never made her a list or anything. She just notices things. God, why couldn't she just be an absent stepparent, one who always worked or didn't really care? It would be so much simpler. To love Rebekah would be to betray her mother, and she'd never do that. Besides, she has no interest in starting over a year and a half before she leaves for college.

In the kitchen with its exposed brick and dark metal and white walls washed with sun from the skylights above, Oscar sits on one of the leather barstools eating his afterschool Fluffernutter sandwich. He's changed from his uniform into a pair of sweats and a white T-shirt.

"Still eating like a five-year-old, I see." Laney pulls a new bag of Takis out of the pantry and plops in the stool beside him.

"Still bitching at my mom like a pubescent middle-schooler, I hear."

"Whatever."

"She's just trying to be nice."

"I know." Laney's voice rises. She suspects she was in the wrong, but she'll stick her face in the garbage disposal before she lets Oscar see that. "She's just so . . . here all the time."

"It's the worst, isn't it? A parent who cares?" He uses the tip of his finger to get peanut butter off the roof of his mouth. "Speaking of parents. Before he left for golf, your dad asked me to tell you that if a detective calls, you are not to talk with him. At all. Whatsoever."

"Has a detective been calling?"

"I have no idea. But your dad did a lot of hand gestures that made the whole conversation very intense. I couldn't possibly replicate them."

"Try."

Oscar shoves the last bite of sandwich into his mouth and flails his arms around, one finger pointed, with an expression of solemn duty on his face. Laney can't help but laugh.

"She does have a sense of humor!" Oscar says.

"Don't get used to it."

"I won't." Oscar narrows his eyes. "Hey, sorry about school sucking so bad this week."

"It's not your fault."

"I'm still sorry."

"Well, I'm sorry the love of your life is dead."

Oscar laughs. "Summer was not the love of my life. The inspiration for my longing, perhaps."

"What does that mean?" Laney shoves a handful of Takis in her mouth, not bothering to wipe the corners of her lips.

"She was the girl I could never have, and as such, completely safe. And that, Elaine. That, is poetry." He rests his palms against the quartz countertop to give himself leverage to stand. "Good luck with your calculus homework. It's impossible, and the answers are not in the back of the book."

Laney gives him a thumbs-up and eats another handful of Takis. The answers are never in the back of the book, not for math and not for life. She wishes they were, because then maybe she wouldn't be so torn about working with Cora, Grace, and Adam to find Summer's killer. If she sticks her nose in where it doesn't belong, it could look suspicious.

Who's she kidding? Of course she's going to do it. If she doesn't, they might find out about her deal with Summer and think it's motive enough for killing her. She's not close enough to them to know whether they'd throw her under the bus. She responds to the group chat:

LM:

Ok. I'll start brainstorming.

Laney takes the Takis to her room and shoves her headphones back over her ears to fill her head with snaps and creaks that she created. Alone, but not lonely. Alone, but free. That's the best she can ask for, isn't it?

Saturday, July 18, three months ago, 10:23 p.m.
Cambridge University Dormitory

*"Hey, Laney? Could you do me a little favor?" Summer smiled at Laney
from where she was propped up in her dorm room bed.*

*Even though their program was only a month long, Summer
had brought her own pillow and quilt to brighten up the space.
According to Summer, people wanted the influencers they followed to
be both relatable and aspirational. And navy dorm blankets weren't
aspirational.*

*It was the second week of ISSOS at Cambridge, and Laney still
wasn't quite sure how to take Summer. She'd started to sense a pattern.
For every gram of kindness Summer showed, there was always a little
favor expected in return. Even before her mom's death had changed her
forever, Laney had never been the girl who had tons of friends. Still, she
knew that a series of reciprocal favors wasn't friendship. It was a business
transaction, and she was tired of it.*

"Pretty please?" Summer prompted.

*"What do you need?" Laney sighed and swiveled her desk chair
around to face Summer. She was trying to format new audio clips for her
production class, but whatever.*

*"I'm about to post to my story, and at home, I use a ring light. But it
was obviously too big to pack when I flew out here. Could you hold this
lamp, like . . ." She shoved a desk lamp into Laney's hands. "Yeah, like
right there. Perfect. Don't move."*

"You know they make mini ones for your phone—"

But Summer had already tapped her phone's screen and pasted on a bright smile. When she spoke, her voice was a hint brighter than her everyday tone. "Hiiiiiii, everyone! It's me, SumSum! It's past ten here in jolly old England, and I had a revelation today I had to share with all of you!"

Laney wasn't sure when Summer would have time to have a revelation, because their days were jam-packed with activity from breakfast at eight until after dinner at six. She barely had time to pee, much less contemplate the universe. It was great—no time to worry about her dad's wedding or listen to the family counseling podcast her dad had sent her about blended families. He couldn't even be mad she wasn't listening to it, because she was doing extra school.

"You guys know I'm all about self-love and self-acceptance, etc. and today, during my meditation time, I imagined myself running past all of the old versions of me who were unfulfilled, the old versions of me who only wanted to make other people happy, the old versions of me who ate lunch in the library because I didn't have anyone to sit with."

Laney schooled her face to hide her skepticism. Or tried. There was absolutely no way that Summer was ever the girl who ate alone, even in middle school. Summer's Instagram was full of fake modesty like that. Oh, I was wait-listed for ISSOS, but here I am, living a dream!! It was a load of BS. When you had money like Summer's family obviously did, you didn't get wait-listed. But Summer was smart. She knew that the world loved a good underdog success story.

"When I got to the end of the road, I saw that I had overcome my problems, and all the old versions of me were there, surrounding me, cheering me on. And you can have that, too! Be your own squad before you let anyone else distract you. Love you all the most. Mwah!"

Summer ended her livestream and chucked her phone on the end of her bed. "I'm exhausted."

Laney shook her head and laughed as she handed Summer back the light. "Unbelievable."

"What?"

"Nothing." When Summer raised an eyebrow, Laney shrugged. "I can't believe people buy the live-your-best-life visualization crap you're peddling."

Summer crossed her arms over her chest. "Excuse me?"

"You eating alone in the library?" Laney said as she climbed the ladder into her bunk. "Come on."

Summer stood so she was just below eye level with Laney on the ladder. "Fine. You caught me. Sometimes I embellish things to make myself more relatable. To give people something realistic to aspire to. I'm such a terrible person."

"I'm not criticizing." Laney pulled herself into bed. "It's working for you. Clearly you're making bank. Props."

"It's not about the money. Believe it or not, I care about my followers."

"I never said you didn't."

"Just because you don't care about anyone—"

"Whoa." Laney put her hands up in front of her. How had the conversation turned so quickly? "I care."

"Really." It was a statement, not a question, like Summer didn't believe her. When Laney didn't answer, she nodded. "You know what, you're right. We don't know each other."

"No." Laney pressed a fist to her eyes. She really did care, sometimes so much it was a physical pain. The thing was, she didn't know how to let herself feel it, because the last time she really loved someone, she'd lost her. Everyone—especially her dad, who was about to move on in the biggest way possible when he married Rebekah—seemed to think that three years was enough time to get over her mom's death, but it wasn't. "I *shouldn't have teased you about something you care about."*

"It's fine." Summer hopped off the ladder. Laney could feel the bed shift as she climbed into the bottom bunk. "Clearly we both have some damage."

"No kidding," Laney said.

Being vulnerable wasn't her thing—it terrified her—but that was exactly what she decided to be. Maybe it was because she couldn't see Summer that she had the courage. Maybe it was because her mom's death was always at the forefront of her mind, ready to spill out anyway. Either way, Laney told Summer about her mom's car accident, about how she was exhausted driving home after her twelve-hour shift at the hospital, about the truck her mom drove into.

Summer listened so quietly, Laney wasn't sure she was still awake when she finished talking. Then Summer cleared her throat. "Sounds like you guys were close."

"We were."

"And you had thirteen whole years with her."

Laney buried her face in her pillow. "It wasn't enough."

"You don't get how lucky you are."

"How am I lucky?"

"You had a mom who cared so much about you that three years later, you still miss her. Having someone to miss makes you lucky."

And before Laney could process the depth of sadness in Summer's voice, Summer rolled over so the bunk creaked and turned out her light.

FIFTEEN

Adam Mahmoud

Wednesday, November 4
4:31 p.m.

Adam parallel parks his Jeep three spots behind Picante, a cherry red food truck with a giant jalapeño painted on the side above the slogan *Sauce at your own risk*. Grace works there every Wednesday after school and most Saturdays. He's dying to know what the detectives talked about this morning at her interview. School was the wrong time to ask. Too many people listening who would give their left kidney for the gossip. And yeah, he could have texted, but he can't read Grace's facial expressions over text.

Tonight, Picante is parked near the donut shop on Highland Avenue, one of Grace's favorite locations because of its proximity to a bus stop on the same line as the bus she takes from school. Adam likes Highland Avenue, because even though he's lived in LA his entire life, there's something about the way the palm trees frame the white buildings, the way the street stretches all the way to the hills like a perspective drawing that's appealing. He's not obsessed with celebrities like most of his classmates—some of his classmates *are* minor celebrities with bit roles on the Disney Channel or are kids of major stars—but he's not immune to the possibilities that the Hollywood sign represents. Wealth. Fame. Success. Who wouldn't want those things? Who wouldn't want to be remembered one day as a somebody instead of just another guy who did okay?

Adam gets in line to order. Grace doesn't notice him at first, because she's too busy adding pickled red onion to the top of the famous shrimp tacos that always saturate her red Picante T-shirt with the smells of ocean and burn-your-mouth-out hot sauce. Behind her, steam rises from the grill where her boss, Sofia, face flushed from the heat, sautéed marinated steak. It smells like heaven—if heaven were built out of Cali-Mex.

When he gets to the front of the line, Grace blinks in surprise. "Oh. Hey, Adam. I thought you had lacrosse practice?"

"Coach cut our training short. His wife called."

"She having the baby?"

"Sounds like it."

"So no more practice this week? Nice."

Normally, Adam would love a break from fall lacrosse. Games were all scheduled in the spring, so fall was for training—practice shots to take, laps to run, weights to lift—all time he could be using to build up his Twitch channel. But according to his parents, universities cared about athletes, not gamers, and they didn't work overtime for Adam to ditch college for video games. They didn't understand the money he was on the verge of making, the fact that if he succeeded, they'd never have to put in extra hours again.

Now, though, Adam craves the mindless repetition and physical exertion of lacrosse. If he works his body hard enough, his brain can't think about Summer.

"So what can I get you?" Grace asks.

A conversation. Reassurance. Adam takes a deep breath. "One chicken, two steak, all the toppings."

"Sure."

Grace takes the cash he hands her, makes change, and turns away to prepare his food. He's just about lost hope that he'll get a few minutes to talk to her when she hands him the paper carton of tacos, pico de gallo drizzled with lime crema spilling from the top onto their hands.

"One second." She holds up a finger, then calls over her shoulder to her boss, "Mind if I take my fifteen, Sof? The line isn't too bad."

"Yeah, honey, go talk to your . . . friend?" Sofia raises one eyebrow at Adam, then hands Grace a steak taco wrapped in foil. "And you eat something, too. You look pale."

They go to Adam's Jeep to sit. When Grace is nestled in the front seat, knees pulled up to her chest, she flicks his ear. "You're an idiot."

"What are you talking about?"

"You think I don't know you're here for details about my police interview?"

"That's not true." Adam tries to keep a straight face, but as the tension flows out of his body, it's replaced by giddiness. Being with her is good for him. She reminds him of simpler times. "I really needed tacos."

"Well, don't let me stop you from eating them." Grace stares at him until he takes a bite of steak taco. It's so normal it hurts. "Hey, what did you think about Cora's text?" she asks.

Adam swallows his bite. "What does she think we're going to do, aside from drawing more attention to ourselves?"

"I don't know, but Cora's a loose cannon. Better to know what we're getting into, don't you think?"

"Won't it look worse for us if we butt in? Why not just let the police do their jobs? You going to respond?"

"I already did," Grace says.

Adam's phone is still on silent from school. He yanks it out of his pocket and reads the texts.

LM:

Ok! I'll start brainstorming.

GG:

I can try to get the video Harrison took during the party

CP:

Yayyy! Thanks! 🖤 I'm going to talk to Avalon ASAP.

LM:

👍

Just seeing Harrison Cartwright's name gets under Adam's skin. Grace is way too good for that guy. No, there's nothing inherently wrong with him, but Grace needs to be with someone more thoughtful, someone who understands her anxiety, someone who's willing to go out of his way to be there for her to listen when she has a bad day. Someone like . . . him?

"So you're still going to hang out with Harrison?" Adam asks. "Even with the hair? And the camera? Even after . . ."

"I do need to get the video." Grace folds her arms across her chest.

Adam has to watch it, or he's going to royally piss her off. It's rare for Grace to lose her temper, but when she does, it's intense. "I just think it's safer to stay out of it."

Grace pulls the foil off her taco and takes a bite. Kicking off her flip-flops, she rests her feet on Adam's dashboard. "No one's making you help."

What Grace doesn't realize is that all she'd have to do is ask him. He'd do anything for her, and it's both terrifying and electrifying. After breaking up with Summer, he thought maybe he'd have the chance to tell Grace how he feels—how when they're in a room together, he instinctually knows where she is even when he's talking to someone else, how he sometimes goes to the park hoping to run into her, how much he regrets not seeing her, really *seeing* her, in the first place. And now everything is complicated again by Summer's death.

For now, he settles for asking about her interview. "How *did* it go for you today . . . with the detectives?"

"Ha!" She points a finger at him. "I knew it."

"Were you seriously going to leave me hanging?"

"Yup."

"Heartless."

Grace laughs, but her face quickly grows solemn. "The detectives seemed to think I was the one who wrote the new posts on Summer's account."

"Why?"

"Because . . ." She pauses to take another bite of taco, holding one hand under her chin to catch any juice so it doesn't stain her work shirt. Adam's seen her use the strategy before. She's stalling, because inside, she's freaking out, and she doesn't want her freak-out to spill out. It has nothing to do with tacos. "Harrison told them I had the password to her account."

Heat rises in Adam's chest. Screw that guy. "Do you have it?"

"She gave it to me when she had appendicitis."

This is bad, Adam knows. Summer didn't just give her password out to anybody, so if Grace has it, chances are good that she's one of the only ones.

"I also asked them how Summer died," Grace continues.

Adam rests his forehead in his hands, leaning so far forward his tacos almost dump out of their carton. It's not like he thinks that Summer will be magically resurrected, but there's a part of him that doesn't want details, because details make it more real. "What did they say?"

"That it was nicotine poisoning. They think she maybe drank the stuff inside an e-cigarette." Grace nods at him, her calm facade wavering when he widens his eyes. She curls her legs to her chest. "I really think we should talk to Harrison, because he—"

"What do you see in that guy?" Adam lets his annoyance color his words.

"He's actually really sweet. Maybe a little much sometimes, but—"

"Sweet? For all we know, he killed his sister!"

Grace stiffens. "For all you know, I did."

"C'mon, Grace. You know what I mean. Harrison is a douche bag. He isn't right for you."

"Why do you care?" She gets out of his car, her face flushed. "I'm with someone else, and suddenly you have opinions about who I date? You had years to care." Grace slams the passenger-side door closed and backs away from the car. The top is off his Jeep, so Adam hears her clearly when she says, "Harrison is nice to me. He wants *me*. Go home, Adam, and leave me alone."

Adam regrets saying anything. "Grace, wait. I'm sorry! I didn't mean to—"

But she turns her back to him and goes to the Picante truck. He watches as she pulls her silky hair into a ponytail, squares her shoulders, and returns to work like nothing happened. Like he never happened.

Adam drives home on autopilot. He finds his apartment empty. Not a huge surprise since his dad works late most weeknights, and his mom takes the twins to ballet, but when he opens the fridge to grab a can of Coke, he finds a note his mom left for him on the door.

Adam—You have an appointment with Detective Mwanthi tomorrow at 7:30 a.m. Let's please talk when I get home.

He doesn't want to talk. All he wants to do is log into *Mythos* and lose himself for a few hours, be someone whose monsters can be slain, monsters that look like actual monsters with dripping, sharp teeth. Those are easy to deal with—one good chop with a digital sword, and they disintegrate. But in reality, monsters wear human masks. They go to school and work, they have friends. They could look like Cora or Laney or Grace or him, and the detectives know it.

He groans and responds to the group text, the only thing he knows to do right now to get Grace back on his side.

AM:

I'm down. Let me know what I can do to help.

The_Summer_Cartwright

Let's talk about getting out of our #ComfortZones.

.

If I had to pick my biggest #fear—and that would be a challenge, because if I'm being real, there are a lot of them—it would be the fear of stagnation. Of never growing or changing or becoming someone other than who I am now. Don't get me wrong, I'm not hating on myself. You guys know I'm all about #selflove!! 🩶 But I don't want to stay the same forever.

.

I rep some AMAZING brands (huge shout-out to @PowerBoost, @TheAccessoryBar, and @CutieBox) and I've partnered with tons of great companies, but I got to thinking, what if I branched out to helping other influencers . . . influence? And as weird as it sounds, my first project has nothing to do with #fashion or #decor or #wellness or any of my other hobbies. It's 100 percent out of my comfort zone!!

.

So please meet @ManofMythos. He's a—drumroll please—professional #gamer looking to build his following here on IG! For this whole week (I know, right??!!), you can find the link to his Twitch channel in my bio. He'll stop at nothing to win! 💪.

.

So maybe this week, get a little out of your comfort zones and give @ManofMythos a follow. I've never met him in person, I have no idea what he looks like because his whole persona is that he plays silently and wears a mask, but word on the street is that he's a snack. I like to imagine him with killer green eyes. But who knows? That's the fun of it, right? The #mystery? AND he's totally coming to my Halloween party! Anyway, let's be real, when you first log into #Mythos (because I do my research!!), the theme song playing while the avatar of that toga-wearing warrior flexes is such a vibe. 🔥 Swiiiipe for pics of said warrior. #HottieWithABody

.

As always, you guys are adorable, keep sending those sweet DMs, and I love you five-ever.
SumSum 🖤

ɯ 💜 ▶

SIXTEEN

Grace Godwin

Thursday, November 5
7:07 a.m.

Grace has never experienced a silent car ride with her mom, but this morning is something special. While she drives Grace to school in her battered fifteen-year-old Corolla, Gina talks a mile a minute about everything from cuticle care to a new recipe she found for traditional Russian borscht. They aren't Russian. They don't own a blender. But sure, blended beet soup for dinner sounds great.

"You're quiet this morning," Gina says.

"You're not."

"That's a little sassier than the Grace I'm used to."

"Sorry." Grace leans her head against the passenger-side window. Part of her regrets agreeing to help Cora figure out who killed Summer. Maybe Adam is right and distance from the case is the way to go, though after their argument last night, she doesn't want to admit that he has a point. "I'm just tired."

Even though Grace is desperate to sleep, her dreams are haunted by Summer. Not by the Summer who lay dead on the bathroom floor, not even the Summer whose face was known by five million people.

Grace is haunted by the eleven-year-old Summer who found her drinking lemonade at the mall food court and gave her a pair of dangly leather earrings from the two-pack she'd just bought, because she thought Grace had the perfect neck for them and she knew Grace couldn't afford them herself. She's haunted by the Summer who stood on tiptoes to kiss Adam. By the Summer who was genuinely happy when Adam's arm was around her. She's haunted by the Summer who shed her hard exoskeleton when they were alone at the beach, who waded up to her knees in the ocean and let the waves spray her legs until her denim cutoffs were speckled with water spots. Who sometimes almost told Grace the things that made her vulnerable, things that Grace knew instinctually but wanted Summer to be able to say out loud. Like, *I'll never be good enough for my family,* and *I don't really know who I am outside of the person I've created online,* and *I don't know what I want out of life, but it's not this.*

Grace is haunted by five years of friendship destroyed by two mistakes. She's haunted by the knowledge that even before the mistakes, their friendship was already fundamentally broken and flawed, so that the harder she worked, the more desperate she became to be the perfect friend, the more she pushed Summer away. She'd become needy. Summer hated that.

"Are you not sleeping well?" Gina takes her eyes off traffic to press a worried hand to Grace's forehead. "You don't feel hot."

"I'm not sick, Mom."

"Let's get some fresh air in here." When Gina rolls down her window using the hand crank, they're hit by a blast of exhaust from the truck in front of them. It makes Grace's head ache more than it already did. "Anything I can do to cheer you up?"

"I'm really okay."

"We could get coffee on our way. There's a drive-through on—"

"No thanks. I'm cutting caffeine."

"Since when?"

Since her heart palpitates at random times, stopping for a beat, then hammering harder to make up for it. "It's for swim team. Coach thinks it'll help my times."

"Oh, I know! We could play the three things game."

Grace freezes. "Why?"

"Just for fun!"

They haven't played the three things game since Grace was in middle school, but it used to be their go-to car activity. Their goal was to list and explain the things they would each bring from their apartment if they had to leave right then and they could only take three. Snacks and clean underwear were givens. The three things game was all about the extras. For example, when Grace was eight, she always picked Pippi the hippo (in case she needed snuggles on the road), *A Wrinkle in Time* (her favorite book), and the little album that had her only baby picture, her tiny little footprints in ink, and the curl of hair from her first haircut. Memories were important to her. Still are. Pasts are elusive when your family motto is "Always forward, never back."

Gina hums under her breath. "I'd bring that snow globe you bought me for Christmas last year, the one from Santa Monica. And my curling iron. And . . . hmmm . . ." A car lays on its horn when Gina slows to a crawl. She gives them the finger out the window and slows down more until the car zooms around her, almost clipping her bumper. "I hate LA people."

"We're LA people."

"We are not. We might live here for now, but we're not the same."

A panic bubble starts to form in the back of Grace's throat. No. This can't be happening, not again. Her chest squeezes until it's hard for her to breathe. "Oh my god. Is that what this is about?"

"What?"

"Are we moving again?"

"Not right now. But I was thinking . . . maybe in the summer—"

"I'm not moving before my senior year!"

"No need to freak out."

"Clearly there is!"

Gina's eyes grow shiny with tears around the edges. "Don't you want a fresh start after all this? Everyone here knows who you are. It's only a matter of time before your picture gets picked up by the media—"

"I'm a minor. They aren't allowed. You said that."

When Gina puts on her blinker to turn into the parking lot of WW Prep, Grace grabs her backpack from the floor by her feet and flings open her car door. She doesn't want to leave LA. She likes it here, her job, her school. And yeah, things are tough right now, but wouldn't leaving be running away again?

"Just think about it," Gina says.

"I'm not leaving, Mom. The Excellence Grant—"

"I don't give a damn about the grant!"

Grace flinches. "What?"

"What is it anyway? A few thousand dollars? You think money is more valuable than your life—"

"Here I have a chance at a life!"

"People live well all over the world, Grace—"

"But *my* people are in LA." She can't breathe. She can't. Oh my god, she can't leave again, not when she feels so normal sometimes.

Adam is here, and she needs him in a way she can't quite wrap her mind around, even if he does only see her now because Summer is dead.

Gina's eyes shine brighter. "I'm not enough for you? Is that what you're saying?"

Grace knows exactly what to say to make her mom feel better. It only takes three words. *You are enough. You are enough. You are enough.* But she doesn't say them. For almost three years, she's worked herself half to death to qualify for the Excellence Grant, to make sure that her résumé is padded with swim team and honor society and every AP class the school offers so that she has the same chance of going to college as her classmates with money.

Grace slams her car door closed without saying good-bye. Behind her, she knows her mom's heart is breaking, but she doesn't turn around to confirm it. If she turned, she'd run back to the car to give her mom a hug, to say the words. But the thing is, Gina *isn't* enough for Grace forever. She can't be. Gina thinks life is like an Etch-a-Sketch. Draw until you run out of room, then wipe the slate clean and start over. But life should be a museum of memories and experiences and friends, collected and stored with care.

As she stands on the steps of WW Prep watching the Corolla pull away, Grace's phone buzzes. Three texts from Harrison, one after another.

HC:

Hey, babygirl. You busy after school?

HC:

I really need to talk to you.

HC:

Want to come over for dinner? It's cool with my parents.

Grace types no, then erases it. Then types sure and erases that, too. She doesn't want to hang out with Harrison after school, but she also knows how important it is for her to get the video footage from the party from him.

With her mom's words echoing in her ears—*I don't give a damn about the Excellence Grant!*—Grace responds to Harrison.

GG:

I'm free now. Want to grab coffee?

HC:

You sure?

GG:

Yeah. Pick me up by the west side doors at school?

HC:

I'll be there in 10.

The_Summer_Cartwright
#BestieBrag #BookDeal

.

Okayyyy, just had to take a minute here to brag on my bestie G again! 👯 Many of you saw (and liked!!) my announcement post yesterday about my upcoming debut #memoir All Your Likes Can't Buy Me Love, out in March from @SwiftEaglePress! You guys may not know that not only is my bestie a cutie pie (back off boys . . . she's dating my brother!!) but she's also a total #genius.

.

So of *course* I asked her to proofread a chapter or two of my book! She was soooo excited to read the chapters about her! Haha! She has so many great thoughts about her chapters, things I should add or take out, not to mention great feedback on my style. I think I shocked her with my writing skills! 🤓

.

Literally, I *pray* that all of you have a bestie as awesome as mine. I can only hope I'm as good of a friend to her as she has been to me. Don't worry, @ohmygodwinGrace I have major plans to pay you back! 😎 #FriendshipGoals

.

XOXO,
SumSum 🖤

₪ ❤ ▶

└ ○ OCTOBER 6, ONE MONTH AGO

PART 4

#RealOrNothing

SEVENTEEN

Adam Mahmoud

Thursday, November 5
7:28 a.m.

A dam accepts the cup of coffee Detective Lombardo offers him and hands it to his mother. She took extra time with her makeup today and is wearing her lone pantsuit instead of her usual cartoon-print scrubs in an effort to look professional. Adam's in his school uniform, freshly ironed and tucked, his student leader pin fastened to his lapel.

Even though Adam assured his mom there is no reason for her to worry, she isn't stupid. She knows how it looks that Adam and Summer broke up less than a week before her death, but as she sips her coffee at the table in the middle of interview room two, Adam can tell she has relaxed, at least a little, mostly because Mwanthi struck up a conversation about the Egyptian origins of the last name Mahmoud and told her all about his family in Nigeria. Adam, on the other hand, is tense. Even though he told Cora he'd help, he woke up this morning more certain than ever that the best course of action is to stay as far away from the investigation as possible. He doesn't care if Cora feels like being Nancy Drew.

"Let's jump in, shall we?" Mwanthi presses the button of his recorder. "I will need to record, but this is just a formality. Info gathering."

"It is?" Adam prepared himself to be grilled, to have the detectives certain that he is Summer's killer.

"It's clear why your photo was in the new post on Summer's page. The two of you dated. You broke up. It would be weirder if you weren't there."

Adam's mom leans forward. "Then why do you need a recording? What will you do with it?"

"It's for our records. We need to build a time line of the night of Summer's murder. Every piece of information is helpful."

"So . . ." Adam pauses. "You don't think that I—"

"Not in the slightest," Lombardo says. She sits at the table across from Adam's mom and smiles reassuringly. "We have other, more interesting suspects."

Does she mean Grace? Because as much as Adam is relieved to not be a suspect, he doesn't want her to be one either. Adam knows Grace, knows her inside and out. They've been friends since the first day of sixth grade when he invited her to sit with him on the bus because she was new to LA and didn't have any friends yet. It would take a strong motive for Grace to even criticize someone, and what motive did she have? Summer wasn't mad at Grace for what happened, not really. She was mad at Adam. It had been all his fault.

"All right." Mwanthi grips his knees with both hands. "For the record's sake, did you have any motivation for killing Summer Cartwright? Motive doesn't mean you did it. Just that you could have had reason, so don't hesitate to tell the truth."

"No," Adam says. It's a lie, but how could the detectives possibly find out about the other thing? "I broke up with her."

"Yes, I have that in my notes. Great. Were you surprised to still get an invite to Summer's party?"

"Not really. She liked drama."

"Speaking of drama, did Summer know that you're Man of Mythos?" Mwanthi asks.

Adam hesitates. "Not at first? But yeah, by her party, she knew."

"Did you ask her to boost your account?"

"No, she did that all on her own. She felt like her account was getting stagnant, and she needed to show varied interests." All Adam wants to do is crack his neck, then his knuckles, but he read somewhere that it's a nervous habit and he doesn't want to seem nervous, suspect or not. Anything Summer did served her own purposes. It didn't matter that he had been her boyfriend at the time. If she hadn't wanted to boost his account, she wouldn't have.

"Right. Next question. Are you surprised to find out that Summer died of a heart attack?"

"What?" Adam blinks. "I thought it was nicotine poisoning."

Lombardo raised an eyebrow. "Have you been talking to Grace?"

Shit. Is it bad that he and Grace hung out, that she told him about the poison? His mom pinches his knee under the table, and he knows what it means. Watch it. Be careful.

"It's not a crime to talk to Grace," Lombardo says. "It's understandable. You were both there, you both found Summer."

"You've been friends for some time as well. Is that correct?" Mwanthi consults his notebook.

"That's correct," Adam says. "And yeah, we talked a little last night."

"On the phone?"

"No, I met up with her at her work."

"You two ever dated?"

"No." He glances at his mom's blank face. If she had her way, Adam would never have dated Summer in the first place and would be half-married to Grace already. He knows she's not happy with the way things turned out, but there's also a part of her that's reveling in her *I told you so.* "Grace is like my sister."

"More coffee, Mrs. Mahmoud?" Lombardo asks.

"Thank you, but no. I need to get to work soon, and my son needs to be in class. Are we almost finished?"

"Almost," Mwanthi says. "Just a few more questions. Now that you're single again, Adam, you have no interest in pursuing a relation ship with Grace? It would be convenient. Summer out of the way, you could move forward with no baggage."

Adam folds his arms over his chest, ignoring his mom's second knee pinch. "I'm in high school, man. It's not like a divorce."

"All I'm saying is that I get the feeling that breaking up with Summer might have been a lot messier than you're saying. Why'd you dump her anyway? She seems to be the type of girl you hold on to."

"We were just too different. We wanted different things."

"Such as?"

"Like . . . when I first started dating her, she wanted me to stand out, be the homecoming king type of guy. And I thought I wanted that, too." It was exciting for a while, all the attention. Being a some-body, the guy who everyone said hello to in the hallway at school. Even the teachers had been nicer to him, like he was the moon reflecting the glow of Summer's sunshine. "But the pressure . . ."

"Too much?"

"Yeah. People looking at you all the time, pretending to be someone I'm not . . . I hated it."

Lombardo rests her chin on one fist. "Think you broke her heart?"

Adam considers. "Honestly, I don't know. I hurt her, but she could have had anyone. If she hadn't died, she'd probably be dating someone else already."

"All right. Last few things." Mwanthi looks up from his notebook. "In my notes here, I have that you arrived late to the Halloween party? Why was that?"

"Traffic was rough. I was in the middle of a raid in *Mythos*. And . . . I don't know. I think a part of me questioned if I should even show up. I didn't want to play into Summer's drama."

"I told him not to go." Adam's mom clutches her purse in her lap like a shield. "Why go to a party thrown by a girl you're no longer seeing? But he insisted."

"I didn't want to be a jerk. Summer and I still had to go to school together, you know? Keep the peace?"

"Understandable," Mwanthi says. "So you arrived, then what?"

"I talked to Grace for a bit, said hi to Summer, got some food . . . then we saw Summer's new post and thought she was setting us up for a murder mystery party."

"We?"

"Grace and me."

"What was your first thought when you found Summer in her bathroom?"

What had he thought once the initial panic had subsided, once he knew for sure that she was gone and not just passed out? It's strange how that evening can be both stamped in his mind forever and feel so vague it's like it never even happened.

"I thought," he says slowly, "that Summer would hate everyone looking at her when she was like that."

Monday, October 26, 3:15 p.m.
WW Prep Courtyard

Summer texted Adam during seventh period.

SC:

Meet me in the courtyard after school?

He told her he had lacrosse practice, but she was adamant that she needed to see him, that it was important. When she breezed out of the building after the last bell rang, shirt already untucked, her leather bag slung over one shoulder, he forced himself to smile at her like everything was normal instead of eroding like the cliffs alongside the Pacific Coast Highway.

In the sunlight, her hair was gold and lemons, and her lip gloss was shiny. When she met him where he stood under one of the red oak trees, he reached for her hand. She took a step back, her eyes radiating hurt. He flinched. She hardly ever looked like that.

"What's going on with you, Adam?" she asked.

"What do you mean?"

"You've been keeping things from me. I know you have."

Adam's stomach dropped. What did she know? That he was thinking about breaking up with her? About what happened with Grace? When had he let his life get so damn complicated? A year ago, he hadn't had any secrets, and even though he'd felt like he was becoming an extra in Summer's life, at least the background was safe.

Summer held out her phone, open to her Instagram page. "You unfollowed me? What the hell?"

He winced. While stuff like that didn't seem like that big of a deal to him, he knew how important it was to Summer. But with five million followers, he hadn't thought she would notice. "It was just . . . getting hard, you know?"

He was tired of watching her live online as a whole different person. She'd changed over the past year, almost like achieving her dreams was slowly poisoning her instead of making her happy. Now she wore as much of a mask as he did playing Mythos, *so much so that he had started to lose track of who Summer really was. Maybe she had, too.*

"Hard?" Her voice was louder than she probably knew. Or maybe she did know that other students in the courtyard were starting to stare at them. A few guys from the lacrosse team. Oscar over on a bench by the parking lot. Blossom texting at a picnic table, her AP Lit book open in front of her. Grace beside her, her face stricken. "Oh, okay. Well, I'd hate for you to have to work or sacrifice literally anything at all to support your girlfriend."

"I just want to have a normal relationship. I'm tired of faking happy with you. Can't we hang out sometimes without you posting about it?"

"It's my job to post about it. Sorry if that makes you so unhappy." Her jaw clenched tightly, and Adam knew that for once, he'd hit her at her core. Who was Summer if not The Summer Cartwright, the perfectly imperfect girl millions of people followed? Who was she if it was just the two of them together? "There's nothing I can do about that, Adam, and you know it. The book—"

"You already sold the book. You just have to finish it, so why not take a break from the show?"

"Show?"

"Stop posting everything online and just live for a second."

"Are you ashamed of me?" she asked. "Is that what this is about?"

"No, of course not." Adam reached for her again, but she moved even farther from him.

"Because I've forgiven you a lot."

He crossed his arms. What did she mean by that? He'd been far from perfect—he knew that—and Summer didn't deserve to be treated the way he treated her. But this pressure, this always wondering if she meant what she said or if there was a layer of passive aggression . . . it was too much. "I can't do this anymore."

"Do what?"

"The fighting. I feel like I'm walking on eggshells all the time."

"If I'm so hard to be around, then maybe we should just break up." Summer wrapped her arms around herself. Her gaze was defiant.

As much as Adam could see he was hurting her, the thought of not having to live the lie anymore was like an antidote to the expectations that had little by little been killing him. So instead of arguing with Summer or begging her to forgive him and agreeing to be better like he usually did, he nodded.

"Maybe we should break up," he said.

For the first time ever, Summer only stared at him, her mouth open, but behind her eyes, there was a loneliness so deep Adam almost told her never mind, that he still loved her. He didn't want to be the guy who hurt her, not when she looked so fragile. Adam glanced toward the picnic table to gauge Grace's reaction, but she was frantically gathering the textbooks and highlighters she'd taken out to study with Blossom.

"Are you for real right now?" Summer said. "My party is in, like, a week. All my sponsors expect—"

"Look, I'm sorry." He ran a hand through his hair to get it out of his face. "I'll still come to your party, but I need to focus on school and lacrosse, and—"

"And Mythos?" She spit the words angrily.

He sighed. She really did know. "Summer, I—"

"At first, I didn't know why you didn't just tell me about your Twitch channel, because I could have boosted it for you, but now I know." She smiled, but it was a bitter expression that flattened her mouth. "I know all about what you do."

Adam's heart raced. Was she threatening him? Would she do that? Were the others right about what they said at Griffith Park the other week? He and Summer had dated for a year, and even though he knew she wasn't always nice, she'd never struck him as cruel.

Just as that thought ran through his mind, panic washed away the anger on her face. "I'm sorry. We can figure this out, can't we?"

"Look . . ." Adam had always been attracted to Summer's edge, to her ability to make him wonder what she was thinking even when they'd been together for months. Summer was exciting, a mystery. But maybe excitement was less important than understanding. He thought of Grace. The idea of patching things up with Summer again when he knew he loved another girl was just too much. Adam was nervous about what Summer would do if he ended things, but what other choice did he have? "Summer, you're great. It's just that . . . there's someone else."

Summer cringed at his words. He took a step closer to her. What did he think he could do to make her feel better? Hug her? Pat her on the shoulder? He didn't know how to break up with someone, because he'd never done it before.

"You think I'm surprised?" Summer asked. "You think I'm stupid enough to not know?" Even though she didn't break eye contact with him, he knew she was very aware of all the people listening. "Fine, Adam. Go die in obscurity with your someone else. Screw you both. I can do so much better."

And as she walked away, Adam couldn't catch his breath. Summer could make his life hell, and she wouldn't hesitate. How could he stop her?

EIGHTEEN

Cora Pruitt

Thursday, November 5
7:50 a.m.

Cora goes to the gazebo in the WW Prep courtyard instead of straight to homeroom. There's too much to do, too little time to do it in. Now that the others are on the same page, she needs to pursue her Person of Interest Number One. Avalon James.

It's unseasonably warm—in the eighties—so Cora peels off her burgundy school jacket before she nestles on the wooden gazebo bench, legs pulled up beside her. She doesn't usually come here in the mornings, because no one else does and being alone means missing social opportunities. She has to admit, though, it's peaceful. The air smells like freshly cut grass clippings, and she's got a great view of the rugby team playing shirts versus skins.

She takes out her phone. Avalon is, like, really great actually, so Cora feels a little bad for turning her over to the police as a suspect. A few months ago, right before her makeup line dropped, Avalon asked

Cora to start a closet account for her, too. Cora wanted to, but when Summer heard . . . well, she just wasn't comfortable with it.

Cora squashes her regret. It's not like she's accusing Avalon of anything. Far from it. If nothing else, it gives her the opportunity to defend herself.

Cora hits Avalon's name and the call button. The phone rings twice before Avalon answers, her husky voice everything Cora wishes hers could be. No one makes fun of sexy, smoky voices like they do high-pitched ones.

"Cora! Hi!" In the background, there's the murmur of voices, of liquid pouring, of dishes clattering. Avalon must be getting breakfast. "I was just thinking about you."

"You were?" Cora isn't used to people remembering her existence at all, so it feels nice for a change, which kind of sucks because now she feels even worse for calling.

"Yeah. You doing okay after everything that went down at the vigil the other night? I couldn't believe it when I saw your face in that post. Ridiculous."

"I'm fine." Cora tucks her feet beneath her on the wooden bench, careful not to scuff the leather of the flats she paired with her uniform knee highs. "A little freaked out, I guess."

"Understandable. So what's up?"

"I was just wondering . . . if I could ask you a few things about . . . um . . . you and Summer?"

Avalon pauses for a few beats too long. "Why?"

"Well . . . I'm just trying to figure out who could have it out for me. Like, why list me in the new post, right? And I know you and Summer were kind of close at one point?"

Avalon clears her throat. "I hadn't talked to her in months, Cora. I'm not sure I'm the best—"

"I saw you talking at the party."

"After what she did to me, she didn't even have the decency to take a selfie with me so I could prove that we're cool. To get my following back up again."

"I knew you had to shut down your Instagram account for a while, but—"

"Do you know how much money I lost because Summer *cancelled* me?" Her voice caught on the word.

"She never asked anyone to stop buying your makeup. She told me she just felt like she had to be honest."

"That's the thing. You don't get it, Cora, because you're still so . . . I don't know. Innocent. You don't get how the world works. If Summer had told her followers to cancel me, everyone would have thought she was a hater or racist or whatever. But the way she did it, she still got to be the sweetheart. She just had to be honest? Sure. 'Oh, everyone, look at this gross hair in my lipstick. Let me pull it out slowly so it's extra nasty. Poor Avalon tried so hard, but I can't recommend an unsanitary product.' Bullshit. She loved every second of it."

"Why would she love trying to end you? That doesn't make sense."

"Jealousy? No one was offering her a makeup line. Maybe the drama of it. I don't know, but I do know she could have chosen to just let it go or message me privately. But instead, she chose to make it a huge deal."

"Oh." Cora's stomach lurches. Summer had scored her an extra PR pack of Avalon's makeup, which made Cora feel really special. She'd even commented on Summer's post about the lipstick from her closet account, because she'd felt she had to back what Summer was saying. "I'm sorry if I—"

"I'm not mad at you. You got caught up in it. It happens. But twenty-four hours after that post, my makeup line was dead." Avalon's voice is more sad than bitter.

Cora feels as guilty as Summer in Avalon's fall from grace. She's thought about it a lot, about how she owes Avalon, but she can't think about that now when she has to focus on clearing her own name. As she looks out over the rugby field trying to figure out how to respond to Avalon, one of the guys knocks someone down hard enough that the coach blows his whistle to stop the game. He probably got the wind knocked out of him. But maybe that's what Avalon felt all those months ago when all her planning, all her dreams for a makeup line for all skin tones, foundations for every color, beautifully pigmented eyeshadow that popped on dark skin, came to absolutely nothing. Because of Summer.

"Did you offer to send new lipsticks?" Cora asks.

"Obviously, but no one reached out. It was too late. I lost sponsorships, money. By the next morning, I'd lost over a hundred thousand followers. People kept tagging me in hate posts and posting reels of themselves going to put on lipstick and finding, like, an entire cat worth of hair in the makeup with the *Psycho* violins in the background. Which . . . I know sounds kind of funny, but it ruined me. No matter what I did or said, no one was willing to give me a second chance. Or almost no one. But that second chance turned out to be bullshit, too."

"Second chance?"

"I wrote some stuff in a college workshop . . . like a screenplay or whatever? It was a murder mystery centered on influencers, not like based on me and my experiences, but using them. My contract, though . . . I should have had a better lawyer look at it. Whatever."

Cora's gut lurches. She doesn't want to throw Avalon under the bus, not after everything she's already been through, but she's scared. What if the police arrest her?

"Why did you go to Summer's party, then? If Summer hurt you that badly?"

The line grows quiet. "Listen, you're great and all, Cora. Really, I'm rooting for you. But I have to know . . . why are you asking me all of this?"

When the coach gives a hand to the downed rugby player and one of his teammates claps him on the back, Cora hangs up on Avalon without saying good-bye or thank you or anything else. Because how do you tell someone that you're planning to push them down instead of pick them up?

You don't.

Saturday, October 31, 7:33 p.m.
Summer's Halloween Party

Cora opened the door to the walk-in closet. Summer's closed bedroom door dulled the throbbing music and voices, and the quiet created a sense of isolation that Cora both loved and totally, totally hated. Like, it gave her a chance to pull out her phone camera to take pics—good—but it also added to the existential crisis she'd been having, the heavy feeling of loneliness that followed her around—bad.

She didn't want to get caught, and with the front half bath out of service for the evening, the risk was high. She'd seen multiple people wander back into this hallway looking for the second bathroom, but that worked in her favor, too. She could claim to be lost if anyone found her in Summer's room. "Oh, I was just looking for a more private bathroom! Female stuff! Ahahahahaha!"

That would work with anyone but Summer. Cora didn't want to see her for more reasons than one. Earlier, when she'd thrown her arms around Summer's shoulders to say hello, Summer had peeled her away with a look that made her want to sink into the floor or hide in the broken-toilet bathroom all night.

"Don't crinkle the silk," Summer said, then turned back to her conversation with a guy named Miles who was a huge influencer on TikTok with, like, two million followers who obsessed over the videos he posted of him stunting in high places.

Don't crinkle the silk. That had been it. After the personal invite Summer had given her to the party. After Summer boosted her account.

After all Cora had done for her. Don't crinkle the silk? She was more worried about her dress than Cora? All her fantasies about being friends with Summer crumpled like . . . well, silk beneath an unwanted hug.

Because Summer owed her for being so mean, Cora slid a pair of Tory Burch flip-flops into her tote, then pushed aside a clump of hanging shirts to see the bag shelves behind. Oh my god. Summer had the brand-new Birkin? The camel-colored pebbled leather one. They cost fifty thousand dollars. Cora's dad would've never ever in a million years considered buying her a Birkin bag even though he could have afforded one because of, like, investments and 401ks and saving up all his money, because whoever died with the most was the winner. Having money but not being allowed to spend it was worse than being poor.

Part of Cora was annoyed, because it was totally not fair, but another part of her wanted to be Summer, wanted to curl her shiny hair but not too much so it had the perfect beachy wave, to have that something that made everyone want to be near her. Why did Summer attract when Cora repelled?

She was snapping a few photos of the Birkin bag and Summer's casual dresses and sandals—she'd find the links online to post to her closet account so Summer didn't know she went through her actual closet—when she lifted a box and found Summer's laptop beneath it.

She shouldn't have snooped. It wasn't her business, and besides, the laptop was probably password protected, but she couldn't help herself. Summer was literally at her fingertips.

She lifted the lid. To her surprise, Summer didn't have a lock screen, and the Notes app was still open to her latest document. Cora checked the timestamp—last edited today at 1:36 p.m. As she scanned through it, her eyes widened. Was Summer for real? The document seemed to be drafts of new Instagram posts with excerpts from Summer's book. Cora had thought the book would be cuter—pics and Instagram how-tos paired with her already written posts—but this was a lot. If Summer told these stories in her book, if she even posted a snippet . . . Wow.

And Summer wrote these today? It looked like she was planning to post them on her Instagram, one a week for the next few weeks. Why was she suddenly so willing to destroy her friends?

Before Cora could read through all of them, she heard a low groan from outside the closet. Was someone coming? Panicking, Cora slid the closet door all the way shut with her foot and peered through the slats to see if anyone came in.

Nothing.

Then she heard a thud. Should she take her chances and dart back to the living room before someone found her sitting half-draped in a cashmere sweater she knocked from the shelf mostly-accidentally-but-a-little-on-purpose? She rolled the sweater into a tight tube and slid it into the bottom of her tote, too.

"Sum? You in here?"

Through the closet slats, Cora watched as Harrison poked his head into Summer's room. He glanced around, huffed in annoyance, ran a hand through his beautiful hair, and left. Good thing Cora didn't risk it for the biscuit. Ugh, she needed to stop saying that. It was so cheugy. Summer would never say things like that.

After another minute, there was no more thumping, so Cora quietly slid the closet door open. She needed to hurry.

She grabbed a lipstick from the nightstand and dropped it into her bag beside the flip-flops and sweater. It was Chanel. Who could blame her?

NINETEEN

Grace Godwin

Thursday, November 5
8:03 a.m.

The Beanery buzzes with people ordering and working at industrial-style tables. Open shelves on the walls overflow with vining plants and local roasts for purchase, and colorful tiles in pink and green and baby blue dot the otherwise white walls. Grace loves it here—good music, good people, good coffee, good vibes—though she's never come at this time on a weekday and didn't expect it to be so crowded. Then again, she's never cut school. How would she know what the Beanery is like this early in the morning when she's usually swimming laps?

Grace shoves her hands in her blazer pockets while she waits in line with Harrison to order. She's cold. Also, when her hands are busy, Harrison can't try to hold them.

"Did I ever tell you that the guy who owns this place won a coffee roasting competition in Austria last year?" Harrison asks.

Grace smiles weakly up at him. "No. That's awesome."

Harrison did tell Grace this the last time they were here together, but she doesn't want to make him feel bad when he's struggling. Everyone has compulsions, coping mechanisms. Maybe his way of coping is being the guy in the know, and if that helps him, great. His eyes are red, and he's got massive dark circles that age him from eighteen to late twenties. Even though he and Summer weren't especially close, she was still his sister. Her death reweaves the fabric of his life, and for a long time, that fabric will just feel torn.

After they got their coffee—a decaf honey latte for Grace and a straight double shot for Harrison—they grab a booth in the back where there's more privacy.

"Thanks for ditching school for me," Harrison says.

"Of course. You sounded upset." Grace feels a pang of guilt. She didn't ditch *for* him. If it wasn't for the fight with her mom, she'd be in first period right now. Just thinking about missing school twists her stomach into knots. There goes the Excellence Grant—not like it matters if she and her mom are going to move again. Not like her mom cares. "You hanging in there?"

"No. I don't know how to do this."

"Me either."

"My mom is so focused on funeral planning that she's not talking about any of it, and my dad's so worried about the police making an arrest ASAP that he's constantly on the phone with lawyers. I'm starting to wonder if he cares about catching the killer, or if he just needs to see someone punished. He's talking about suing."

"Suing who?"

"Who knows. Anyone he has a legit lawsuit against."

That did sound like Mr. Cartwright—more focused on winning than his own daughter. Grace sips her latte, breaking the heart pattern the barista poured into her cup with steamed milk. "I know you miss Summer. Me too."

Harrison sighs, then knocks back his espresso in a gulp. "That's the worst part. I'm not sure I do miss her. Not like I should."

If she and Harrison have nothing else in common, they have this. In the last few months, Grace has mentally restructured all her interactions with Summer—the earrings when they first met, the beach days, all of it—and started to wonder if she ever knew Summer at all.

Grace reaches out to touch Harrison's hand. She knows she's leading him on, but which is worse? Leading him on or leaving him alone in the days after his sister's death? "We don't have to talk about it."

"No, no. It's fine. I should say it out loud, rob the feelings of their power." Harrison rubs his eyes. "The thing is, in some ways, Summer being gone is almost . . . a relief? For the first time in my life, my dad needs me. He's talking to me. It sounds awful."

"No, of course not." It does sound awful, but who is she to judge?

"My dad made everything a competition between Summer and me. Who could get the best grades, get into the best college, have the most successful career. One time he threw my baseball glove in the garbage, because I walked three batters in a game. He told me Cartwrights don't attempt things they can't win. Another time, he told Summer she needed to lose five pounds if she wanted people to like her, no lie, and she lost it by the next week. Like, tell me how that's healthy? When we were little, my dad used to count our Halloween candy to see who made out best. It was never me. Even now with Sum's book . . . it's probably just gonna be more successful than ever."

Cold pools in Grace's stomach. "What do you mean?"

"Even though my dad is trying to push back the release date while he gets an injunction to kill it altogether, Swift Eagle is bugging him for more content, asking stuff like, did Summer keep a diary offline? I think their marketing team is going to promote her book hard."

"I didn't think it was still coming out, not after . . ."

"The ever-spinning wheels of capitalism, giving voice to Sum beyond the grave."

Grace can't help but think that Summer would have loved the notoriety. If she could have found a way to fake her own death just to watch people mourn her at her own funeral, she probably would have done it. What will the others think when they find out that Summer's book is still coming out? Will they freak out? And how will Grace deal with the aftermath? At least she has until March to figure it out.

"Summer was good at winning, even as a little kid," Harrison continues. "I could never compete. So I stopped focusing on winning and started focusing on figuring out what's real. What's authentic? Because I sure as hell know my parents' life isn't it."

For the first time ever, Grace kind of likes Harrison. Genuinely. In his search for authenticity, Grace has often found him fake, but she gets it now. In some ways, Grace has always been Summer's anti-competitor, which is probably why they stayed friends so long. Grace never wanted what Summer wanted. And if Summer got what Grace wanted without even trying, well, Grace always kept that to herself. If Adam wanted Grace, too, he'd had years to do something about it. But he never did, not until it was too late.

"So now," Harrison says, "I feel like the only way to make up for my own feelings is to do everything for Summer. The vigil. A memorial video for the funeral. I'd do anything to catch the person who hurt her, because maybe then Summer and I could call it even. Ironic, huh? To be in the debt of a dead person?"

"Maybe I can help with that." Grace modulates her voice, trying not to sound too eager. This was her chance. "The finding out who killed Summer part, I mean."

"How?"

"Any chance you still have the video footage from the party?"

"It's still a raw file on my camera."

"Could you format it so I could watch it?"

"Why?"

"I was just thinking . . . maybe there's something on there that would help us figure out what happened to Summer, you know?"

Grace has never been a manipulator. That was Summer's thing, not hers. But she knows she's manipulating Harrison's emotions when she squeezes his hand and smiles at him, and it makes her feel like a spy. An evil one who works for Adam and Laney and Cora. But what if Cora is right? What if the only way to avoid arrest is to give the police more suspects? Grace isn't stupid enough to believe that the detectives don't suspect her.

"Yeah, okay." Harrison squeezes her hand back. "I'll rip it to my laptop. Want to come over tomorrow night for dinner?"

Grace swallows her initial *ugh* before it shows on her face. "Sure. Okay."

"Seven?"

"Might be more like eight since I have to work. That okay?"

"Yeah. We eat late anyway."

Grace drinks the last of her latte. She really should get back to school, but she takes a second to text the group. Meeting Harrison tomorrow night to get video from party.

Is it possible that Harrison is right about Summer's book still coming out? The only thing Grace wants to do less than watch the party video is have dinner with the Cartwrights, but she has to.

She's using Harrison, manipulating him the way Summer used to manipulate her, but maybe this time the end would justify the means.

Friday, May 29, 4:05 p.m.
The Cartwrights' Loft

*"Here." Summer handed Grace a fat Cuban cigar from her father's
humidor. "One for you, and one for me."*

*It was the last day of sophomore year, and Summer had dragged
Grace into her father's office, the one room in the Cartwrights' loft
Grace had never entered. The office was also the one room that wasn't
an homage to minimalism. Quite the opposite. The lights were heavy
brass, and the art so expensive that one piece had its own security camera
pointed at the frame. Matching sets of leather-bound books that no one
would ever read lined the shelves.*

"I don't want to smoke this," Grace said.

*"We aren't going to smoke them. My lungs are a temple. We're just
going to take pics with them like we're celebrating school being out."*

*"We are celebrating school being out." But Grace still clamped the
cigar between her teeth and tried to find a balance between the cigar not
falling on the floor and her not biting the end off.*

*"Pics or it didn't happen." Summer held her phone out on selfie
portrait mode and snapped a few different angles with the cigars between
their lips.*

*"Can we put these away now? If your dad comes home, and we're in
here—"*

*"Fine. But he's on set today, so he won't be home for hours." Summer
rolled her eyes, stuck both cigars back in the humidor, then sat with her
feet up on her father's desk. "What do you want to do now?"*

"Lay out by your pool?"

"Meh."

"Beach?"

"Too many tourists lately."

"Beanery?"

Before Summer could answer, Mr. Cartwright flung open his office door. He always entered rooms, never just went in like a normal person. Grace's stomach leapt into her throat. He wasn't on set after all, and she wasn't sure what he'd do if he thought they'd been going through his stuff. Her eyes flicked to Summer, who jerked her feet off the desk like she'd been caught committing a crime. Her face looked frozen, and for the barest second, Grace thought she saw real worry in the flare of Summer's nostrils.

Mr. Cartwright's eyes darkened when he saw Summer at his desk. "Get the hell up from my desk and—" He reached toward her like he was going to grab her arm and drag her out of his office. But when his eyes landed on Grace, his entire demeanor changed. He smiled a full smile that showed all his top teeth. "What are you two doing in here? Causing trouble?"

"Just showing Grace your new Bowling." Summer gestured at a modernist landscape on the wall—was there a tremble in her hand?— then hopped to her feet. "She's super into oils."

"Do you paint, Grace? I didn't know that."

"Uh. A little?" Grace prayed that he wouldn't ask her a single question about color-mixing or brushstrokes. She had no idea what turpentine did. She hadn't painted since elementary school. "Not well."

Summer stood from the desk and took a paper out of her backpack. "At the end-of-the-year ceremony today, I got the award for best in the debate class." She showed him the certificate.

Mr. Cartwright barely glanced at it. "Wonderful."

"It's a really big class. There are seniors in it."

He drew out a cigar from his humidor. "Nothing like a good Cuban to relax after a long day. Don't tell your mother." And when he winked at them, snipped off the end, and lit it with a silver lighter from his pocket, Grace suspected that somehow, he knew they'd taken out cigars, and he wanted them to know he knew. "What about your other classes? What awards did you win in them?"

Summer's face fell, the hint of hope that Grace had seen there only seconds before gone. "Debate is the only class I got an award in."

"Then you'll excuse me if I withhold my excitement until you do something worth celebrating." He opened his laptop and started working, a clear dismissal.

"We'll leave you alone," Summer said. "Sorry."

Mr. Cartwright didn't even look up.

Summer gestured for Grace to follow her out of the office and down the hall to her room. When she closed the door behind them, Grace told Summer her concerns about Mr. Cartwright knowing what they'd done. The anger simmering beneath his cultivated surface of ease scared her. What was he like when no guests were around?

"My father doesn't notice anything about me unless it comes via notarized letter." Summer flops backward onto her bed with one arm over her face. "Don't worry about it."

Grace sits beside her. "Are you okay?"

"Why wouldn't I be okay?"

"You just seem . . . I don't know . . . upset about your dad or something."

"I haven't bothered caring what he thinks since the third grade when he stopped coming to my stuff."

But Grace leaned forward and studied her. She could tell Summer did care. A lot. "Does this have to do with Stanford, or—"

Summer sat up quickly, an angry line carved between her eyebrows. "I already told you, Grace. I'm fine. You're just reading into this because you have daddy issues. Sorry, but you do."

Something was up, though. Grace could tell. "Are you worried your dad is mad that we were in his office?"

"My father will never know we held cigars, Grace. Calm down. It's not like we did anything wrong."

Grace knew Summer was right, but there was something about Julian Cartwright that made her nervous, something in his eyes that scared her. A sense of power, of entitlement, paired with a dark humor that kept her guessing. He'd never said anything harsh to her, never done anything that should make her feel uncomfortable, but she was still uncomfortable around him. She could swear Summer was, too. "I just wonder if—"

"I went through the entire filing cabinet at your apartment—the one in your kitchen?—and you never found out, did you?"

"What?" Grace stopped breathing. "When?"

"Like, two weeks ago. You were in the shower and your mom wasn't home, so I was bored."

"Did you . . ." But Grace couldn't finish her thought. If Summer hadn't found out her Big Secret, telling her one existed would only have pushed her to keep looking. Summer traded in appearances, in knowledge, in having the upper hand.

Summer frowned. "You've been keeping secrets. I would have understood if you'd bothered to tell me."

"I was scared." Grace curled her legs up toward her chest.

"Of what?"

"I don't know." Of Summer telling people. Of her not caring. Of everything, just everything, being ruined forever.

When Summer smiled, her smile was her father's. Satisfied. Powerful. Cold. "Don't worry, Gracie Grace. Your secret is safe with me."

Grace took a deep breath and tried to force herself to stay calm, to not panic, even though hundreds of fun facts were exploding inside her brain as it tried to cope. Even though her palms were sweaty, and she felt like her lungs would pop if she couldn't get more air inside them.

Over the last couple of months, Grace had noticed Summer changing, growing quieter, more introspective. Something wasn't right. But the more Grace tried to be there for her, the more distant Summer became. And the more distant she became, the more Grace wanted to be the perfect friend, never needing anything, always ready to listen should Summer need to talk. But she couldn't keep that up forever.

Except . . . she kind of had to, or Summer could ruin her life.

The_Summer_Cartwright

#NEWS #LifeUpdate

.

Some of you guys may have heard the big news—my first book is coming out with @SwiftEaglePress next March!! OMG!! Cue explosions and fireworks! 🎆 🎆 🎆 🎆 🎆 Can't believe I'm finally allowed to announce it after months in the works! Yay!

.

My **#memoir** All Your Likes Can't Buy Me Love is a tell-all about my life, the good, the bad, and the *tragically* ugly. It's everything you've seen on my IG page, gathered and organized into one place, plus MORE! There are pics from my childhood, stuff I wrote on things I care about or find interesting, plus exclusive tips on how to build a successful IG page. Not to mention the whole story of me and my so-called friends. All of it. It gets a smidge sexy, gotta warn you, younger followers! But it's also a cautionary tale about who you should trust. (Hint: absolutely no one.)

.

Here's the blurby **#blurb** from Goodreads! ⬇️

.

Sixteen-year-old Summer Cartwright seems like she has it all—the fame, the platform, the talent, the closet—but in this dishy memoir, she reveals that friends can be frenemies, girls can be wannabes, and guys don't always have good intentions. If you like the Bachelor and Gossip Girl, you'll be captivated by Summer's frank tales of love and betrayal. Is it possible to really have it all?

.

Catchy, no?? And no one, absolutely no one in my life is safe from being included. It's a #TellAll, not a #TellSome. Telling all isn't always nice, but it is always interesting, amiright?

.

XOXO,
Summer Angelica Cartwright 🖤 (S. A. Cartwright? Summer A. Cartwright? Gah, picking an author-y name is hard. Leave your votes in the comments!)

₪ 🖤 ▶

TWENTY

Adam Mahmoud

Thursday, November 5
11:22 a.m.

In fourth period study free, Adam is completely unproductive. He has plenty of math homework spread out in front of him. That's not the issue. It's quiet, but not too quiet since, unlike study hall, study free allows group work and quiet conversation, so that's not it either. It's not even the stares and whispers from the students who think he probably killed Summer. He's weirdly used to that after three and a half school days of it.

Light streams through the media center windows, highlighting the shelves of books and the glass-walled innovation lab in the corner where the entrepreneurial students plan marketing schemes with Expo markers. Through a door in the back of the room, Adam can hear muffled singing. The video production class must be recording the audio for the chamber choir's annual music video.

The issue with Adam's productivity is Blossom Vasquez, seated

across the table from him instead of in her usual place at one of the
iMacs the yearbook students use for photo editing. The way she
glances around the room instead of doing homework on the iPad in
front of her is a clear indication that she has something private to talk
to him about, but they aren't close like that. However, Blossom's end-
less curiosity, paired with her inability to pick up social cues, means
she doesn't care if they're close or not. Adam has info. She wants it. Is
it possible she doesn't realize or care that the last thing in the world he
wants to do right now is talk about Summer's murder?

After his police interview this morning, Adam knows he needs to
work with Cora to find new suspects, if only to protect himself and
Grace. Blossom may be digging for info, but she also may be able to
help.

"You'll never guess what happened last night," Blossom whispers.

Adam closes his textbook and manages to keep his sigh internal.
"What?"

"Detectives called my mom." Blossom leans forward to whisper.
The purple highlight at the front of her dark hair falls across her face.
"They asked her for my camera SD card with all the pics from the
party. Who knows if I'll get it back."

"Did they have a warrant?"

"Nah, but, like, my mom isn't going to say no, you know? The
good news is that they don't have it yet. My camera was out with me,
so my mom told me to drop off the card today after school."

"What did Grace say when you told her?"

"Ummm, I haven't told her. She's like one piece of bad news away
from a mental breakdown."

Adam didn't think Grace was that bad, though she'd always been
good at hiding her real feelings. He blows a puff of air from his cheeks.
The detectives probably want the photos to continue building an

accurate time line of events from the night of the party. The problem is that Adam left out a few little details in his interview. Nothing earth-shattering . . . but those pictures could make him look bad.

"I loaded all the pics onto my Google Drive so I wouldn't lose them," Blossom says.

By the way she leans forward with her elbows on the table between them, Adam can tell she wants him to ask about the pictures. Because then, she can tell him it's a secret, so then he'll beg, so then she'll be able to roll her eyes and show him "as a favor to Grace." It won't be the first time they go through this whole song and dance. Blossom was in his biology class last year, and at Grace's behest helped Adam pass his final. Blossom is loud about being in the running for valedictorian, the type of girl who, even though she's fluent in Spanish and could crush every test without studying, takes German because she'd rather be trilingual than have an easy class.

Adam gives in. "Anything interesting in the pics?"

"I probably shouldn't tell you. You're a suspect."

"I am not. Come on, Blossom."

"You're suspect number one online."

"Good thing the internet can't make arrests. Are you going to tell me or what?"

"Fine," Blossom says. "I'll do you one better and add you as a collaborator. Not sure if there's anything helpful? But in the last few pics of Summer, she looks sweatier than I've ever seen her, definitely in need of some blot paper for her forehead if you know what I'm saying."

"You think she had already been poisoned then?"

"That's for sure how she died? Poison?" Blossom's eyes light up. "I mean, I figured as much, but it's good to have confirmation. I took plenty of pics of her eating stuff." She opens her Google Drive on her iPad to show him the pics. "You should probably know there's a whole series of you with your arm around her helping her walk toward the kitchen. Timestamped eight thirty-ish."

Adam curses under his breath. Part of him has been hoping that no one noticed him leave the main room with Summer, or at the very least that if it came up, he could blur the truth a little, tell the detectives he just walked her to the door of the kitchen or something.

"She already wasn't feeling well," he said. "I took her to get some water."

"When I saw it happening, I thought, oh my god. *The* Summer Cartwright, California's sweetheart, is totally trashed. Gotta document this moment in history. But when you guys found her dead . . ."

"She had been drinking."

"Not that much."

"Why are you telling me this?"

"You have to admit the cops could build a compelling case against you if they got ahold of these."

He scrolls to the last few photos and finds the ones of Summer leaning heavily on his arm. It only shows her from the back, but in a few, Adam glances over his shoulder like he's checking to make sure no one sees them leaving together. Which is exactly what he was doing, but not for the reason detectives might assume. He didn't want Grace to see him and Summer together and think that they were getting back together. He'd meant it the day he broke up with Summer when he said there was someone else.

Before weighing the outcomes of what it would look like to Blossom or to the cops if they found out, Adam highlights and deletes the pics of him with Summer before handing her iPad back. Maybe she won't notice.

"Thanks for the heads-up," he says.

"Any friend of Grace's or whatever. Look, you didn't hear this from me . . ." Blossom lowers her voice even more. "But when I saw you and Summer go into the kitchen, I followed you guys a minute later. Not a fan of sober guys walking out of the room with drunk girls, you know what I'm saying?"

"I would never—"

"That's what every guy says, yet one in six women gets raped. You do the math. Anyway, by the time I got to the kitchen, Summer was drinking a big glass of water, and you were gone. She was kind of pale, so I asked if she wanted something carby to eat to soak up the alcohol."

"What did she say?"

"She lost it. Started yelling at me to put away my camera. She said she was fine, so leave her alone. I didn't want to make waves, so I was like, Okay girl. You do you. You know?"

Adam nods. "That was Summer."

"She didn't sound drunk. I thought maybe she'd gotten a stomach bug or something and didn't want me to see her vom." Blossom waits as the chamber choir pours out of the production room, a few of them singing a squawky high note and jabbing a red-faced girl at the front of the group. When they're gone, Blossom continues. "Anyway, on my way out of the kitchen, I found a trash can to throw away my gum. It was mostly empty, because there were other trash cans by the dance floor. But at the bottom of this one, there were, like, a crap ton of PowerBoost wrappers."

Adam narrows his eyes. "And?"

"Just saying, what if someone poisoned her bars? It would explain why no one else got sick from the party food." The bell rings then, ending the period, and Blossom gathers her things. "Think about it."

On his way to lunch, Adam opens Instagram. Tons of people were at the party. Who's to say someone else didn't post something? The police would look through those pics eventually if they hadn't already. When he types in the hashtag Summer created for the evening—#SumSumDoesHalloween—a few hundred pics pop up.

He scrolls through as he walks, not finding anything until his finger accidentally taps Summer's account. And it's not shut down anymore.

Did the detectives reactivate it, or is the person who wrote the new post during the vigil getting ready to strike again?

Saturday, October 31, last week, 8:34 p.m.
Summer's Halloween Party

The DJ cranked up the volume on the new Cardi B song that everyone had stuck in their heads. The lights flashed in time with the beat. After making her welcome announcement, Summer hopped down off the DJ stand, wobbling on her ridiculous heels. Before Adam could reach her to steady her, she was intercepted by Avalon James. He'd met her at a party last year. Tonight, she wore her hair in waist-length box braids, and her green dress formed to her curvy body like dragon scales.

"You're trending top one hundred! Congrats!" Avalon's smile was forced as she handed Summer a bottle of water. "You seemed thirsty."

"Yeah, thanks, Avalon." Sweat stuck a strand of blond hair to Summer's forehead, and before her eyes seemed to register Avalon at all, she gulped down the entire bottle. She didn't wipe away the water droplets that clung to her upper lip. "Though top ten would be better."

"Maybe by the end of the evening you'll be there. Thanks for inviting me." Avalon held out her phone. "Selfie?"

Summer just stared at her.

"Thanks for talking to your . . ." Avalon paused. Summer clearly wasn't listening, clearly was scanning the room for something or someone else instead. Avalon's eyes darkened. "Never mind. Have fun." As she walked away, Adam thought he heard her mutter, "Thanks for nothing ever."

Summer stood alone in the crowd, blinking harder than usual. As much as part of Adam would have loved to say screw you *and never talk to her again, something seemed off with her. Her under-eyes were shadowed, and beneath the glitter, her cheeks were pale.*

He pushed past a crowd of seniors to get to her. "You feeling okay?"

"Is it hot in here?" She fanned herself with one hand. "It's really hot, right?"

"Do you want to step outside for a minute to cool off?" He hated how concerned his voice sounded, like he was her boyfriend still taking care of her. Old habits die hard.

"There's a fan in the kitchen. God, I feel so weird. Is it possible to develop, like, a shellfish allergy when you're sixteen?"

"You think the lobster's hitting you wrong?"

"Or something. I'm like . . . a little . . . dizzy maybe?"

He wrapped an arm around her shoulder, hoping that Grace didn't see them together. When he glanced over his shoulder, though, she was nowhere in sight.

In the kitchen, Summer leaned against the marble countertop and pressed a hand to her forehead. "Maybe I'm just dehydrated. Too busy to drink water, didn't want to mess with my lipstick, you know?"

"Makes sense." Adam grabbed a glass from the cabinet beside the sink and filled it with water. "Drink this."

Summer took a long sip. "Such a gentleman."

"Look, you know that you and me . . . we can't—"

"Oh, I'm well aware, Adam. Give me credit for a little self-respect."

"Not trying to make things worse."

"Ha! Too late for that. You broke my heart, you know. You're the only guy who ever has. Proud of yourself?"

"I'm sorry. I wasn't thinking. I should have picked a different time to—"

"Not the day you dumped me at school in front of everyone. That was humiliating, but you know me. I bounce back. I mean the other time."

"You . . . What?"

Adam knew exactly the day she meant, but he didn't know how she knew about it. Did Grace tell her? Did someone see? Thinking about what happened made Adam feel sick, not because he regretted it, but because he'd thought maybe Summer would never find out. That he could take it to his grave. Still, the idea of him breaking her heart was ridiculous. Stainless steel hearts didn't break.

"Once a cheater, always a cheater, right?" Summer locked eyes with Adam and raised one eyebrow. "Right, Adam?"

"What are you—"

"You and I both know what I mean." Summer drained the rest of her water. "In fact, I think a lot of people are about to know. You've been so special to me, you get an entire chapter in my book. You're welcome."

Adam took a step toward her. "I never meant to hurt you."

She smiled, and despite the sweat on her forehead, the glisten in her eyes, her smile was made of nails and ice. "So glad you came tonight. Enjoy the party."

Adam knew a Summer dismissal when he heard one. When he went out the back entrance of the kitchen to the hallway that led to the Cartwrights' bedrooms, heat spread from his chest to his limbs.

Adam had never hated anyone more than Summer Cartwright. Except for maybe himself.

TWENTY-ONE

Elaine Miyamoto

Thursday, November 5
2:07 p.m.

When Laney gets called to the office between seventh and eighth periods, she wants to run away instead, head for the hills and live off locusts and honey like that guy John the Baptist whom she learned about in Sunday school in Sacramento. WW Prep rarely does office calls over the intercom, and she hasn't done anything to get called to see the headmaster. The last time she heard her name over an intercom was in eighth grade. When she got to the front office that day, her father was waiting for her with the news that her mom had been in a car accident coming home from her shift at the hospital. She'd been too tired and had fallen asleep at the wheel. Her little Prius slammed into the back of a tractor trailer, and it was completely Laney's fault.

Laney's therapist says that when situations start to feel familiar, they can bring back deep emotions, even if at their core, they're totally different. That must be why she's feeling this nagging, pulling sense of dread going to Headmaster Norton's office today.

His office is eerily like the one where she got the news of her mom's death. The same SWIM YOUR OWN DIRECTION! fish poster is behind his desk alongside a bunch of pretentious-looking diplomas and certifications that mean zilch to her. But her father isn't the one waiting. It's Detective Mwanthi, his hands shoved deep in his pants pockets and a warm smile on his face. Laney doesn't trust that smile.

"What's going on?" she asks Headmaster Norton.

He pushes his leather chair back from his desk and straightens his thin-framed glasses. "Detective Mwanthi would like to ask you a few questions, Elaine."

"Sorry." Lancy squares her shoulders. "My dad says I'm not allowed to answer any questions unless I'm under arrest. And in that situation, I have to have a lawyer with me. Am I under arrest?"

"No, you're not." Mwanthi leans forward to rest his hands on his knees. "But we spoke with your father, and after assuring him that you're not currently a suspect, he is willing to allow Headmaster Norton to stand in as your appropriate adult."

Laney narrows her eyes. "How do I know you aren't lying?"

"Lying would only make anything you say inadmissible in court. Besides"—Mwanthi slides a paper across the desk to Laney—"your father signed a waiver. He faxed it over this morning."

All Laney needs to hear is the word *fax*. Her dad refuses to email anything important, even though fax machines are the woolly mammoths of tech. "Okay. I guess."

"Should you become uncomfortable, Elaine, you are welcome to return to class at any time," Headmaster Norton says. "Would you take a seat, please?"

Laney considers insisting that she's already uncomfortable—it wouldn't be a lie—but maybe it's best to get this over with at a time when she doesn't have to worry about her dad interrupting her every three seconds. Besides, information is reciprocal. Maybe she'll find out something, too.

She sits in the chair offered to her. "Shoot."

"Let me see here," Mwanthi says. "According to my records, you arrived at the party just before seven with your stepbrother, Oscar?"

"Right."

"And he was on Summer's list?"

"No, but I didn't want to go alone. I didn't really know anyone who'd be there, and since Oscar and Grace kind of know each other from swim team, she let him in."

"Interesting. Did she let in many people not on Summer's list? I'm just trying to get an accurate idea of who was there."

Laney shrugs. "You'd have to ask her."

Mwanthi moves through a few more baseline questions—where Laney was during the party, what she saw that might have seemed strange, etc.

"Everything seemed fine, until it wasn't," Laney says.

"And when was that?"

"The whole murder mystery thing was a little weird, I guess. But really, I didn't think anything was wrong until we found Summer dead."

Seeing her lifeless body, her legs twisted beneath her, the writing on her face . . . It was surreal. Part of Laney still believes it can't be true. She was so shocked to see Summer lying there that night that she reacted poorly. She knows that. Disbelieving laughter bubbled out of her mouth, and she just . . . stood there laughing. Honestly, she's shocked she's not the prime suspect, just from that reaction. Had someone mentioned it to the detectives?

"Were you and Summer close?" Mwanthi asks.

"We roomed together at ISSOS, and her parents sort of know my stepmom from her country club, but that's it."

"Sort of?"

"They ran into each other at lunch sometimes. Rebekah played tennis with Mrs. Cartwright once or twice."

"I hear your goal for the future is to attend film school at USC, correct? To study movie production?"

"Yeah, with a focus on sound artistry." When Mwanthi looks at her quizzically, she clarifies. "You know, like sound effects? Those are added in post-production."

Headmaster Norton pushes his glasses farther up his nose and interrupts. "The USC program is highly competitive, but here at WW Prep, we pride ourselves on one of the highest national acceptance—"

"Of course," Mwanthi cuts in. "But from what I hear, many colleges are moving to a test-blind system. A letter of recommendation from someone in the business would certainly help, wouldn't it?"

Laney knew this moment would come. Should she tell Detective Mwanthi about her deal with Summer? If she doesn't and it comes out another way, she'll look guilty for sure. Blackmail is motive for murder. But what if the police don't need to know? No one besides Summer can prove what she did, and Summer is dead.

"Mr. Cartwright wrote me a college recommendation letter, if that's what you're asking," Laney says.

"I've spoken extensively with him in the course of this investigation, and he mentioned that yours was one of only two he has ever written. Any idea why?"

"Ever consider that I'm freaking talented?"

Mwanthi smiles. "So many are."

They stare at each other for a moment while Headmaster Norton anxiously shuffles papers on his desk. He's the last person who'd ever admit the heavy role favoritism plays in acceptance into good colleges, but he might as well add, *We help students make connections!!* in the school brochure. Of course students get into the best schools based on their own merit, but when everyone is equally awesome, how do you stand out? Julian Cartwright is a successful, well-known USC alumnus. A recommendation from him matters. It just does.

Mwanthi waits.

"Summer talked to him for me when we got back from England," Laney says.

"That was nice of her."

"Yup."

"But you weren't close? Did you do anything for Summer in exchange?"

He's dangerously close to the truth. "I helped her study sometimes."

"Because you wanted to?"

"I didn't mind. Usually."

"Usually?"

"I mean, yeah, I kind of felt like I owed her after she talked to her dad for me. And Summer was annoying as hell. I've never met anyone more obsessed with herself, what her hair looked like, what her body looked like. . . . More than once I wanted to be, like, Suck it up, buttercup, you're never going to have an ass like Kim Kardashian. Kim Kardashian doesn't even have an ass like Kim Kardashian."

"Did she ever threaten you? Make you feel like if you didn't listen to her, there would be consequences?"

Headmaster Norton stands. "This strikes me as a rather inflammatory question, Detective. As Elaine's adult presence, I—"

"You're right, of course. My apologies." Mwanthi smiles at Laney pleasantly, like he knows more than he's letting on. The problem is, if she asks, then it only proves she's not telling him everything.

"I think this conversation is over for today. Elaine." Headmaster Norton gestures to the door of his office. "It's time for you to return to class."

"Of course." Mwanthi stands with Laney. "But you should be aware that Summer had a series of prewritten Instagram posts scheduled for the upcoming weeks to support her book launch. I get the feeling you factor heavily in her memoir."

And as he nods at Headmaster Norton and leaves the office, Laney is completely frozen. If anyone finds out what Laney really did for Summer, she'll be screwed. The detectives won't let the scheduled posts drop, will they? And how much did Summer include in the posts?

The_Summer_Cartwright

#BookTeaser 😎 📖 😎

.

OMG, only a few months until my **#memoir** All Your Likes Can't Buy Me Love comes out from @SwiftEaglePress!!! Gah! In anticipation of **#LaunchDay**, my editor has given me permission to post some little snippets to whet your appetites.

.

This first teaser is from chapter 4 of my book, and some of you will think I've lost my mind sharing this. But I've realized recently that I'd rather fail on my own than succeed by being fake . . . with myself or with you. So get ready to see the real, raw, unedited Summer in my book. **#NoFilter #AndIDontMeanFaceTune**

.

Anyone who knows me knows that my whole childhood, my parents' dream for me has been for me to go to Stanford University. The plan is for me to major in something fancy-pants like international relations or ecogastronomy. In the family photo albums, there are baby pictures of me wearing the Stanford Tree on my onesies, and every year, we'd fly up for at least one game. Did the pressure to be the best, to be a Cartwright of the first order, stress me out? Obviously. I still wanted to make them happy, because

I was naive enough then to think I could ever accomplish that. Here's the problem—there was no way I'd ever get in. Why, you ask? I am the worst test-taker of all time. That's where Elaine Miyamoto, Ms. SAT 1541, came in.

.

Is it reckless of me to spill this tea to the world? Maybe. But like I said, #RealOrNothing.

.

Past the point of no return,
SumSum 🖤

₪ 🖤 ▶

TWENTY-TWO

Grace Godwin

Friday, November 6
8:02 p.m.

After work Friday night, Grace buzzes the Cartwrights' loft and tries not to look at the rotting jack-o'-lanterns sagging on their stoop. They remind her too much of the Halloween party. The sky is gray with fluorescent lights—LA skies are never truly black—but she feels like she's fallen in a dark ocean where she can't swim.

"Come in. Dinner's just about ready," Harrison says when he opens the loft door. The saucy smell of something Italian wafts through the doorway. Sometimes Mrs. Cartwright cooks, but Grace doubts that's the case tonight, not with everything she's been going through. If Grace had to bet, she'd say they brought in Janine, their sometimes-chef, for the evening.

As Grace ducks beneath Harrison's arm into the foyer, she catches his scent, too. Aftershave and minty ChapStick. He's wearing fitted jeans and a green Henley T-shirt, and his blond hair is a little damp like he's just gotten out of the shower. She smells like beef tacos, but whatever. It's not like she's trying to impress him.

"I made brownies for dessert," he says.

"You baked?"

"I am a man of many layers."

"But are your cakes?"

"Come back for dessert another night, and you can see for yourself."

The whole exchange is flirtier than Grace intended. The thing about Harrison is that he's insanely fun to flirt with. Blossom is right about the hotness quotient—blond hair, trim body, eyes that are always interested in what she has to say, which feels like a straight-up power trip. Grace's fleeting moments of attraction to Harrison don't have much to do with his appearance, though. Maybe it's the fact that he's passionate about something. Sure, his passion is videoing people authentically eating cereal, but at least he hasn't affected the blasé nothing-is-ever-interesting attitude that most people their age have. But she suspects the real reason has to do with how much he wants her. It's a little raw, vulnerable. He tells her exactly what he wants, and that's sexy for a people pleaser. It would be so easy to make him happy.

Harrison gestures for her to follow him into the living room, which is back to its usual state of pristine whiteness. The couches are undraped, the *Phantom-of-the-Opera*–style chandelier is nowhere in sight.

"Make yourself at home," Harrison says. "I ripped all the videos to my computer so we can go through them after we eat. Let me check on dinner."

"Did Janine cook tonight?"

"Nah, I did, nothing fancy, believe me. My parents have been kind of weird about outsiders coming over." He leans closer to Grace.

"They're both checked out. Mom barely leaves her room, and Dad barely leaves work, so I'm just . . . I don't know. Hanging out, I guess."

Grace feels sorry for him and, like yesterday morning, likes him a little more. She's always thought of Harrison as a one-note kind of guy, but his mourning Summer, putting together her vigil, and cooking—what is it, spaghetti?—for her is endearing.

"Are your parents okay with me being here?" she asks.

He shrugs. "You're part of the family."

God, that should make her feel so good, but it aches instead. Her whole life, she's been desperate for a big, happy family. Not that she doesn't love her mom. She does. But it's not the same as having siblings and cousins and a dad who's around. It's part of the reason why Grace was drawn to the Mahmouds in the first place. The twins were babies when she first met Adam, and their apartment was always chaotic. But at Adam's place, there was so much genuine joy in being together.

Being an unofficial part of the Cartwright family feels like a shadow of that, especially after the last few months with Sum. Not to mention that Mr. Cartwright was far from the father figure Grace wanted.

When Harrison goes into the kitchen to check on dinner, Grace wanders into the dining room and is surprised to find Miranda Cartwright seated at the table. Of course Mrs. Cartwright would be out of her room at this of all times. Why didn't Grace just stay put where Harrison left her? Mrs. Cartwright's skin is a shade whiter than usual, whether from sadness or a lack of bronzer, and she's wearing a black silk dressing gown.

She turns her wide blue eyes on Grace. "Aren't you going to sit?"

"Oh. Thanks." Grace joins her at the table, but her stomach is in knots. She hasn't talked to Mrs. Cartwright since a few weeks before Summer's murder, and facing her now feels impossible. There's something about her expressions, the way she's a grown-up, more rigid version of Summer, the way her eyes are heavy-lidded, the way her mouth presses into a cold line like a statue that the chairs make. Grace want to turn on her heel and run away. "How . . . uh, how are you?"

"I'm alive," she says, her eyes hard enough that Grace wonders if alive is the right word. "And you?"

"Um. I'm okay. Actually, I'm . . . kind of a wreck? I miss Summer." Grace's shoulders tense until they feel like rocks. She wants to leave now. Coming in the first place was a horrible idea, videos from the party or not.

"Yes, I'd imagine so." Mrs. Cartwright stands from the table, pausing long enough that Grace feels caught in her blue gaze, like Mrs. Cartwright has weighed her and found her wanting. "My husband should be home any minute."

"Working late?" Grace can feel herself about to digress into absolute verbal diarrhea, talking to fill the air. But what do you say to a woman whose daughter was murdered?

"He's meeting with Swift Eagle Press about Summer's memoir."

"Right. I heard that was still happening. That's . . . Wow. How do you feel about it?"

"Her story deserves to be told, I suppose. Though I'd rather keep her to myself for once."

Grace blinks, surprised. She always thought Mrs. Cartwright loved Summer's fame. In the background, Grace hears the front door open. She is suddenly overwhelmed with the need to find out as much about the book as she can before it's too late. "And Mr. Cartwright? How does he feel about it?"

"How does he feel about what?" Julian Cartwright paces into the dining room from the foyer, drops his suit jacket over a chair, and kisses his wife on the cheek. It should be endearing, but it's sterile somehow. Maybe it's the light that never reaches his eyes. "Hello there, Grace."

"Hi, Mr. Cartwright." She tries not to squirm in her chair, especially since she knows from experience that the chairs make a horrible, leather squirping noise. "We were talking about Summer's book."

"Ah. Have you read it?"

"No." Which is kind of true. She's only read the one chapter. It's not like she could mark it as read on Goodreads. "Have you?"

"Snippets."

Grace forces herself to stay motionless, to not jiggle her foot or pick at her nails or anything else that would give away her nerves. Has he read the chapters about her?

"What a shitshow," he continues, pulling a decanter from his liquor cabinet. "I just talked to them about taking chunks out. My minor child wrote it. I should have more control over the content."

"You don't?"

"I was busy the day Summer signed her contracts. I sent her with my lawyer. My own fault—if you want something done right, do it yourself."

"What . . ." Grace pauses. To her left, Mrs. Cartwright stares out the window at the line of cars crawling across Century City. To her right, Mr. Cartwright pours himself two fingers of scotch and watches her so closely she feels like an amoeba on a slide. "Um. What did you want cut out of the book? If you don't mind my asking?"

"You know how teenagers are. Family drama that was skewed by her hormones." He sips his drink, then laughs a little. "I'm sure you feel the same way about your mother. Nothing's fair, etc."

"I guess. Sometimes." Like when her mom decides it's time to move and doesn't let Grace have a part in the decision-making. Still, what strikes Grace most in this moment isn't that Summer raged against her family in her memoir. That doesn't surprise her at all. What surprises her is how calm Summer's father is when his daughter hasn't even been buried yet. The funeral isn't until Sunday.

This dinner is going to be the most uncomfortable ever. Grace glances at the laptop Harrison left open on the living room coffee table. If she could just get the videos, she could leave. She doesn't know how long she'll last making polite conversation with the parents of her dead best friend, and she doesn't want to pretend to be into Harrison when she's not. It's wrong and fake, and she's never been fake.

"I'm gonna change," Mr. Cartwright says, then offers a hand to his wife with a half-smiling, half-scoffing snort. "And you should, too."

Silently, Mrs. Cartwright follows her husband down the back hallway toward the bedrooms as Harrison pokes his head out of the kitchen. "Only a few more minutes."

"Take your time," Grace says.

This is her chance. She darts to the couch, hits enter on Harrison's laptop, and relaxes when it opens his Google Drive. Before she can change her mind, she emails a zip file of the videos to herself, then deletes the sent mail from Harrison's outbox.

From the hallway, the Cartwrights' low voices murmur, and in the kitchen, Harrison taps a spatula or something on a pan. She's got to get out of here before she melts from discomfort. She's never been good at knowing what to say to people who are sad, because whenever she's been sad, she's mostly had to stuff it down and deal.

"Hey, Harrison?" she calls into the kitchen. "I am so sorry. But my mom just texted me. She locked herself out of the apartment again and needs me to let her in. You know how she is."

"Aw, seriously, babygirl?" He comes around the corner from the kitchen wearing an apron—an apron!—and again, Grace's heart squishes a little. Why does he have to be so human all of a sudden? "I can call her a locksmith, no need for you to go."

"I have to."

"But—"

"I'm sorry."

He folds his arms across his chest. "Fine. Okay."

And before guilt has time to creep its way through Grace's body so she changes her mind and says yes to whatever Harrison wants, before his parents reemerge from the bedroom, she leaves.

It's not until she's on the bus that she sees the text from Adam with an address at the bottom.

AM:

> Meet at Laney's in an hour? Bring the video footage if you can.

Saturday, October 31, last week, 7:18 p.m.
Summer's Halloween Party

Grace clutched a clipboard in the Cartwrights' foyer. Of the almost fifty people on the list, only four or five were missing. She felt weird being the party population controller, like a stereotypical mean girl telling less cool people that they couldn't sit at her table. Not that she'd had to turn anyone away yet, thank goodness. The only not-on-the-list person to show up so far was Oscar, and Grace knew him from swim team, so it hadn't seemed like that big of a deal to let him in. Aside from his sarcastic commentary in history class, he was harmless.

The DJ blasted Dua Lipa, and with everyone distracted by the music, the lights, the food, the . . . too-muchness of it all, no one cared what Grace did. So before she had time to overthink it, she tucked her clipboard behind the giant potted snake plant and pushed through a cluster of influencers whom Grace suspected were demigods or sexy vampires to the hallway that led to the back of the Cartwrights' loft.

She had to find the early draft of Summer's book. According to Harrison, Summer had printed a copy of her latest draft and was keeping it somewhere in her room. Ever since Summer had asked her to proofread a chapter last month, Grace had dreaded the book's release. But maybe Summer had changed her mind about some of the stuff in it? She had been mad after their fight, but mad enough that she'd put the Big Secret in her book, knowing it could ruin Grace's entire life? Two weeks ago, Grace would have said absolutely not, but with the way Summer had been acting lately—distant, too nice, too polite—she wasn't sure anymore. Plus, when they'd hung out just a few days ago, Summer had made a point to tell Grace she wouldn't lie in her book. Why had she felt the need to say that?

So while everyone at the party shout-sung "Levitating," Grace slipped into Summer's bedroom. Street lamps cast long, rectangular shadows through the blinds onto the carpet, but the darkness didn't bother Grace. There was only one place Summer would keep something as important as her book.

The music throbbed dully as Grace slid a decoupaged box from beneath Summer's bed. It was full of photos and handwritten notes—a box of Summer's favorite memories. Grace picked up a Polaroid of her and Summer at the beach jumping above the waves with their arms over their heads. Their bikinis were bright against their August tans. Seeing it made Grace feel nauseous.

A thick stack of paper took up the entire bottom of the box. The cover page read All Your Likes Can't Buy Me Love. *Not for the first time, Grace wondered what Summer's family thought about her writing a tell-all about her life. Were they as nervous about it as Grace was? When Grace's mom had heard the news about the book deal, she'd pointed one finger at Grace and said, "Not for you. Okay? It's called discretion. Use it."*

Grace had maybe five minutes before Summer noticed she wasn't at the front door and came looking for her, so instead of searching for a chapter that could possibly contain the Big Secret, she flipped to the table of contents and found the chapter she'd proofread a few weeks ago. If Summer had edited it, maybe the Big Secret wasn't in the book either.

The chapter was titled "Burn It Down."

What she read in the light that spilled through the glass french doors turned her stomach. It was the same stuff she'd read before, no changes, proving that, deep down, Summer still hated her.

Want to know about the day I decided to burn my life and everyone in it down to the ground? The day old Summer died, and new
Summer was born, not like a phoenix from the ashes of my old life,
nothing that triumphant. More like the day I was reborn in a new
dimension where truth is told and trust is unheard of.

To begin.

No one, not one single person, knows the real me. That's what
I realized that night at dinner with my parents and Harrison when
I tried telling them that I didn't really want to go to college. Like,
for real? There are so many ways to make a living right now without
college, but my dad was all, *It's not just about future careers. It's
about connections, Summer.* Well, screw you, Dad, I can connect
online.

Then I told them that I'd tell the truth in this memoir, the whole
truth. I'm not going to make my life rainbows and sunshine where it's
not. You readers deserve the truth, the whole truth, and nothing but
the truth about the Cartwright fam.

First of all, my family feels like I'm not myself online. When will
they realize that the place I'm not myself is with them? I'm sick of
wearing the mask of perfect daughter, successful progeny, beautiful
doll that lives on the shelf of my dad's display case. I'm sick of editing
myself to make other people more comfortable.

So I flipped my dad the bird that night, ignored him when he
yelled at me to sit my ass back down in the chair and stop crying or
he'd give me something to cry about, and left dinner.

I didn't even think about where to go. My bestie and BF live across
the street from each other, and there have been plenty of days when I
needed them both, so I just shot them a text and met them in the park
near their buildings. It's always been a huge perk of them growing up
together.

So that's what I did. I didn't hear back, but I figured, whatever. At least one of them will be home.

But they were both in the park when I got there. And when I saw them, I died a little bit inside. People always think I'm immune to hurt and heartbreak because I have five million followers, because I'm pretty or whatever. Like, I'm not going to lie, I know I'm pretty. I know I have a lot going for me and I'm probably privileged, but I'm also a human being with feelings and love to give.

So when I saw Grace Godwin and Adam Mahmoud on the swings—

The hallway light flicked on as Grace turned the page. She froze in the yellow glow that spilled beneath Summer's door. Who wandered away from the party? What if they saw her?

Her mind raced a million miles per hour. What if she got caught in here? Her palms sweated, her chest tightened. Coming back here had been a bad idea, so bad. She and Summer had just gotten past their fight. Grace was doing so good not mentioning anything that could cause tension between them again, even on the days when she wondered if Summer had ever really forgiven her or if she was faking to make it seem to the world like everything was okay. And despite this chapter, maybe they could be okay?

But deep down, Grace knew that was wishful thinking.

She had to get back to her spot at the front door. Now.

That was the only thought in her mind when she dropped the file back into the box, shoved it under the bed, and bolted into the lit hallway just as the doorway to Harrison's bedroom started to open.

"Grace!" he said. "What are you doing back here?"

"Hey, so sorry! I went into that front bathroom, and it wouldn't flush!

It almost looked like it had overflowed a little, so . . ." She shrugged.

"Oh great. Guess I better block that one off."

"Might be a good idea." She smiled at him.

As she walked back down the hallway with measured steps so Harrison didn't think she was upset, her brain churned. Summer hadn't edited the chapter about her and Adam, so she must still be mad about what happened. She had every right to be. But was she mad enough that she'd include the Big Secret in her memoir? It's one line in the book that convinces Grace that the answer is yes: Want to know about the day I decided to burn my life and everyone in it down to the ground?

Grace stationed herself back at the door and tried her best to pretend like nothing had happened, but she knew the truth—Summer wouldn't hesitate to torch Grace's entire life as she knew it.

PART 5

#BurnItDown

TWENTY-THREE

Elaine Miyamoto

Friday, November 6
9:57 p.m.

Laney's not sure what she was expecting when Adam texted her to ask if they could meet at her house to review photos and video from the party, but it wasn't a four-way staring contest with Adam, Grace, and Cora in her living room. Though maybe she should have expected that. They aren't friends—well, other than Grace and Adam kind of. The rest have nothing in common except for Summer herself.

For all Laney knows, one of the others is a psychopathic killer, and she's next. She's glad Oscar insisted on crashing the party, even if he is eating all the Flamin' Hot Cheetos, just in case Cora pulls a shiv out of her purse and Laney needs him to call the cops.

Grace blinks first. She adjusts her feet so the soles of her sneakers aren't touching Rebekah's white-white sofa. "So . . . should we . . ."

"Yep," Adam says. "I have the pictures on my iPad."

But Laney holds up one finger as her dad comes into the room, still in his work khakis. She doesn't want to deal with explaining to him why they're all together. Earlier, when she mentioned she had people coming over tonight, she told him it was a study group for chemistry. She has the text book in her lap.

At least her dad isn't on social media. In sixth period, Laney found a meme of her own face—a pic someone took at the vigil of her shocked eyes and slack jaw—with the caption, *That moment when you realize you're a million percent screwed.* Another version read, *When you realize the final project you haven't started is due in ten minutes, and it's 50% of your grade.* There were probably more, but Laney turned off her Wi-Fi.

"More snacks, anyone?" Laney's dad asks now. "There's water, sparkling water . . . popcorn, plenty of chips and salsa."

"We'll be fine, Dad," Laney says. "I promise to feed and water them."

Oscar looks up from where he's sprawled on the overstuffed love-seat. "And I'll chaperone. No making out on my watch."

Laney's dad gives her and Oscar both a look. "I'm heading to bed, then."

Laney still isn't used to the fact that when her dad goes to bed, he's going to Rebekah. It's gross.

Cora helps herself to one of the schmancy candies Rebekah leaves out in a cut-glass dish. Laney suspects the candy is like her stepmom's seashell soaps—you don't actually use them, you just look at them. "I'll go first since I'm the one who kind of called this meeting. I talked to Avalon James. She hates Summer, like, a lot. So I say she's a valid suspect. Right?"

"Oh, come on," Adam says. "She and Summer hadn't even talked for months."

"Besides, does she really hate her? Or is she just bitter?" Grace says.

"Because there's a difference. We shouldn't jump the gun."

"Calling out suspicious behavior isn't jumping the gun," Laney says. So typical of Grace, always trying to find the best in people. How nice. Everyone likes Grace for that, but Laney would rather be mean than be in jail. She twists to pop her lower back, but it's too tight.

"Want my two cents?" Oscar asks.

"No," Laney says.

"He was at the party, too," Adam says. "Maybe he can help."

"He was too busy flirting."

Oscar smiles. "For your information, I'm an excellent multitasker."

"Fine then, Sherlock. What's your value add?"

"Only that police are looking for someone with means, motive, and opportunity, right? And the four of you have all those things. E-cigarettes aren't hard to get ahold of. With a decent fake ID, you could buy them yourselves, and let's be real. We all know someone trying to quit smoking, right?"

"What about motive?" Adam asks.

"For god's sake, Adam." Laney is sick of lying to herself. "After that night at Griffith Park, it's abundantly clear that we all have motives. Let's move it along."

"But actually killing Summer?" Cora says. "That's way too—"

"Sweet Cora." Oscar pats her on the shoulder. "Nearly everyone at school probably has a motive for killing Summer. And someone did."

Grace twines and untwines her hands, then clears her throat. "There's something you guys should know. Summer's book is still coming out. Harrison told me this morning."

Shocked silence falls over the group. If Summer's book comes out, Laney's chances of film school—of any decent school—will evaporate.

"What?" Cora's voice squeaks. "No one told me that it was—"

"We're screwed," Laney says. "Big time." That day at Griffith Park, each of them admitted that Summer knew things about them. They basically had to, because Summer had given them all dirt on one of the others. It was genius, really. That's how Summer was. Like a steel-jaw trap for an animal, she stroked egos until people opened up to her, then when she needed to, she used the information to break them.

Oscar taps his nose. "Excellent, Elaine. I admire your brutal acceptance of reality, though perhaps not totally screwed. You all had means, yes. Motive, apparently. Now opportunity. From where I was sitting on the couch, I had a perfect view of the hallway leading to the bedrooms. You went back there, Grace. Alone."

Grace's eyes widen. "I didn't—"

"But you did, my friend. You did. It was just after Laney and I arrived. You ditched your clipboard and slipped out for, what, maybe five, ten minutes?"

"If you'd let me finish," Grace says. "I was going to say I didn't do anything to Summer. When I came back, she was still alive."

"Poison takes time."

"Look," Adam says. "We had to use the hall bathroom. I'd be willing to bet that lots of people went back in that hallway. I did. I hydrated. I had to pee. So yeah, I guess I had opportunity, too."

"Is this supposed to make us feel better, Oscar?" Grace asks. "Because it doesn't."

Oscar sits up straighter. "You don't see it? This is good. If it looks like all of you could have killed Summer, then as far as the police are concerned, none of you did. They have no way of proving anything beyond a shadow of a doubt."

Laney has to admit Oscar is right. "I wonder how many other people, I mean aside from us, had the opportunity?"

"Can I borrow your computer?" Grace gestures at Laney's laptop, which she left out on the coffee table. When Laney nods, Grace logs into her email and clicks on a video file. "I got Harrison's video footage."

The five of them spend the next hour scrolling through Blossom's pictures and Harrison's video from the party. Most of the video is Harrison's version of an authentic take—lots of unflattering angles, drunken ramblings, and a clip of Summer giving him the finger. But in the background of a few shots, they do see people going into the back hallway. Grace. A random couple who lean against the hallway wall to make out. Adam. A girl who seems lost. Avalon. Laney.

"Harrison was back in that hallway, too," Grace says. "Though obviously not on video. I passed him leaving the bathroom."

Cora sits up excitedly. "So there are at least two people with motive and opportunity aside from us who could have poisoned her and written on her face. Literally millions of people can vouch for the fact that Summer's page hurt Avalon, and—"

"So because Summer blew up Avalon's career, now she's a killer?" Adam asks. "You're just going to destroy her life even more than Summer already did?"

"I'm just throwing out ideas." Cora crosses her arms over her chest. "And Harrison is Summer's brother. I'm sure there's some reason he might want to kill her."

"Dark. I don't want to kill my sisters," Adam says.

Cora's chin juts out defiantly—Laney's pretty sure she doesn't do well with differences of opinion—so she jumps in to diffuse the tension. "I might kill Oscar if he keeps leaving toothpaste dribble in the sink," Laney says.

Oscar clutches his chest. "You strike at the heart, Elaine."

"I don't know," Grace says. "I mean, Summer and Harrison *were* competitive. Their dad was always pitting them against each other, but I don't know if that's a motive?"

"So what then?" Adam looks at each one of them in turn. "You want to go to the police? Get ourselves even more involved?"

Cora shrugs. "Maybe? But my dad says the court of public opinion is the most important court to win. We need to get the internet on our side."

Laney has to admit to herself that Cora might be right. That post on Summer's page majorly screwed the four of them, but if they could get people to stop posting those awful memes and making accusations, maybe they'd be less in the spotlight. Maybe people would start posting about other suspects. That couldn't be a bad thing.

Cora's confidence wavers when no one answers her immediately. "Don't you guys think?"

Saturday, October 31, last week, 9:15 p.m.
Summer's Halloween Party

Laney saw her opportunity to slip away from the living room when
everyone was distracted with Grace's murder mystery announcement.
Laney wasn't the type of girl to wait around, a damsel in distress, for
someone to save her. She had always been into the idea that the princess
can get herself out of the damn tower. For months now, Summer had
been holding Laney's letter of recommendation from her father over her
head. Laney, don't be ridiculous. You can't even apply for early action
yet. Of course I'm going to give the letter to you. There's just one
more little favor. . . .

There was always one more little favor, all connected like branches on
the tree of the first favor that got Laney into this mess. The thing she had
done to get that letter would destroy her if it got out, and Summer knew
it and used it. That was what happened when you made a deal with the
devil.

But Laney was done with little favors. She wanted her letter.
According to Summer, her dad had written it back in September. So
where was he keeping it? His desk? Somewhere else in his office? Laney
planned to find out. If she found it, she wouldn't need Summer anymore.

"Gotta pee," she told Oscar, who was distracted by the girl in
the princess gown. If he kept this up, their first date would be at a
Renaissance festival. They'd share a turkey leg and maybe some saliva.
Adorable.

"Have at it," he said.

Julian Cartwright's office was easy to find. Glass-paned french doors separated it from the back hallway, and through the doors, Laney could see a desk framed by paneled shelves filled with leather-bound books.

Laney opened the door as nonchalantly as she could. Look like she belonged, and no one would question it. But where to begin? The desk overflowed with paperwork, and there was a huge filing cabinet in the back corner. Laney sifted through the papers on the desk, opened and closed desk drawers aimlessly. There was no way she'd find the letter in this chaos of paperwork.

Then Laney saw a worn book sitting on the cushion of a leather chair. It was Faust. It had been required summer reading for AP Lit. The corner of an envelope stuck out the top. Laney opened the book and slipped out the envelope. It wasn't sealed, so she pulled out the paper inside.

It was her recommendation letter. A good one. Words like stunning talent *and* compelling artistry *caught her eye. It was real; it existed! She slid it in the waistband of her shorts. That was it, then—Summer had no power over her. Laney didn't let herself think about the fact that Summer still had major blackmail on her, that Summer could fill a chapter of her book with what Laney did to help her. As she left the office and headed to Summer's bedroom to search for murder mystery "clues," she didn't let herself think about the highlighted passage the letter bookmarked.*

"Who holds the devil, let him hold him well. He hardly will be caught a second time."

TWENTY-FOUR

Adam Mahmoud

Saturday, November 7
12:35 a.m.

After leaving Laney's house past midnight, Adam and Grace park in the lot of her apartment complex. Instead of getting out of the car, Grace unbuckles her seat belt and asks, "Can we hang out? Just for a little bit?"

"Sure." Adam's mom will already be in bed, and his dad is pretty chill about him being out late, as long as he texts. He shoots him one now to say he's with Grace.

"Summer's funeral is Sunday," Grace says.

"Yeah, I heard." It would be a small service for family only, followed by the burial. He wasn't invited. Why would he be? Still, it feels like he should be there. "Are you going?"

"I kind of have to. Harrison asked me to come."

A jolt of sharp jealousy hits his gut. What is it about Harrison that Grace likes? Why Harrison and not him? He knows how heartless it is to be thinking about stuff like that so soon after Summer's death, but he can't help himself. Things are going well with Grace, so as much as he wants to ask, he doesn't. "You going to be okay?"

She shrugs. "No."

"I'm sorry."

"Do you ever wonder if we'll ever be okay again after all this?" She curls her knees to her chest. "Like, can we ever be the same people we were before Summer, or are those people gone forever?"

"We won't be the same again, that's for sure. But . . ." Adam takes a moment to consider. "I think maybe one day, we'll be okay. We had lives before Summer, you know?"

Grace smiles and takes the hand he was resting on the car's gear stick. She squeezes it, then lets go so quickly, he wonders if he imagined it. "I hope you're right."

What starts as conversation about tonight at Laney's and at Summer's funeral and the investigation shifts to reminiscing about middle school and all the times they did stupid things at lunch, like combine the leftover drinks at the table to create one nauseating mixture that, for five bucks, someone would drink.

"Remember when you first moved here?" Adam asks. "How quiet you were? I could barely get you to tell me your name."

"So embarrassing."

"The whole bus ride to school, you just looked at me with those big cartoon eyes—"

"Shut up. I do not have cartoon eyes." Grace laughs. "And people are just more reserved in Rhode Island. East Coast vibes."

"Is that where you're from? Why did I think Ohio?"

"I was born in Rhode Island, but we moved after my parents got divorced. I lived in Ohio before LA. A few other places in between. You knew that."

"I didn't!" It's hard to believe that after all these years of being friends with Grace, there are still things he doesn't know about her. "Where did you like living the best?"

"LA by far. Though in Rhode Island, there was this marina near our house? Sometimes on Saturday morning, my mom would take me to get doughnuts, then we'd go look at the boats. She'd ask me where I'd sail if I had the chance." As she talks, her voice grows slushy with sleep.

They trade stories about their lives, most of them starting with "remember when": *Remember when we tried out for the sixth-grade play and both got cut because you got stage fright and bolted, and I refused to be Prince Charming unless you were Cinderella? Remember when you got sent to the nurse, then the principal's office in seventh grade because Kyle M. dared you to do parkour in the cafeteria, and you broke a table?*

Then, out of nowhere, just when Adam thinks they might both doze off, Grace asks, "Do you regret it?"

He doesn't have to ask what she means. He thinks about it all the time, that ten minutes. It was the end of September, and after dinner with his family, Adam went for a walk to clear his head. He had read some pretty messed up stuff about himself online, serious stuff that he couldn't talk about with anyone. He walked until his street dead-ended in the playground. Throughout the years, either the park had gotten crappier or maybe WW Prep had made his standards higher. The chains on the swings were rusty, the sun had bleached the red plastic slide pink, and the sandbox was more gravel and weeds than sand.

But at the playground, Grace sat on a swing, pushing it side-to-side with the toe of one sneaker. Her long hair hung loose, and with no makeup on and in a pair of black sweats, she was middle school Gracie again. His entire body relaxed when he realized that he could tell Grace what he was going through. She was the only person in the world that he knew without a shadow of a doubt wouldn't judge him. And it was in that moment—that exact moment when she looked up and saw him—that he knew he was in love with her.

Not Summer. Grace. It had always been Grace. It took his breath away.

He sat on the swing beside hers and pushed it sideways so he bumped into her. She laughed. Bumped him back. This was what he'd always wanted and hadn't known he wanted. Simplicity, nights spent watching the sun setting behind the city, understanding. He didn't care about being a somebody, about massive success on Twitch or in college or about being the guy Summer could be proud of in public. With Summer, Adam was always playing a role that he didn't want to play anymore.

With Grace, he could just be Adam, and he was enough.

So the next time their swings bumped, he grabbed the rusty chain, pulled her close, tangled one hand in her hair, and kissed her. After a second of hesitation, she kissed him back. Their kiss was desperate, like they both knew it only existed in that fragmented moment and could never happen again.

And it never had, because Grace started ignoring him after that. Even after he'd broken up with Summer at school.

That kiss changed everything between them, maybe forever. It changed him. Was Summer right when she said, *Once a cheater, always a cheater*? Was that who he was now? Had Summer been talking only about him and Grace, or did she know about the other thing he'd done?

So, does he regret it? For right now, at two in the morning in a dark parking lot outside Grace's apartment building, he answers Grace honestly. "I don't know."

She nods. "I don't know, either." Then she opens the car door and runs up the outside stairwell to her apartment.

The_Summer_Cartwright

✨#TrustYourself ✨

.

I've been thinking a lot in the last few days about #SelfTrust. You guys know I've always been about #SelfLove—take that bubble bath, make that leap, eat that ice cream, let go of that guilt and shame. You are beautiful. You are amazing. You are YOU. 🫠

.

But self-trust is a little different. If I had to define it, I'd say it's the ability to listen to your gut when it tells you something, even if it seems extreme. Like leaving that party when something feels off, or trying again when the first try almost broke you. Like cutting someone out of your life completely when they break your heart so badly you can't breathe. Your peace is worthy of protection.

.

Other people might call you insensitive or ruthless. They might not get it. But I'm here to say without a doubt that you should go with your gut, wherever it leads, even if you have to walk in the dark for a while to find the light again, even if you end up alone. Screw the people who screwed you over. They don't love you, so why should you care about them? Keep walking, keep going, and if you're brave enough, take the shortcut and light the whole damn path on fire. 🔥 🔥 🔥

.

Love,
SumSum 🖤

₪ 🖤 ▶

See all 2,731 responses

L.Miy2006 You do you, girl! 🔥 Just don't let yourself get burned!

LittleHulkie31 If you have something to say, just say it @The_Summer_Cartwright. 😕 This post came off suuuuper passive aggressive . . .

SumSumsCloset OMFGGGG! @The_Summer_Cartwright you are the MOST inspiring ever!! #goals

G-Money$$ Want to make $1200 a week? @ me and comment ME!! 💰💵💰

OhmygodwinGrace Love you @The_Summer_Cartwright! Thanks for sharing this!! Xoxo

The_Summer_Cartwright @LittleHulkie31 I'm sorry, are you a person or a cartoon character? @OhmygodwinGrace you know you inspire me. This post wouldn't be here without you and A. #AllTheHeartEyes

CloudiaJay You losers who stalk this page need to get a life.

The_Summer_Cartwright @CloudiaJay feel free to unfollowwww! 🌚 All the love . . .

TWENTY FIVE

Cora Pruitt

Saturday, November 7
9:30 p.m.

Cora checks her phone for the twentieth time. Still no text. She wants to hurl her phone across the room. Instead, she slides her diary from beneath her mattress and scribbles in it until her frustration subsides and she can think more clearly. Probably, she should stay off social media, too, because there are, like, a ton of new pages popping up on Instagram all about solving Summer's murder, and according to popular opinion, either she, Adam, Grace, or Laney definitely killed Summer. For a while, some people wanted to pin it on Summer's dad, probably because he's one of those men who looks totally suspicious, but then people pointed out that he and his wife were out of the country when Summer died.

After the four of them met last night, Cora was positive that things would be different—that they would be a team, *friends* even—but she hasn't heard from any of them all day, which doesn't work with the

Mystery Inc. vibes she's been storyboarding in her head.

If she were here now, Summer would want Cora to figure out what really happened that night at the Halloween party, wouldn't she? Cora can almost hear her voice in her ear. *Screw the others, Cora. You're the only sophomore I invited to my party, and there's a reason for that. You're the only one I trust. You have to figure this out. Please. Please.*

Cora is home alone tonight. Her parents went out to some fund-raising gala (Wells in Africa? Funding for pediatric cancer research?) even though they couldn't care less about any of the causes. Donating makes them look good, and appearances are everything. Amanda's spending the night at their aunt's, because their mom doesn't trust Cora to take care of Amanda if she has a seizure. She messed up the one time. Once! But whatever.

With no one to distract her, Cora's freaking out. After reading through thousands of comments online, she's pretty sure it's too late to convince the Instagram community to pick a new suspect to obsess over. She can't stop thinking that the first person to be totally honest with the police gets the best treatment, so why not her? She can tell them the whole conversation the four of them had in Griffith Park, and since she'd be the one to come forward, they'd be way less suspicious of her.

She'd be screwing the others over. She sees that. But Laney's been rude to her ever since they met, and Adam only cares about himself and Grace. He completely shot down her idea about Avalon. Besides, she was the one to get up and leave that day in Griffith Park, the one to tell the others that their conversation was messed up. Not Adam. Not Laney. Not Grace. Her. So she doesn't really care if she screws them over, especially with how awful they treated Summer.

Grace, though . . . she's always been nice to Cora, saying hi to her in the hallway when other people walked right by. So thirty minutes ago, Cora fired off a text to Grace asking her if she was freaking out as much as Cora right now.

But that was thirty minutes ago, and Grace left her on read. She couldn't take two seconds to respond? Nothing? At first, Cora worried that she did something to upset Grace, but now, she's just pissed. If Grace won't respond to her texts, Cora will go to her.

She slides her feet into flip-flops and throws a sweater over the tank top she wears to bed. Even though she's only got her learner's permit, she's a great driver, and if she follows the speed limit and makes sure her headlights are on, who's going to pull her over? When Summer shared Grace's contact a few months ago when she was in the hospital to get her appendix out, her address with apartment number was included. Cora's mom's minivan is in the garage. The keys are on the kitchen counter. She'll be back long before anyone gets home.

Twenty minutes later, Cora circles the block in front of Grace's apartment building until she finds a spot by a playground to park the minivan. She wrinkles her nose. This is where Grace lives? Litter lines the gutters in the street, and the air smells vaguely of fry grease and urine. Less than a block away, a highway overpass intersects the neighborhood so she can hear cars whooshing by. She can't imagine Summer ever coming here.

She checks her phone. Still no text. Apartment 3B it is. The windows are lit, so she's home.

Cora almost goes to the buzzer to call up to Grace's apartment, but when someone goes into the building across the street, she follows them in. Maybe from a top floor window, she'll be able to see into 3B.

She's rewarded for climbing four flights of stairs with a clear view into Grace's living room. Two figures—Grace and her mom?—sit on a gray couch, heads bent together like they're watching TV. Grace isn't doing anything important. If she had wanted to respond to Cora, she could have. She chose not to.

Cora's chest fills with rage. Here she is, worrying about what to say to the police so she doesn't screw the others over, and not one of them gives a shit about her.

Well, fine. Tomorrow, she'll go talk to the police and tell them everything she knows. About the conversation in Griffith Park, about Summer's Instagram, all of it. Screw Laney and Adam. But especially screw Grace.

As Cora watches, the two embrace, so happy, so comfortable. So not lonely like Cora is.

Cora's mom never spends time with her. No matter what she does, her mom thinks she's irresponsible. She's not strong like Amanda, not confident like Summer, not nice like Grace. And even though she tried on all those attributes at one point or another, none of them stuck. She'd say that people underestimate her, but no one cares about her enough to give her a second thought.

Some people have everything, and other people have nothing. And it's. Not. Fair.

Friday, February 21, 9:30 p.m.
Cora's House

Cora chucked her pencil onto the kitchen table, annoyed. It rolled until it stuck in the crack between yellow tiles that decorated the tabletop. Her mom was hitting the Tuscan theme hard enough that their kitchen looked like an Olive Garden. It disgusted Cora. And this homework . . . What was even the point of algebra anyway? Her teacher liked to go on and on about how they wouldn't always have calculators in their pockets, but, like, she had a cellphone? And the most math she'd need to do on the fly would be calculating 30 percent off at the Nordstrom's winter clearance sale.

It was Friday night, her dad was working late to make tons of money, and her mom was volunteering away her guilt at a charity auction raising funds for desks for underprivileged schoolchildren in Guatemala.

Cora was under strict instructions to stay home and watch Amanda. There was no way Summer Cartwright would be sitting in the kitchen doing equations when the world was out there. She was probably at a party or having a movie night with her friends or taking a moonlit beach walk with Adam Mahmoud and they'd sit on the sand and make out and the cops would interrupt them and tell them it was a public beach and they'd laugh about it and have great stories to tell their future children. Ughhhhh, perfection.

Meanwhile, Cora would tell her future children about math. She had to get out of the house.

"I'm going out for a little bit," Cora called to Amanda, who was

*baking cupcakes in her fluffy slippers. She had to repeat herself louder,
because Amanda had her earbuds in listening to some disturbing podcast
about an old lady who hid bodies in her basement. God, it must be nice
to be not-quite thirteen, when it didn't matter if you didn't have plans
on a Friday night.*

*Amanda took out an earbud with her hand that wasn't covered in
flour. "Now? Mom said—"*

"I'm losing my mind. I need some fresh air."

"You're going to get in trouble."

*"No, I'm not, because I'm going to be back before she gets home from
the auction."*

*"Where are you going?" Amanda cracked an egg into her mixing
bowl, then dropped the eggshell into the garbage disposal.*

"I don't know. Just out."

*"No guarantee these cupcakes will be around when you get back."
Amanda held out the bowl of buttercream frosting that was waiting for
the first batch of cupcakes to finish cooling.*

"You're going to eat two dozen cupcakes in the next hour?"

*"I'm hungry." Amanda screwed up her lips, and for a moment, her
pleading eyes almost swayed Cora. She looked so young. "Please don't go?"*

*But Cora had to know what Summer was up to tonight. How exactly
did people like her live? Summer's house was a fifteen-minute Uber
ride away. She wouldn't knock or anything, just . . . see if she could see
Summer through a window.*

*For the briefest moment, it crossed Cora's mind that watching
Summer through a window was creepy, but she brushed it aside. She
wasn't going to do anything creepy to Summer. Watching never hurt
anyone.*

*Twenty minutes later, Cora stood on the sidewalk outside of
Summer's building looking up at the lit windows on the top floor.*

Because the building was only five floors, Cora could still glimpse a few rooms in the Cartwrights' luxury penthouse loft. This neighborhood was so different from her own with its blaring traffic sounds, horns and motors and thumping bass from car radios. Since the Cartwrights owned the fifth floor penthouse, Cora couldn't see more than lit windows. The dark window on the left was Summer's, the lights probably off because Summer was out so she didn't need them, and Summer was the type of person to care about the environment and her carbon footprint, which Cora totally admired.

When someone tapped her shoulder, Cora jumped, like, three feet in the air. She whirled, sure it was a mugger and ready to give up her purse even though it was brand-new. Then it occurred to her that muggers usually don't tap people on the shoulder, and by the time that registered, Summer Cartwright was already raising an eyebrow at her. Because it was such an ingrained habit, Cora did a quick fashion sweep of Summer and decided her high-waisted jeans, embroidered at the hems and pockets with astrological signs, were totally random but Summer pulled them off.

"Are you spying on me?" Before Cora could decide how to answer, Summer laughed at her. "Oh my god, you're such a freak, Cora."

"What are you doing out here?"

"In my own neighborhood?"

"Right." Cora winced. "I was going to buzz your loft, but—"

"Whatever, weirdo. But since you're here and clearly my biggest fan, help me with something." Summer grabbed her arm and dragged her to a nearby bench.

"Um, okay?"

"You're the one who just started that closet page, right? You tagged me in your first post last week."

"Yes?" Was that the right answer? Did it make her seem desperate? She had no idea.

"Let me pick your brain. What would you want me to post about next? Like, what content are you looking for?"

Cora chewed her lip and considered. Out of the corner of her eye, she could see Summer watching her. It felt like a test. "A post about staying fit when school gets busy?"

"Played out."

"Best sweaters for winter?"

Summer groaned and stood up like she was ready to leave. "How many times can I write the same thing? No one's life changes with the right sweater."

"Or . . ." Cora racked her brain for a fresh idea. "Finding your identity when everyone is pressuring you to be someone else? Like . . ." She could tell Summer was about to walk away and was desperate to keep her attention. "Like ripping off the mask of who everyone wants you to be?"

Summer considered. "Not bad for a stalker."

"I wasn't—"

"Of course you weren't." She held out a hand to help Cora up. "So if you were going to write that post, how would you start it?"

"I could . . . I don't know . . . write up a draft for you?" Cora's heart accelerated when she realized what she'd implied—that Summer couldn't write it herself.

But Summer shrugged and said, "Okay. Text it to me tomorrow?"

"Sure."

And as Cora ubered home, her head resting against the cool glass of the car window, she saw her chance to live. Maybe it wouldn't be her own life, but living vicariously through Summer had to be better than just being Cora.

TWENTY SIX

Adam Mahmoud

Sunday, November 8
10:19 a.m.

After closing the door to his room just after two a.m. he was still wide awake, so he spent a few hours playing *Mythos*. It wasn't the best time of night for streaming—fewer followers were on, especially since it was five a.m. Eastern Time—but it made him feel like he was accomplishing something at least. Not to mention that sliding on his gold Zeus mask made him feel like he was Man of Mythos. Not Adam. He didn't have Adam's problems or concerns. He could just defeat the Hydra, strike at its heart instead of uselessly chopping off heads like it felt like he was doing in real life. Defeat one problem only for two more to grow back.

Yesterday, he spent the entire day trying to distract himself by playing with his sisters and helping his mom with her annual fruit canning and watching the UCLA game with his dad. It worked in little spurts—for a minute or two, he'd forget about Summer—then reality would come crashing back, more painful than ever.

Today, though, when he wakes up around ten, he doesn't want to ride the waves of emotion with his family as an audience. Across town, Summer's funeral is beginning, and he'd rather be alone. He can't handle Lia and Samia's shrieks of laughter, can't handle his mom's solicitous questions about how he's doing—no how he's *really* doing—can't handle his dad's raised eyebrows when he asks about Grace. At home, Adam has tried to hide the stress of the investigation from his family, but he's cracking. He needs to go out.

Grabbing his keys from the hook by the front door, Adam drives to the Beanery with his copy of *The Scarlet Letter* from American Lit. Maybe he can get some homework done if he has coffee and lots of it. Aside from the adrenaline-induced productivity on the day after Summer's death, he hasn't done any all week. His teachers are starting to get on his case, especially since the terms of his scholarship state he has to keep a minimum 3.0 GPA.

He snags a table in the back, one of the ones where the booth backs extend to the ceiling for added privacy, and opens his book to the bookmark. Two hours later, he's three pages further, and all three of those pages were describing the same rosebush. There's probably some sort of important symbolism there he should be annotating for class, but he has no clue what it is.

Just as he's about to give up, someone slides into the seat across from him. Before he looks up from his book, he notices her smell, cloying perfume masking the sharp bite of tequila, Miranda Cartwright's poison-of-choice.

Slowly, he tucks his bookmark back inside *The Scarlet Letter* and tries to prepare himself for whatever might be coming. Miranda watches him with bloodshot blue eyes. Her usually upright posture is bent, and her ever-present sunglasses push her blond hair back from her forehead. She's wearing all black.

Miranda taps a red nail on his book. "One of the first books to acknowledge that women pay while men get away. That's what my English teacher told me when I was your age."

Adam doesn't know what to say to Miranda—what do you say to someone after she just buried a daughter?—but he feels for her. She did lose Summer only a few days ago. He can't imagine what state his mom would be in if something happened to him or his sisters.

She folds her hands on the table in front of her. "Summer's funeral was this morning."

It takes him a moment to decide what the best response would be. "You must miss her."

"Of course I do."

"I miss her, too."

It's the truth. When you date someone for a year, no matter how it ends, there's always a part of you that misses them. The bad times fall away in their absence, leaving a dulled glow of positive memories. Like the time he and Summer skipped homecoming sophomore year to go mini golfing in Santa Monica, she in a mid-thigh-length white dress, he in khakis and a white shirt rolled to his elbows. They laughed themselves silly and got out of their Uber at a red light to take a kissing selfie in the middle of the road, much to their driver's dismay.

Miranda taps her fingers on the table. Her eyes are even redder than they were a second ago. "We also found out this morning her publisher changed the release date for her book."

"Really?" Adam allows himself to feel a moment of relief. Maybe this could buy him time to—

"It comes out next month."

"Like, December?"

"The week before Christmas, with an added section about her murder at the end written by a renowned mystery novelist. The speculation surrounding her death translates into book sales. Nothing like a good dead girl to make the holidays bright." Her laughter is bitter as she stands. "When I saw you over here, I figured you might want to know. Considering."

"What is that supposed to mean?"

"The preorders are massive. It's a guaranteed *New York Times* best seller."

"What do you mean, you figured I might want to know?"

"Just that you're about to be famous." She puts her dark sunglasses back on her nose and heads toward the door. But when Adam follows her, desperate for clearer answers, she stops. "I want you to know this, really know it, Adam. If you hadn't left my daughter, if you'd still cared about her, she would be alive today. I hope that haunts you."

When she pushes open the door to the Beanery with her shoulder, Adam close behind her, the world explodes in a burst of light. Or at least, Adam thinks it does for a moment. When his vision clears, he sees the hoard of paparazzi, their cameras pointed at him. Someone must have called them. Miranda? He knows what it looks like, what the headline will read:

"Ex-Boyfriend of Murder Victim Torments Her Mother in Her Time of Grief."

Or "Teenaged Murder Suspect Stalks Mother of Victim, Wife of Studio Head."

Or "Sixteen-Year-Old Mahmoud: One of Four Suspects in Summer Cartwright's Murder. Is Her Mother Next?"

He puts a hand in front of his face and retreats back into the Beanery. *Considering.* He can't get that word out of his head. Does that mean Miranda Cartwright read Summer's book? And if so, does she know what he did?

By the time Adam sneaks out the back of the Beanery and cuts through an alley to his Jeep, he doesn't even care what garbage the tabloids come up with, not when Miranda Cartwright might have a point. If Adam hadn't broken up with Summer, maybe she would still be alive.

The_Summer_Cartwright

#NaturalConsequences 👀

.

In my upcoming memoir All Your Likes Can't Buy Me Love, which comes out in March (available for preorder as of November 1!! See link in bio), I discuss life, love, success, and betrayal—no holds barred. No one in my life is off-limits.

.

Why, you ask? We all make choices, and we have to live with them. I totally get that sometimes, accidents happen, but when we decide to do something on purpose, the consequences are our payment, right? And one natural consequence is the world finding out your true colors.

.

So to begin, please enjoy this excerpt from chapter 3: "The Doodle That Did It."

.

I've heard all my life that girls fall in love with men who are like their dads, and honestly? Gross, amiright? Like, no, thank you. When I started dating Adam Mahmoud, the idea never even occurred to me. He's an athlete, no interest at all in the movie business or fame, which was a breath of fresh air. Then I found out about his Twitch channel. Not because he told me. Because I figured it out on my own.

.

At first, I was like, noooo, there's no way Man of Mythos is my boyfriend! But the more I watched, the more I started to realize that it is, in fact, him. But it was the doodle that did it. At lunch, pretending like I was being all cute or whatever, I drew a sunshine on the inside of his wrist with my red pen. Guess what showed up in the video? I didn't care that he played on Twitch. We all need hobbies. But it bothered me that he didn't tell me about it! I was his girlfriend!

.

Then, after doing some digging, I found out Adam Mahmoud is a huge cheater. . . .

.

More details to come. Better buy the book to find out what he did! Let's just say this: It gave me the creeps, because turns out, I was dating a younger version of my dad after all. 😱

Love,
SumSum 🖤

₪ 🖤 ▶

LAST EDITED OCTOBER 31 AT 1:46 P.M.

TWENTY-SEVEN

Grace Godwin

Monday, November 9
9:57 a.m.

Monday morning, Grace slogs through the first two periods. Sunday was the hardest day of her life. Summer's funeral, even with the few attendees holding tight to their celebration-of-life fake cheer, was long and sad. Grace has never felt more terrified than the moment when Summer's casket was lowered into the ground and shovelfuls of dirt were poured over it.

She thought she might suffocate. She still might.

At the beginning of third-period Chemistry, the school secretary calls Grace's name over the intercom. She's never been in the head-master's office before, not at any school, and her brain can't help but fly through all the reasons for calling her. Headmaster Norton might want to talk to her about losing the Excellence Grant, or maybe he found out she skipped school without permission Thursday morning. Worst of all, it could be that the detectives are on campus to talk to her. It's all over the school that they pulled Laney from class Friday while Grace was out with Harrison, and now, Laney is rising in the murder polls people keep posting on Instagram.

"Leave your books here," Mr. Miller says when Grace starts to pack up. "I'm sure you'll be back soon. Get notes from . . ." His gaze sweeps the room. "Laney, you have good handwriting. We'll copy your notes for Grace at lunch."

Laney gives Mr. Miller a thumbs-up, but when he turns his back, she mouths *Don't be stupid* to Grace. It's the closest to an overture of friendship Laney has ever made to her.

When Grace gets to Headmaster Norton's office, her worst fears are confirmed. Both Detective Mwanthi and Detective Lombardo wait in the cushioned chairs facing the headmaster's big wooden desk. The only chair left for Grace is a plastic one dragged in from a classroom.

"Sorry to pull you out of class like this, Grace," Detective Mwanthi says. With one shined black shoe crossed over his opposite knee, he looks more at ease than ever, and his ease terrifies Grace. Not that she knows much about detectives in real life, but on TV, they're always most at ease when they already know the answers to the questions they're going to ask. "Headmaster Norton here says your teachers will gladly let you make up your work."

"You aren't a suspect at this point, Grace," Detective Lombardo says. "We don't have our sights set on anyone. We're just trying to get some answers."

Headmaster Norton clears his throat. "I called your mother immediately, of course, to let her know that the detectives wish to speak with you. She would like to remind you that if you feel as though you need a lawyer—"

"Got it." Grace shifts from one foot to the other. "So . . ."

"Have a seat," Detective Lombardo says. "This will take a few minutes."

Mwanthi uncrosses his leg and leans forward, his eyes intent on Grace as she sits in the cold chair. "This morning, early, we had a visit at the station from one of your friends. Cora Pruitt. She had some interesting things to share about a conversation she had with you in Griffith Park. It would have been a few weeks ago. Do you recall the day I'm speaking of?"

"Um." Grace's heart accelerates.

"Grace?"

"Yes. Sorry. I remember."

"According to Cora, you had a conversation with her, Adam Mahmoud, and Elaine Miyamoto relating to Summer Cartwright and her book, and in this conversation you insinuated that the only way Summer wouldn't spill your secrets would be if she were dead."

Grace's palms start sweating, and she barely keeps herself from wiping them on her pants. She remembers that day in Griffith Park, obviously. Summer asked to meet her there to pose for a few pics for a post she'd planned on friendship. What a joke. Even though it felt weird going all the way to the top of that hill for a pic, Grace didn't have the right to even ask for Summer's rationale, not after she'd kissed Adam on the swings. Intense guilt gnawed at her stomach every time she thought about it. She would have done anything Summer asked, no matter how ridiculous.

So she went to the park. Summer wasn't there. Instead, Grace was left with a text from Summer cancelling their plans and a conversation with Laney, Adam, and Cora that could only have been a setup. Summer wanted them to figure out how much she knew. Who started the discussion about Summer's book? About their secrets?

Grace swallows hard and forces herself to make eye contact with

Mwanthi. "I know that conversation was super dark and awful, but we didn't mean anything by it."

"Did you, in fact, say those words?" Mwanthi asks. "That 'the only way to be sure Summer won't spill our secrets would be if she was dead'?"

"Not those exact words." Grace should stop talking. She should lawyer up right now, but there's something about the way Lombardo is watching her, dark eyes blank, head tilted to one side, that reminds Grace of Summer herself. Whenever Summer looked at her like that, it was because she didn't believe her. Grace saw a lot of that look in the weeks leading up to Summer's death and seeing it again in Lombardo . . . it made Grace desperate to prove herself.

"But you insinuated it?" Mwanthi asks.

Headmaster Norton clears his throat. "Remember, Grace, you can ask for a lawyer. You can stop speaking at any time. In fact, I rather think that—"

"Haven't you ever been super pissed at someone and said, 'I'm so mad, I could kill her,' but not actually meant it?" Grace asks.

"Sure," Lombardo says.

"That's all it was. Yeah, it got out of hand. It was ill-advised. But it's not like I was actually planning to kill Summer."

Mwanthi finishes writing something in his notebook, then nods. "Fair enough. I do have to ask, though. What did Cora mean . . . secrets?"

"I have no idea." Lies. Lies, lies, lies, lies. Her face would give her away, but she couldn't tell the truth, not without ruining her life.

"I think you do. And if I had to guess based on a post about you Summer scheduled for next week, it has something to do with Adam Mahmoud."

Grace's shoulders sag with relief before she catches herself. That's all they think it is? Adam? She's happy to tell them all about the kiss if it means she can avoid talking about the other thing.

"Is he right, Grace?" Lombardo asks. "It's better for everyone if you tell us the truth now. We will find out one way or another."

"I liked Adam before he started dating Summer. Is that what you want to hear?"

"If it's true."

"It is."

"Why didn't you say something to him then?"

Grace shrugs. "He's been like my brother since middle school. What was I supposed to say? I love you?"

"Do you?" Lombardo asks.

"Do I what?"

"Love him?"

And even though Grace told herself she'd tell them the truth about this at least, she hesitates. Because how do you tell someone the truth if you don't know what that truth is?

"I don't know," Grace admits to the detectives finally. "But he kissed me in September."

"While he was dating Summer?"

"Yeah. I didn't think Summer knew at first, but . . ."

"But?"

"She was weird around me after that. Maybe I was imagining it?"

"Or"—Mwanthi leans forward to rest his elbows on his knees—"maybe you weren't, and you killed her so you could be with Adam."

"What? Oh my god, no." Anxiety hits her like a hundred volts to the wrists. She opens and closes her fists to release the tension, but it doesn't work. "Look. Adam and Summer . . . they were temporary. I've always known that. I told myself I'd wait it out until college, give myself time to figure out if I really did have . . . you know . . . feelings for him. Besides, Adam and Summer had already broken up when she died."

"Maybe you saw them together at the party. Maybe they were getting back together."

Headmaster Norton stands from his seat behind the desk, startling Grace. She forgot he was even in the room. "Detectives, this line of questioning is becoming inflammatory. I must insist—"

"Cora only told you so you won't investigate her," Grace says. Her voice is desperate, and she knows it. "She was obsessed with Summer, like out of control obsessed. Summer told me she caught Cora watching her loft once. Seriously, you have to—"

"Thank you, Grace." Lombardo smiles. "But Headmaster Norton is right. We're finished for today."

"You may return to class," Headmaster Norton says.

Grace doesn't want to leave until she knows the outcome of her interview, but Headmaster Norton's secretary ushers her into the hallway. Her wrists still jolt from the electricity of anxiety, and her heart races, making her chest feel tight. She's got to chill out. She can't let herself fall apart. As Detectives Mwanthi and Lombardo give a final wave to Headmaster Norton and follow her from the office, Grace takes a long drink from the water fountain. The bell rings ending third period, and burgundy blazers pour into the hall. Voices drown her, so many it's like that time Summer dragged her to a Tibetan sound bath relaxation class and wave after wave of gonging washed over her until her mind stopped thinking about Mount Everest or the fact that 47 percent of the world's drinking water filters through Tibet, and was quiet.

Her mind is quiet now. Chillingly so. She can see how this might play out.

Any minute, Headmaster Norton will call her mom. If she isn't

wrong, she's the detectives' suspect number one. She needs a lawyer, which her mom will have to help her with unless she wants a
crappy public defender. If Grace's name leaks to the press, her mom
will be packing the car for a fresh start, even before the end of this
school year. Or, before her mom can rip her away from her friends,
the detectives will arrest her for Summer's murder. Based on recent
headlines, the mayor and Julian Cartwright are pressuring the LAPD
for an arrest. Stat.

Once Mwanthi and Lombardo turn the corner at the end of the
hall, either unaware of or immune to the stares of hundreds of curious students, Grace heads to the C-wing back door that connects the
academic building to the athletic center. There is no way she's going
to be able to focus for the rest of the school day, and she's already
screwed her chances at the grant, so as she pushes through the back
door toward the athletic building, she texts Adam.

GG:

Can we leave school? Please?

He responds in less than a minute.

AM:

Absolutely. Where are you?

GG:

In front of the athletic center.

When Adam pulls up five minutes later, the doors on his Jeep
are open so she can swing inside before he's completely stopped.

His striped tie hangs loose around his neck, and his button-down is untucked.

"Let's go." When Grace sticks her backpack by her feet, she realizes she doesn't have her chemistry book to do her homework. She'll get a zero if it's not turned in on time, which bothers her for less than a second. Maybe homework doesn't matter anymore. Maybe this tincture of dread distilled with vinegary panic is too much chemistry for any one person to handle anyway.

"Where to?" Adam asks.

"Anywhere but here."

"You good?"

"Not even a little."

Adam knows her well enough not to push before she's ready to tell him. Instead, he gives her a half smile and pulls onto the palm-lined drive that leads to the school's main entrance. He's the last person she should talk to—for all they know, the detectives are watching them right now, not to mention the fact that when he kissed her in September, he broke her in ways she can't explain—but he's the first person she wants to talk to. Her chest is tight with what-ifs and regret. Maybe her mom is right. Maybe a fresh start wouldn't be the worst thing in the world.

After a few minutes, Adam parks at a 7-Eleven far enough away from school that they won't run into any seniors grabbing off-campus lunch.

"Want to get taquitos?" he asks. "Since we're so classy?"

Grace laughs, surprising herself. "God, yes."

"They should be nice and cold by now. Kind of hard."

"Just the way I like them."

"Crusty taquitos heal all wounds, I think. Speaking of wounds—"

She holds up one finger. "Taquitos, then words."

Inside 7-Eleven, Grace is assaulted by the smell of old hot dogs, and blue raspberry Slurpee residue sticks her shoes to the linoleum floor. When she gravitates toward the back where the taquitos slowly rotate on a metal rack, it takes her a moment to realize Adam isn't behind her anymore. She turns around to tease him about getting distracted by the candy aisle, but he's staring at the *LA Times* on the newsstand.

His picture is on the front page beneath a headline that reads "Heartbroken Mother of Murdered Teenager Begs Police to Arrest Daughter's Ex-Boyfriend." In the photo, he's pushing through the door of the Beanery behind Miranda Cartwright, one hand outstretched like he's trying to stop her. His hair blocks most of his face—otherwise, the press couldn't include the picture since he's a minor—but the implication is clear. According to the media, Adam is suspect number one.

Grace skims the first paragraph of the article, which includes a summary of the investigation to date and a quote from Miranda Cartwright herself. "My daughter was a beautiful soul. She deserves justice, even if justice means a child goes to prison. He is old enough to face the consequences of his actions." Beneath the quote is speculation that "the ex-boyfriend" may have been involved in the drug trade.

Touching Adam's elbow, Grace whispers, "I'm sorry."

Adam doesn't turn, but his fists ball tight. "This is bullshit. Drugs? Why, because I'm Black? Because I don't live in their part of town? I don't even drink. The Cartwrights have always had it out for me, ever since the day I first met them. I. Don't. Do. Drugs. And I didn't kill Summer."

"I know you didn't."

He takes in a deep breath and lets it out slowly, then wraps an arm around her shoulders. "Thanks. I know you didn't either."

Grace could cry when he gives her a quick squeeze. All she wants to do is wrap her arms around his waist and bury her head in his chest. Instead, she steps out of his embrace. "I swear if you don't feed me taquitos as promised—preferably the pizza-ish ones—in the next three minutes, I will stage a French Revolution–scale rebellion. Liberty! Fraternity! Taquito-ry!"

"Nerd."

"You just think I'm a nerd because you don't get the joke."

"I get it! I'm not actually on drugs, remember?"

"I mean . . . the newspaper said—"

"Too soon."

Grace nudges Adam's sneaker with hers. "Come on."

They eat outside on the cleanest part of the curb between the muddy gum wads and oil spots, feet stretched over the gutter as cars rush by. Between bites, Grace tells him about her interview with the detectives, about what Cora told them.

"I think she's stressed," Grace says. "The pressure—"

"Cora threw us under the bus to make herself look better."

"Well, mostly she threw me under. She told them that I was the one to bring up killing Summer."

Adam starts to stand. "That little—"

"Stop." Grace yanks him back down. "I *am* the one who brought it up."

"You didn't mean—"

"I know."

"Maybe the LAPD should be looking at Cora. Maybe she heard Laney talking about the nicotine that day and decided to kill Summer, and she can't handle the guilt."

"What possible motive could Cora have?"

"Who knows? Maybe she wants to become the new Summer.

Maybe there's something in Summer's book about her, too."

Grace shrugs. "Maybe. But we can't prove anything. We don't have the book."

Adam runs a hand through his hair. "This whole time, I've been all about leaving things alone. Just letting the police take care of it, but we can't sit around while Cora screws you over."

Grace considers for a moment. "Apparently there were scheduled posts on Summer's Instagram, excerpts from her book. Probably for marketing."

"Have you read them?"

"No. I didn't know they existed until Detective Lombardo said something about them." Grace eats her last bite, washing it down with a swig of Coke. Her phone dings. Grace flinches when she sees it's a text from her mom.

MOM:

How was the interview?

Grace shoots a quick text back to say it went fine, that she didn't say anything stupid, and a few seconds later her mom responds to tell her the police want to talk to Grace with her there next.

"Everything okay?" Adam asks.

"The detectives want to talk to me with my mom present."

"Why?"

Is it possible to avoid thinking about something until it just goes away? Because the only logical answer is that they think she killed Summer and want to officially question her as a suspect. The thought makes her feel dizzy and sick, like her taquitos might come back up any second.

"Can we talk about something else?" she asks.

"But—"

"Please?" She scoots closer to him until her leg brushes his.

Adam leans back on his hands. "What should we talk about?"

"I don't know. Anything. The price of oil. Coffee farming in Peru."

Adam considers. "I don't know anything about coffee farming in Peru, but I did just find out that llamas communicate by humming. Also, they're all diabetic. Did you know those factoids, Gracie? Bet you didn't."

"I'll file them away."

"Thank me when you're on *Jeopardy!* and win fifty grand."

"Done." Bubbles form in her chest, and they aren't painful. They don't have anything to do with the carbonation from her soda. She isn't happy right now—how could she be when her life is falling apart?—but even when her world is crumbling, Grace can't help but try to put it back together. It's who she is. It's who Adam is, too, and maybe that's what binds them, or part of it.

Grace takes another big swig of Coke, loops her arm through Adam's, and rests her head on his shoulder like she used to when they were kids and things were easy. Aside from a porta-potty or, like, inside a dumpster, there's not a less romantic place than the curb outside 7-Eleven. But she cares about Adam hard. In what way, she doesn't know. She's not sure she wants to know, because it's possible that love looks like eating stale taquitos on a curb with someone who can make you laugh even when the entire LAPD thinks you murdered your friend.

But that scares her, because everything is toxic if it's too intense, isn't it? Even love?

Friday, October 31, a year ago, 6:49 p.m.
The Cartwrights' Loft

*Grace rolled her eyes at her own reflection in Summer's gold-framed
bathroom mirror and gave up pinning her hair into a bob. One of these
days, she'd pick her own Halloween costume and dress up like something
easy, like a tourist in a Hawaiian shirt or a Starbucks barista. She and
Summer were going to Avalon James's Gatsby party tonight, and Grace
knew three people who'd be there. If she counted herself. Thank goodness
Summer had finagled an invite for Adam.*

*Summer's Daisy Buchanan costume was perfection—the navy
beading on silver fabric, the fringe, the T-strap heels, and especially
the feathered headband that held Summer's hair into its faux bob. It
made Grace's own maroon flapper dress feel frumpy. Granted, even if
she wore the exact same outfit as Summer, she'd look a little frumpy in
comparison. She'd long ago accepted that. It had to do with leg length
and bone structure and confidence. Still, Grace wanted to look good
tonight.*

*"Did you know that some scholars think Fitzgerald's wife, Zelda, is
the one who actually wrote* The Great Gatsby?*" Grace asked.*

Summer adjusted her fishnets. "Interesting."

*"And he was actually named after his ancestor Francis Scott Key? The
guy who wrote 'The Star-Spangled Banner'?"*

"Wow."

"And—"

"Grace. Stop it with the fun facts and put on some lipstick, will you?

Here." Summer grabbed a tube of deep red from her bathroom and carefully applied it to Grace's lips. "Much better."

"Thanks for asking Avalon to invite Adam." Grace blotted her lips with a tissue. "It's weird not knowing anyone at these parties."

"You know me."

"I know, but—"

"I get it. I talk to everyone, not just you."

"Exactly." Though that wasn't all of it. Lately, being around Adam felt . . . different. Grace could still talk to him like normal, but even just three months ago, she wouldn't have cared if he saw her with no makeup and in her ratty sweatpants. Tonight, she felt a flutter at the thought of seeing him in a pinstripe suit, of seeing him at all.

It was confusing. How do you go from putting your feet in your best friend's lap because it grosses him out to your palms sweating at the thought of sitting next to him at a party?

"What's that face for?" Summer asked. "You look constipated."

Grace laughed. "Nothing. Just . . . thinking."

"About?"

"I don't want to say it."

"Gracie Grace." Summer raised a perfectly filled-in eyebrow. "If you can't say it to me, who can you say it to?"

Summer was right. Weren't besties for hashing out feelings you couldn't explain? Grace groaned and leaned her back against the bathroom counter so she couldn't see her own embarrassed face when she told Summer what she'd been feeling.

"I think . . . I might have feelings for . . ." God, how could she even say it?

"For . . . Spill it."

"For Adam?" Grace covered her face with her hands and waited for Summer to laugh or react at all, but there was only the quiet click of her

curling iron as she touched up the strands by her face.

When she uncovered her eyes, Summer's lips were pressed together, and there was a worry crease on her forehead.

"Say something," Grace said.

Summer set down her curling wand. "Gracie, we both know I have way more experience with guys than you do, right?"

Grace nodded. It was true. She'd never really had a boyfriend, and Summer went through guys like tissues.

"And you believe me when I say that I only have your best interests at heart?"

"Of course."

"Then you have to believe me when I tell you that Adam . . . He doesn't think about you that way, okay?" Summer wrapped an arm around Grace's shoulder. "I can tell. You're his buddy, his sister, but nothing more than that. Don't ruin a good thing."

So that night, Grace swore to herself that she wouldn't let herself feel anything more than friendship for Adam, even if burying her feelings meant that the pressure on her heart was so great it would have to either break or turn to stone.

PART 6

#TheDevilintheDetails

TWENTY-EIGHT

Elaine Miyamoto

Monday, November 9
6:03 p.m.

Laney sits outside by Rebekah's pool while Oscar swims laps. The next meet could determine scholarship opportunities, so even though their pool is way smaller than regulation, Oscar pulls himself through the water, flips, and propels himself off the wall again and again until the sound of his arms pushing water becomes white noise and Laney completely zones out.

The air smells like the hibiscus bushes Rebekah planted along their fence, and the pool has its own mini waterfall. A year ago, Laney would have begged to sit by this pool and not go anywhere at all. Now, though, she's got a raging case of cabin fever. Going anywhere means random people pointing at her and taking pictures and posting them online with #SummerSuspectSpotted.

Even if the police arrest someone else, at this point, Summer has already screwed Laney over for life. Her face is now almost as meme famous as Distracted Boyfriend, which will totally follow her to college. There should at least be a way for her to cash in on it, but nope. She has the distinct privilege of being a pro bono laughingstock. Once Summer's book comes out, she'll be a pro bono villain, too.

It's not fair. There are two sides to every story, but the loudest voice, not the truest one, gets heard. Summer is pretty freaking loud.

Oscar pulls himself out of the pool and stretches himself out on the deck chair beside Laney. Water puddles beneath him. "I'd say penny for your thoughts, but that would be a waste of my money."

"Ha-ha."

"Listen." Oscar turns over on his side to face her, and his face is abnormally serious. "I know you want to work with Adam, Grace, and Cora. I get it, camaraderie and whatnot. But be careful, okay? Secrets are secret for a reason. We all have them."

"What do you mean?"

"Like I told you guys the other night, I had a good view from my spot on the couch at the party."

"And?"

"I watched Grace go into the back hallway, but she didn't just go to the bathroom. She sneaked into Summer's bedroom when she thought no one was looking."

"For real? What do you think she was doing?"

"I don't know. But check this out." Oscar grabs his phone from where he stashed it beside the chair and opens to his camera roll. He clicks on a selfie of him with his Renaissance princess to show Laney. At first, she doesn't get why he wants her to look at it, then Oscar zooms in. In the background, Adam has his hand on Summer's back, leading her into the kitchen. Laney's stomach grows cold.

"They disappeared in there for maybe five minutes?" Oscar says.

"Do you think—"

"And look at this one." Oscar flips to another picture. In it, Cora's standing beside Summer holding a red Solo cup with Summer's name on it in Sharpie while she reapplies her lipstick. "She could have dosed Summer's drink easily. All I'm saying is that people aren't always what they appear."

Laney doesn't know whether to laugh or cry. All of them are screwed. It just depends on which one of them the police decide is most guilty looking. Laney locks eyes with Oscar. "Even you?"

He doesn't smile. "Even you, Elaine. You commented on all of Summer's Instagram posts, always supporting her. You liked every single picture, but I know you hated her."

"I didn't—"

"You did."

"Fine." Laney crosses her arms. "But that doesn't mean I killed her."

"Definitely not. If you were pretending that she was a sweet angel baby, I'd be way more suspicious. At first, your relationship with Summer didn't make sense to me, then I overheard her talking to you at school, something about how if you wanted your letter, you'd get her the answers to the world history test. She was controlling you. What did she have on you?"

Laney hesitates.

"You don't have to tell me," Oscar says. "People deserve to keep their secrets, but you don't have to go through this alone."

Since her mother's death, Laney has become an overthinker, weighing every single word that comes out of her mouth before she says it, thinking through every decision and request she makes. If she hadn't asked her mom to study with her for her biology test when her mom was supposed to be napping before her night shift, she'd still be alive.

Laney killed her mom, and she's borne that unbearable weight alone. Alone, she can't hurt anyone else. No one else can hurt her. But there's something about Oscar's open face, about the way he listens, that pries the story out of her.

"It started at a party at Cambridge," she says.

Oscar listens to Laney's story until the pool lights flip on, casting a blue glow onto the twilit patio. It's getting dark.

"Why would Summer put that in her book?" Oscar asks. "Seems like it would screw her over just as much if not more than you."

"Academic dishonesty is a black mark on any record. No good university will accept me if it comes out. It didn't bother Summer, because after she signed her book deal, she decided not to go to college. With all the college scandal stuff going on in the past few years, she knew if she came clean in her book, people would find it interesting. She's not wrong."

"So you knew this was all in there?"

Laney shrugs. "I assumed. For a while, Summer kept the recommendation letter back from me and kept asking me to do more and more. Get her answers for the history test. Study with her for chemistry. Comment certain things on her Instagram that set the tone for how she wanted other people to comment. It felt like it would never end, so eventually I told her I was done. She told me to say good-bye to my letter. By then, I barely cared, I was so over it all, but when she signed her book deal . . . I knew it could come out and ruin me."

They lapse into silence. Laney grew up going to Mass with her mom, but today, for the first time, she gets the idea of confession, of pouring out your mistakes to another person. Keeping secrets is like drinking poison. Still, she also wants Oscar's reaction. If he judges her, she knows she'll never tell anyone else ever again.

Instead, Oscar nods. "I know you're not supposed to speak ill of the dead, but what a heinous bitch. You didn't deserve the way she treated you."

Laney laughs. Oscar's words don't wash away the self-loathing, but she sees herself for a moment like Oscar sees her—as a human being.

"So what do I do now?" Laney asks.

"You made a deal with the devil," Oscar says. "But maybe Summer did, too. Maybe she knew something dangerous enough that it destroyed her. We just have to figure out what it was."

Thursday, July 23, three and a half months ago, 10:17 p.m. Cambridge House Party

Laney's feet didn't touch the ground when she sat on the brownish futon in Sebastian's flat, and that, coupled with the fact that people were so packed in that Laney felt like she was suffocating, put her in a bad mood. They weren't supposed to go to college parties. She'd never been a Little Miss Perfect, but she also had no desire to get in trouble while visiting a college in a foreign country.

The fact that Summer had even found a college party in the middle of July was a feat, and what was advertised to Laney as a chill evening with a few friends turned into at least fifty people drinking way too much beer and playing flip cup.

Fifteen minutes in, Summer had ditched her to flirt with some guy, and Laney was left wondering why she'd said yes. Another guy tried to sit beside Laney on the futon, but her resting bitch face had clanged into place the moment they walked into the living room. The guy left her alone when she took a book out of her purse. She wanted to leave, but she wouldn't leave Summer behind. That was totally uncool and unsafe at a party like this, especially when Summer had been drinking. Laney didn't love groups of people or parties—she would have rather been recording the sound effects for the slasher flick her production class was making— but she also had a hard and fast rule: You left parties with everyone you arrived with. Period.

So she was super relieved when the guy Summer was with started drunk singing "Bohemian Rhapsody" at the top of his lungs, and Summer found Laney on the futon and asked if she was ready to go.

"Been ready." Laney held up her book, and Summer laughed.

"Let's walk instead of ubering. It's a nice night."

"It's raining."

"Right?"

But Laney did love rain, and she figured the cold water would sober Summer up a little. When they reached the university path along the River Cam, the rain had stopped, and Summer slowed her pace. "College is so not my scene. Isn't the whole point to figure out what I want to do with my life? I've already done that."

"No desire to do the Greek thing?" Laney would have pegged Summer as the girl who already had her sorority picked out.

"And live with that many girls? Please," Summer said. "Besides, I'll never get into any of the schools my parents want me to go to."

"Why?"

"I got a nine-thirty on the PSAT. And I legit tried, like took prep classes and everything."

"You could do the ACT instead of the SAT or apply to a UC school. They don't even look at SAT scores."

"According to my parents, my choices are Stanford or Ivy. It's not about the test content. I just can't take timed standardized tests. I get in my own head." Summer picked up a handful of gravel and tossed it into the river. In the dark, it was impossible to tell if the falling pieces left a ripple or not. "I panic. The words all swim together . . . Ugh. Why am I telling you, of all people, this?"

"I'm not going to judge you."

"You probably got a sixteen hundred on yours."

Not far off. Laney had gotten a 1541, a solid score, but standardized tests didn't matter much when it came to the movie business. Talent mattered. Luck mattered. Who you knew mattered. "If I want to get into

the USC film school, I have to have a stellar audition tape, plus a letter
of recommendation that can take me places."

Summer plopped in the wet grass, careless of the mud on her white
sundress, and thought for a moment. "What if we could help each other?"

"How?"

"You take the SAT for me, I get a letter of rec for you."

Laney laughed. "Would be nice."

"I'm serious. You know who my dad is, right?"

Laney didn't.

"Julian Cartwright? He's studio head at Golden Gate. He's written,
like, one recommendation letter ever, because he's super busy, but if I ask
him, I bet he'll do it for you."

And that was the moment Laney made a deal with the devil, though
she didn't know it then. It seemed like fate, like a door flung wide open.
Summer promised she could get her a fake ID, and Laney agreed. What
she didn't consider was that some doors are meant to open only a crack
at a time, that if you blew a door off its hinges, you could never close it
again.

The_Summer_Cartwright

Summertimeee and the living's easy. 🌞 🍹 🌴

.

Except currently it's not, because of a little fly in the ointment called AP Lit summer reading that I have to get done before school starts in two weeks. It's the worst, and I'm offended my name is involved in any way. What am I reading you ask? A play called #Faust.

.

At first, I was not into it at ALL. The beach was calling my name! Like, come on, I could have been having shaved ice from @KonaIce instead of being stuck with a book in my lap, reading on my patio. Then, the more I read, the more I was like, Hey, this dead German dude and I might be kindred spirits. Like, I totally get where the character Faust was coming from.

.

Here's my takeaway so far: Sometimes you have to make a deal with the devil to get what you want. 😈

.

So with your last summer days, my challenge to you is to live on the edge a little. Take risks. They might just pay off. Spoiler alert: mine did.

XOXO,
Summer Reading (See what I did there?) 🖤

₪ 🖤 ▶

⏱ AUGUST 20, TWO MONTHS AGO

See all 580 responses

OhmygodwinGrace Told you summer reading wouldn't be that bad! You just gotta do it!

The_Summer_Cartwright Yay AP buddies! @ohmygodwinGrace

CallieCo22 Girl powerrrrr! Way to take risks.

JuJuCasagrande Reading on the patio sounds like my ideal day. 😎 Hahahaha! #IntrovertForLife

LACherryBlossom Okay . . . but did you actually finish the play @The_Summer_Cartwright?

TWENTY-NINE

Cora Pruitt

Monday, November 9
7:22 p.m.

Cora is bobbing up to her neck in a strawberry-scented bubble bath when Amanda barges into the bathroom, black trash bag in tow.

"Amanda? What are you doing in here? Get out!"

"I need to talk to you."

The air from the hallway snuffs out two of Cora's candles, changing the light from ambient to almost nonexistent until Amanda flips on the overhead. Which totally destroys Cora's mental vision of a marble bathroom with a soaker tub. Her actual bathroom has a dated beige Jacuzzi tub and an orange oak vanity. Very before-remodel pic.

In the light, Cora can also tell how little her bubbles cover up. Pruitts do not see each other naked. Cora's not even sure her parents see each other naked. As far as she knows, her mom wears a button-down with pearls to bed. When she slides farther into the tub, water sloshes precariously close to the sides, disrupting her bubbles. She wishes her towel weren't on the rack across the bathroom.

"You've been avoiding me all week." Amanda switches off Cora's music and sits on the closed toilet.

"Fine! Talk, then get out!" Bubbles are popping at an alarming rate. "I need some major self-care after this week. You know that."

Amanda is already in plaid pajamas, her hair scraped into a messy bun. "You've been . . . I don't know. Weird, lately?"

"I've barely seen you."

"That's what I'm saying. You've been avoiding family dinners, spending hours in your room alone—"

"I'm just stressed. Hence the need for self-care."

"Then what's this about?"

When Amanda pulls the half-full black trash bag from behind her back, Cora gawks at her. It can't be the same bag, can it? There's no way Amanda followed her out to the Altamontes' garbage can and dug it back out. Why would she? And why would she hold onto it after Cora threw it out a week ago? But Amanda opens the trash bag and pulls out a Chanel lipstick and the sleeve of a fuzzy sweater.

"Um . . . since when are you a trash digger?"

"Since this is the stuff you had on your bed the other day."

"I was cleaning out my room. I read that book about things that spark joy? And—"

"Don't lie to me. I know this stuff was Summer's."

"Leave me alone." Cora sinks into the tub until only her nose and eyes are above the water.

When she reemerges, Amanda crosses her arms. "Did you steal it all? Is that what this is about?"

"I didn't! At least not . . . all of it? I took a few things, but Summer never missed them, and I always supported—"

"Tell me what's really going on, or I'm showing this stuff to Mom."

"Oh my god, for real? You're going to tattle on me?"

Amanda takes a deep breath that puffs out her cheeks. "The detectives came by the house today to ask me some questions about you."

"What?"

"They wanted to know if I ever noticed anything weird about your interactions with Summer."

"What did you tell them?" Cora's heart races. Her relationship with Summer was completely normal, wasn't it? Sure, she looked up to her, but lots of people have role models.

"I told them you liked her style. I don't know if that satisfied them, but . . ." Amanda shrugs. "They're probably going to talk to you again. You know that, right?"

"I'm the only one who told the police the truth. They trust me." Cora shivers, not from any sort of worry, because she has nothing to worry about. It's just that her bathwater is getting cold. "Now will you turn around so I can get my towel?"

When Amanda complies, Cora hops out of the tub, dripping water and suds behind her. She hopes that by the time Amanda looks back at her, she can blink away the first traces of angry tears from her eyes. Even though she wraps herself up tight in her towel, long strands of hair that escaped her bun drip down her back.

"You can turn around again."

Amanda has always seemed like the older sister to Cora, the more responsible one, the calmer one, the one people turn to in an emergency. But right now, Amanda looks young and uncertain.

"I'm worried about you, Cor. Summer's murder investigation hit national news today, not just local. This is big. Everyone is watching. If the police find out about this stuff—" She hefts the trash bag up a few inches. "They might think you killed Summer."

"I was only trying to understand her better. Like, what made people love her the most, you know? I thought if I had some of her things . . ." Cora knows her explanation sounds sad. "Then maybe I could figure out how to, like, capture that?"

"You shouldn't try to be someone you're not."

"I want people to like me."

Amanda stands. "I liked you better when you were just Cora."

Her words are like a punch to Cora's gut, but she knows they're empty words. No one has ever liked the real her. When Amanda leaves the bathroom, Cora calls after her. "Wait! What are you going to do with the trash bag?"

Amanda doesn't look at her as she answers. "I'm going to put it in the dumpster behind the KFC down the road."

"I didn't kill Summer."

Amanda's shoulders heave. "I believe you, Cor."

The_Summer_Cartwright

Uh-oh! #SuspectAlert 👀

.

Today, I got ✨such✨ an interesting DM with a picture of my former bestie Grace Godwin in the principal's office talking to the cops. Check it out! Does this mean what I think it means? Have they set their sights on a suspect?

.

Is my killer really my backstabbing bestie, or is my killer on the loose, laughing at the cops for being so clueless? Everything you need to know to solve my murder can be found in the pages of my book. Who do you think is shaking in their boots waiting for it to be released?

.

My bet's on . . . Well, I hate to give you any #spoilers. That's no fun.

.

Much loooove!
SumSum 🖤

⌐ ○ 12 MINUTES AGO

THIRTY

Grace Godwin

Tuesday, November 10
8:15 a.m.

In the parking lot of the police station, Gina pounds her steering wheel with her fist. "Damn it, damn it, damn it!"

Grace's third interview with the detectives went exactly like she expected it would—they informed her she was a suspect, reminded her she had the right to a lawyer, and then jumped in.

"I should have hired a lawyer already," Gina says. "I just thought . . . I don't even know what I thought. But you will not speak with them again without me and a lawyer present. Got it?"

Grace is pretty sure she responds, but she can't hear herself over the roar inside her mind. For some reason, her memory fixates on Detective Lombardo's shiny slicked-back ponytail, the way the lights in the interview room reflected off her head. The way Detective Mwanthi pressed his palms together like he was praying while he asked her questions.

According to the post Summer scheduled for the end of November, she was going to reveal your biggest secrets in her book. Maybe you couldn't risk her ruining your life. Does that sound right, Grace? The only foods the coroner found in her stomach were water, fruit juice and vodka from the punch, what must've been the lobster crostini, which many party guests consumed, and what we think was a green smoothie. You were the only one in the loft when Summer drank her green smoothie, correct, Grace? It would have been easy to dump the contents of an e-cigarette into the blender when Summer wasn't looking. You admitted yourself that you and Summer had recently argued.

Detective Mwanthi's easygoing manner was gone. His eyes were hard and cold like he'd already decided that Grace killed Summer and he just needed to prove it.

Grace drops her head against the passenger-side window, too exhausted to hold it up anymore. She feels defeated, ready to give up. How many times can she tell the detectives the same story?

"I always knew Summer was trouble," Gina says. "Remember when I told you that?"

Grace hugs her knees to her chest.

"Remember when I told you to be careful and stay out of the limelight?"

"I'm sorry, okay?"

"Because being the center of attention always brings trouble?"

"Mom, I said I'm sorry."

"Sorry doesn't cut it."

"What do you want me to do? Go back in time?"

"That would be great. Yes. And leave your attitude back there. I don't have the energy for it."

A long pause stretches between them as Gina pulls the car out of the police station parking lot into the still-heavy morning traffic on the freeways. Is Grace imagining it, or is her mom's gaze fixated on the far distance, the place where the highway disappears east on the horizon?

Gina takes a deep breath. "Here's how this is going to go. We're going to get you a lawyer. ASAP. And I want you to park your butt at home until further notice. I know you already lost your grant. The school called. No leaving our apartment at all. Not even for school. Not even to see Adam. Do you understand?"

"But that's—"

"You could face real criminal charges, Grace!" Gina leans back to rest her head against the seat. "And have you seen the news today?"

"No." Grace hasn't even logged onto social media, because according to the court of public opinion, one minute she's a killer, the next Adam is. Some of Summer's influencer friends have banded together to convince the world that Grace and Adam killed Summer together, and every time she logs onto Instagram, she's got another batch of hate mail. Things like, *I hope you rot in jail,* and *Better watch your back, or you're next.*

"Your face is everywhere. All over the news," her mom says.

"What? That's not allowed." That's one thing Grace hasn't been worried about. Because she's a minor, the police aren't allowed to release her name or likeness to the press. It's the law.

"It is allowed if the media find the information somewhere already public. Like Summer's Instagram." She keeps talking, but Grace takes out her phone to google her own name. Her mom is right. She's everywhere, all over the local news, pictures of her scowling at the Halloween party juxtaposed with Summer's angelic face.

It's via an article on a local blog that Grace first sees the new post on Summer's account, the one with her full name. It's easy to see how once the media noticed it, they could have sniffed out lots of other information about her. And really, the headline is juicy. Daughter of studio head murdered by her jealous bestie? Posthumous Instagram posts? Total clickbait.

"I mean, we could also just pack up and go." Gina's voice is shrill with panic. "Our lease is month to month. We could—"

"We can't leave. I'm a person of interest."

"You're not under arrest."

"How do you think it would look if we left?" Grace leans against the side of the car and closes her eyes. She wishes she could sleep, just to escape this moment, but there's no way. "It would make me look even guiltier than I already do."

Gina doesn't respond.

As the car flies down the highway, west toward their apartment, not east toward escape, Grace feels like she's in free fall. She knows that falling objects can only accelerate 9.8 m/s2 according to the principle of terminal velocity, but she's breaking records. Last week, she was a valedictorian contender, the best friend of the most popular girl in school, a good daughter, someone who understood herself. Today, she's none of those things.

When they get home, Gina opens her laptop to start researching lawyers that they can afford, and Grace goes into her room to hide, as much from her own guilt as from her mom's wrath.

As she lies in bed, looking up at the Florence + the Machine poster she tacked to her ceiling beside pics of her with Summer and Adam and her mom, she firms her resolve. The only way to show her innocence and get the hell out of LA is to prove that someone else is guilty. And to do that, she needs help. She starts drafting a text.

The_Summer_Cartwright

#BookTeaser 😎 📖 😎

.

One month closer to the release of my debut #memoir All Your Likes Can't Buy Me Love from @SwiftEaglePress!!! I promised you that this memoir doesn't hold anything back, and to prove it, here's a little teaser from chapter 8 entitled "Living (Grace)iously."

.

BESTIE (noun): the person to whom you tell everything, no secrets allowed; the person you call to help you bury gossip or a body; the most trustworthy person in your life

.

But what if you find out that your bestie has been keeping major, life-altering secrets from you? What if you see something she never meant for you to see? Do you keep it to yourself, just suck it up and hope she has a good reason, or do you accept the fact that the trust between you has been broken forever?

.

What did I see, you ask? A few things, actually. But the one that she buried deepest was a little piece of paper shoved inside a filing cabinet.

.

What was on that paper? Guess you'll have to check out my book to get answers. 👀
#RealOrNothing.

.

XOXO,
SumSum 🖤

₪ 🖤 ▶

THIRTY ONE

Cora Pruitt

Tuesday, November 10
9:17 a.m.

Cora hears a strange voice in the kitchen as she slides on her fuzzy slippers. She hasn't bothered to shower or get dressed, because she doesn't plan to leave her house. It's a Hallmark Christmas movie kind of day. After her conversation with Amanda last night, she was way too exhausted to even think about school, and to her absolute shock, her mom agreed to let her take another mental health day. It's so unexpected that Cora's starting to worry about her mom's mental health, honestly.

Now her mom has company before lunch? It's unprecedented.

When Cora gets into the kitchen, she blinks hard because the sight of Detective Lombardo camped at the Tuscan kitchen table while her mom refills the kettle is too strange. An English breakfast tea bag dangles out of the mug Lombardo cups in both hands. Why is she here? Is Cora in trouble? Do the police think she had something to do with Summer's murder?

"Cora." Lombardo sets down her mug and smiles. "Good morning."

"What's . . . um. What's going on?"

"I just have a few follow-up questions from last time we talked. Have a seat."

"Okay." Cora slides a chair out and sits, feeling a tiny bit of relief when her slippers are blocked from view by the table. It's bad enough talking to detectives when she's dressed and put together, much less when she's not wearing a bra under her baggy hoodie. And without her makeup, she feels totally vulnerable, like a little kid or something. Her mom clocks her sloppy appearance and gives her a disapproving look, the one Cora hates. Her mom couldn't have warned her that Detective Lombardo was in their kitchen? God. But that was Mary Pruitt, always assuming her children would be put together all the time like she is, so why bother warning them?

"I know this has been a difficult week for you," Lombardo says when Cora's mom slides a plate of toast in front of her. "Eat, please."

"I'll just be over here waiting for the kettle to boil if you need anything," Cora's mom says. "Tell Detective Lombardo anything she wants to know. You have nothing to hide."

As her mom putters at the counter, conspicuously busy but listening, Cora slides her hands into her hoodie sleeves. She wishes she could hide her face inside it, too, like a turtle. She also wishes Detective Mwanthi were here instead. He's way nicer, probably because he has daughters of his own. He told Cora all about them at their last interview.

But Lombardo doesn't look angry or suspicious today. Her hair is still pulled tightly back, which yanks at her forehead and eyebrows, making her look like she got a bad facelift, but she's smiling.

"Your sister, Amanda, may have told you I talked to her yesterday," Lombardo says. "We wanted her take on a few things. Your relationship with Summer, your behaviors, etc. You understand."

"I guess?"

"Nothing to worry about. She confirmed everything you've already told us. You looked up to Summer. Nothing wrong with that. She did, however, give us something that we found very interesting."

Cora bites the inside of her cheek. "Um. Really? What . . . exactly did she give you?"

Lombardo slides a piece of paper from a file folder in her bag. "Did Summer write this to you?"

It's the note inviting Cora to Summer's Halloween party that Summer shoved in her locker, the one Cora had carried around for days. Where did Amanda find it? Did she leave it out on her desk? In her pants pocket, so it went through the laundry? Cora's hands shake as she gives it back to Detective Lombardo. "Summer left this in my locker last month. Yeah."

"Any idea what she meant by 'what you did' and 'our secret'?"

For a second, Cora almost panics. If Lombardo realizes she didn't tell her everything at the first interview, will she think Cora killed Summer? Then she relaxes. Her father always says that it's all about the spin. The truth can make her look guilty, or it can be no big deal, depending on how she shares it.

"Oh," Cora says, trying to inject breeziness into her voice. She sounds more like a deflating balloon, but she's trying. "She just meant that I was managing her Instagram account for her. If people found out I was the one responding to her DMs, they would have been mad, you know?"

Lombardo narrows her eyes at Cora. "What do you mean, manage?"

"Mostly just responding to comments, replying to DMs. Nothing too big a deal for her, but, like, it was a huge honor for me to get to help her. I learned so much about social media and stuff."

"That's significant. You must have seen quite a bit of her private information."

"Not really? Just the usual stuff from her followers. Fan mail, hate mail, people being stupid."

"Hate mail?"

"She has five million followers. You can't make that many people love you. Some followed to troll her." It was the part of social media that Cora struggled with. She wanted everyone to love her, not just some people, but if she learned nothing else from Summer, it's that love or hate, if people are paying attention, you're successful. Indifference is the poison.

Lombardo checks her phone, and for a second, her impassive face creases with some emotion Cora can't identify. "I have to ask, do you have Summer's password, then?"

"Yes, but . . ." Cora tries to see what Lombardo is typing but can't without being too obvious. "I haven't logged on since her death, I swear."

"Did you know Summer scheduled posts about her memoir?"

Cora shakes her head. "Like marketing?"

"They're sneak peeks of a few chapters. The posts seem to hint that Summer knew certain dark secrets. Do you know anything about that?"

"No, nothing. Sorry."

"Cora, your sister thinks that Summer found out something about one of the others, and that secret got her killed. She's concerned that if you know this secret, too, you could be next."

"Amanda listens to true crime podcasts, like, all the time. She checks the back seat of the car every time she gets in after dark, and she—"

"Nonetheless."

"I don't know some big, scary secret. If I did, I'd tell you. I told you about the conversation in Griffith Park."

"You had access to Summer's account. Maybe there was a threatening message. Maybe you know more than you think you do about one of the others. Any little thing could help. If the killer thinks you know too much, your life could be in danger."

"I'm sorry, but—" Her brain feels like it might explode at any second just trying to process that information. The tea kettle whistles, and Cora's mom takes it off the stove. Cora can't breathe. Does Lombardo really think her life is in danger, that the killer could strike again?

She forces herself to make contact with Lombardo's dark eyes. "I've told you everything I know, I swear."

Friday, October 16, three weeks ago, 5:36 p.m.
Griffith Park

Cora's phone vibrated when she reached the top of the trail in Griffith Park. It was a warm evening, the type with the barest hint of a breeze that tossed the yellowed grass and made everything feel heady and dreamlike. And it was a dream that Summer had invited her along with her boyfriend and bestie to do a photoshoot for her page, some ad for a new leggings brand Summer was repping. Probably she wanted Cora to write whatever post the pics were for, but part of Cora was hopeful that their relationship was shifting from just business to a friendship. Anything was possible, wasn't it?

Cora wiped her sweaty hands on her pants and checked the text. It was from Summer.

SC:

> Hey, SO SORRY, but I'm not going to make it tonight. Something came up.

Cora's shoulders slumped. Or not. Honestly, she was surprised Summer even bothered to text her to cancel. Usually people just forgot about her. She took a deep breath and rounded the corner to the bench where she'd been planning to meet Summer. Instead, the setting sun silhouetted three other bodies against the horizon—one with an arm on the back of the bench, one standing with a wide stance and crossed arms, and one on the ground leaning back on her hands.

Her phone buzzed again.

SC:

> Adam, Grace, and Laney are still going though. It's way past time for all my people to get to know each other. You guys should hang anyway! 😘

When she reached the others, Cora waved. "Hey, guys."

Grace turned around where she was sitting on the ground. "Oh, hey! Cora, right?"

"Yeah." She tried to smile confidently, but her mouth felt wobbly. It was hard hanging out with people in an older grade. Like, she knew it was only one year, but somehow, they seemed to have five years of experience on her.

When Adam and Laney had introduced themselves, Cora sat on the bench beside Laney. "Did Summer cancel on you guys, too?"

"Yeah, we were supposed to do a photoshoot for her Instagram. A post about friendship or something?" Grace scuffed her toes in the dirt at her feet. "That's Summer for you. Did she text you, too?"

Cora nodded.

"Unbelievable," Laney said. "My legs felt like Jell-O from my workout this morning before I hiked all the way up here."

"Did she tell you guys why she cancelled?" Cora asked.

Adam and Grace exchanged a look, like they knew something they didn't want to share. If Cora were Summer, she would not be okay with how close those two were. From what she'd heard, they were über close, the type of friends who never dated because they were "like brother and sister," but still. Hard no.

"Something about a business meeting," Adam said.

Grace shrugged. "Probably to do with her book."

Cora knew she shouldn't say anything about the book, shouldn't reveal that she had insider knowledge, but the idea of sharing something the others didn't know was so tantalizing that she couldn't help herself. "We're all in her book. Did you know that?" The idea of being a part of something as big as Summer's book was seriously amazing. And Cora was part of it in a bigger way than most people knew. She couldn't wait for them to find out. "We'll be, like, famous!"

"Famous or infamous?" Laney asked.

"What do you mean? She wouldn't say anything bad about us." Cora believed that with her whole heart. Summer was a nice person, and there was no way she'd purposely trash them.

"You sure about that? Just last week, I overheard Summer telling her entire study free how obsessed with her you are. She said you're basically her stalker and you—"

"Laney. Stop!" Grace said. "Besides, it's not like you're going to look good in her book, either."

"Wait. What?" Cora tried to shake off the sting of Laney's words. For the first time that she could remember, Laney looked uncomfortable.

"Did she say something to you about me?" Laney asked. "What was it?"

"She had me read some parts . . . I doubt you want me to say it out loud."

Adam cleared his throat. "Look, this stuff . . . no one really believes it. No need to get worked up."

But Cora was worked up, and she had every right to be! She'd known Summer included some things about people that weren't flattering, but those things had really happened. It was real! She had every right to put them in her book. That stuff about Cora being a stalker, though . . .

"You're one to talk, Adam. Summer told me all about you being a huge cheater."

Grace held up her hands. "Whoa. Guys, come on—"

"She said you were so desperate to make money on your Twitch channel that you hacked the game so you always won."

"That isn't true! It's not like I always won. I just . . ." Adam paced down the path a few steps and pressed a hand to his forehead. "She's putting that in her book?"

Cora nodded. She felt a little bad for bringing it up.

"You cheated at Mythos?" Grace asked. When he didn't answer, she prompted, "Adam?"

"I knew someone knew, because it was posted on this Reddit board . . . but I was hoping no one believed it." He paced back up the trail, his breathing heavy. "Look, I barely did anything. It was just . . . the algorithm changed, and not as many people were watching my channel. It's not like I'm better at Mythos than everyone in the world, but with a few little tweaks . . ."

"How did you even know how to do that?" Grace asked.

"Sophomore coding class. It wasn't hard. I just made it so my avatar took two percent less damage with each hit, and suddenly . . . I was the best, you know? Tons of people were watching, I was getting sponsorships. My YouTube channel blew up, too."

The wind unsettled dust from the ground so it swirled around their faces. Cora squeezed her eyes shut until the wind died down, leaving their outstretched legs reddish brown. As Cora watched, Grace traced her name in the dust on her thigh with the initial O beside it—the first initial of her crush maybe?—then brushed it away before the others noticed.

"I need the money. For school, my family," Adam said quietly.

Laney stood. Her eyes were angry. "She had to know we'd find out she was including stuff about us. Like, there's no way she thought we just wouldn't know or care."

"*She wanted us to know she knew,*" Grace said. *Her face was pale.* "*That's why we're all here.*"

"*How could she know we'd talk about it?*" Laney asked.

"*People underestimate Summer,*" Grace said. "*They think she's shallow or ditzy because she's an influencer. But what people don't realize is that in order to get millions of people to obsess over you, you have to be smart. I mean, look at her. She sold a book that's half Instagram posts for almost a million dollars.*"

"*Wait.*" *This was news to Cora.* "*Her Instagram posts are in her book?*"

"*Yeah, I guess so, along with backstories and stuff,*" Grace said. "*The point is, she knows how our minds work.*"

"*And she uses that.*" *Adam's jaw was set bitterly.*

"*Understanding people isn't always a bad thing,*" Cora said. "*It can be good.*"

But as the sun sunk lower, they grew quiet. Why did Summer want them all together? Why did she want them talking about her book? To punish them? To make them sorry?

Against the horizon, the lights of LA began to sparkle as twilight settled on the city. Was Summer screwing with them? Cora wasn't ready to believe it, but at the same time, Summer was hard to read. Cora had spent literal hours trying to figure her out, and she never had. Summer came across as the nicest ever, but sometimes . . . she wasn't nice at all.

"*Can we make her take out stuff?*" Laney asked finally. "*There's got to be some law about violating our privacy. Cora, your dad's a lawyer, right? What would he say about it?*"

"*Um . . .*" *A thrill of pride ran across Cora's shoulders that Laney would ask her opinion, even if she was just a stand-in for her dad's legal knowledge.* "*I think that law only applies if she's lying?*"

Adam kicked at a rock and cursed under his breath. "*We're screwed, then.*"

"Unless Summer has a change of heart," Grace said.

"Or a heart attack." Laney stretched her back. "That would be convenient."

Cora's eyes widened. "That's awful."

"Don't be such a baby. I'm joking."

"Laney's got a point, though," Grace said. "Summer does what she wants. The only way she wouldn't tell our secrets would be if she was dead."

Laney laughed. "Mr. Miller basically gave us a murder tutorial in class today."

"He actually did," Adam noted.

"What are you talking about?" Cora hadn't taken chemistry yet.

Grace spoke up. "There's a page in our chemistry book that talks about nicotine poisoning, like a warning to teens to not be stupid about vaping and e-cigarettes. I guess the contents of one e-cigarette is enough to kill someone."

"The perfect crime." Laney sat up and brushed dirt off her uniform skirt. "Mr. Miller said it would look like a heart attack."

"That's one way to keep Summer from spilling our secrets in her book," Grace said. "Supplies available at your local drug store."

"You guys are freaking me out." Cora's thumbnail was bleeding from her picking at it, and the sight of the blood made her feel a little sick. "I gotta go."

"Cora, they're just messing," Adam said. "Chill."

"I know." She forced herself to laugh. "But I have to be home by six. For dinner." Cora grabbed her dusty backpack and headed back up the hiking path to where she told her mom to pick her up.

She was totally creeped out how easy the others made murder sound. All it would take would be a choice, then another choice, some nicotine, and the sacrifice of a soul. Scary.

THIRTY TWO

Adam Mahmoud

Tuesday, November 10
8:29 a.m.

Tuesday morning, Adam pours himself a bowl of Cheerios and tries to not overthink too much, even though he knows that early this morning, Grace and her mom met with the detectives. He's not sure if it means she's the main suspect, but it can't be good. Part of him is freaking out that he'll never see Grace again because she'll be in jail.

From the living room, Adam hears his sisters giggling, then one of them gasps.

"Adam!" Samia yells. "Your girlfriend is on TV!"

It must be another story about Summer, probably some human-interest piece designed to make her look like an angel gone too soon. Last he heard, there was also talk about a biopic. He wonders who they'd get to play him. It probably depends on if the world decides he's a good guy or not.

Adam joins his dad on the living room sofa, and Lea and Samia grab his legs, pretending to be boa constrictors. Samia, who can't stop giggling, crawls up on the couch to wrap her arms around Adam's face.

"Girls!" his dad says, but it's half-hearted. The whole family has accepted that the twins have more energy than the rest of the world combined, and that's just the way it is. Besides, he's glued to whatever is on TV.

When Adam finally peels Samia's hands off his eyes so he can see, there are two faces on the screen beneath the CNN national news banner. Summer's . . . and Grace's. His heart drops into his stomach. He grabs the remote and turns up the volume so he can hear above Lea hissing like a snake.

"Teenagers killing teenagers?" the too-tan anchor asked. "The question Summer Cartwright's murder poses to the world is this: Is your teen safe engaging with social media? And darker still, how far would they go to find fame on the internet? Back to you, John—"

Adam's dad turns the TV off.

"What were they saying?" Adam asks. "Why was Grace's picture there?"

"Looks like the media knows Grace has been interviewed a few times," he says. "Nothing to panic about. I'm sure Grace will be fine." He wraps his arm around Adam's shoulder, and that's when Adam knows—it's not fine. His dad is more of a show-affection-via-a-firm-nod kind of guy.

Adam's phone buzzes with a text from Laney. He grabs his backpack, says good-bye to his dad, and heads out the door to his car. He wants to get to school ASAP to see if he can catch Grace.

LM:

> Are you watching the news? Did Grace get arrested? 👀

AM:

Just saw it. Not that I know of. This is ridiculous.

LM:

Is it? 🪅

AM:

You don't think she killed Summer?

Adam tosses his bag onto the seat of his Jeep and swings in. Laney takes her time answering.

LM:

I know I didn't kill her. 🙄

For some reason, this response pisses Adam off. There's no way Laney could believe Grace is a killer, and if she doesn't believe it, then what? She's willing to let Grace go to prison for something she didn't do?

Adam's stomach clenches. He's done some messed up things, but now is the time for him to step up. Yeah, if he talks to the police, it's possible that what he did will get out and ruin his gaming career forever. Whatever. Nothing is more important than the truth, than finding out who killed Summer, than protecting Grace.

Maybe today is the day he chooses what kind of man he will become. So he texts Grace with one hand while he's at a stop sign.

AM:

Saw the news. You okay?

She responds seconds later.

GG:

Me too. Not okay . . . but will be. Curled up at home in my fuzzy socks lol.

AM:

You're not at school?

GG:

My mom made me stay home. The interview was 😳 😳 😳

As Adam is pulling into the WW Prep parking lot, he gets another text from Grace, this one with Laney added. Because his first period Pre-calc teacher is super strict about the no cellphone policy, he stays in his Jeep. There's no way he could focus in class today anyway.

GG:

Logged into Sum's account and found the scheduled posts the detectives were talking about . . .

LM:

How screwed are we?

GG:

. . .

GG:

Screwed.

AM:

What do we do?

GG:

I noticed a couple of things that were weird.

LM:

?? Weirder than finding Summer's dead body in her bathroom?

LM:

Weirder than Summer dying in the EXACT WAY we talked about at Griffith Park?

LM:

Bc that's pretty weird. 😳

AM:

What did you find?

GG:

So there are scheduled posts about me and both of you guys. But not one about Cora.

AM:

Really??

AM:

So either Sum didn't schedule a preview post about Cora or someone deleted it.

GG:

Right.

LM:

What was the other thing?

GG:

I'm screenshotting it for you. Hold on . . .

When Adam sees the screenshot Grace sends them—a scheduled post about Summer's father—his stomach lurches. Is it possible?

GG:

I think we need to get together tonight.

AM:

Whatever you need.

LM:

And what . . . do face masks and eat cookie dough?

GG:

Oh my god, Laney. We need a plan.

GG:

I'm going to text Cora, too.

LM:

THAT BITCH? 😡

GG:

We won't tell her what we suspect, but we might need her help.

GG:

Are you in or what????

LM:

Sighhhh. In.

AM:

In. For sure. 👍

Adam sticks his phone in his pocket. Today might last forever, but tonight maybe they'll get some answers. Finally.

The_Summer_Cartwright

Happy #Thanksgiving, babes! 🦃

.

A time for #FamilyAndFood, right? Everyone loves a good 🦃 and stuffing. But what if the people you're eating around the table with are hiding things from you? What if you knew that everyone in your life was hiding things?

.

Okay, I get it. Everyone has secrets. Whatever. But what if these secrets were things that were hurting people? Would you tell or keep it to yourself? If you'd asked me a year ago, I'd have said it depends on who it is. How close are they to you? Like, I was the girl who probably would have helped bestie bury a body.

.

Not anymore.

.

Why? I've decided I can't trust anyone but myself, so I'm going to live for myself, like extreme self-care. 💅 Screw making choices around other people. On that note, please enjoy this excerpt from chapter 10 of my book: "Strain the Water from the Blood."

.

I grew up privileged. I know that. My father's the studio head of Golden Gate, and I benefitted from his money. I'm not denying that. But everything changed when I realized what he'd done to a young writer who had a brilliant idea and the script to go along with it.

.

Maybe he thought if he paid her enough money, Avalon James would just go away. Maybe he thought attaching a bigger name would make it splashier. But my father, Julian Cartwright, is a total #thief. And I doubt this was the first time. 😠

SumSum 🖤

₪ 🖤 ▶

THIRTY THREE

Cora Pruitt

Tuesday, November 10
6:15 p.m.

Cora finishes her thought in her diary and snaps the cap back on her skinny blue Sharpie. She's positive her parents would not be okay with her going over to Grace's apartment, even before the whole murder thing—that neighborhood!—but since Laney's picking her up, they won't care. Probably. Maybe she just won't mention that she's going out.

Tossing her diary onto her pillow, Cora changes from her pajamas into a matching loungewear set she's been dying to show off. She was able to buy it with the money she got from Summer's Closet Instagram. Her mother would've never bought her something so casual and trendy. It's the cutest. She smears on a quick coat of lip gloss and adds a layer of mascara. By the time she grabs her jacket from the hall tree, Laney has texted her to say she's outside.

Amanda stops Cora in the entryway, a mug of tea in one hand, her dark brows drawn in concern. "Where are you going?"

"Just out for a bit. Don't worry about it."

"Cora, you can't—"

"You aren't alone tonight, Amanda. Stop trying to be Mom."

Cora storms out the door, doing her best to ignore the guilt that gnaws at her stomach. She loves Amanda more than anyone, but she's never had a group of friends to ditch her family for. Maybe that's the silver lining to all this, right? Maybe going through something this hard together will bond them.

Laney honks the horn of her silver Civic at the end of Cora's driveway. She rolls down her window. "Let's go."

"I'm coming."

"Your house is completely out of my way."

Cora wants to snap back at her, but she restrains herself. "Sorry."

She swings into the passenger seat, and the two of them ride to Grace's without more than a "Hey, how are you," because Laney's blasting her music. Whatever Grace wants to show her has to be important or she wouldn't have been so insistent on her coming over right then and there. Cora's still mad at Grace for ignoring her, but friends forgive.

When they knock at Grace's apartment, Adam answers the door. He's in sweats with his curls pulled back from his face with one of Grace's scrunchies, which if anyone else did it would look ridiculous, but on him was kind of cute.

"Glad you made it," he says. "Come in."

Grace's apartment is the absolute tackiest. Like, for real, how many magnets can fit on a refrigerator before it just looks like that gum wall in Seattle? None of the furniture matches, and everything is brightly colored, but not like in a boho way? More like in a flea market way. But even Cora has to admit that when she curls up in an old wingback chair, she's comfortable. Laney sits on the floor with her back against the couch, and Adam sprawls on the rug beside her.

When Grace comes in from her kitchen, she's got bowls of ice cream and a shaker of sprinkles. "We know what you told the LAPD, Cora. About Griffith Park."

Cora blinks, and when she speaks her voice is half an octave higher. "I only told them a little."

"Yeah, but you made Grace look like a killer." Adam cracks his knuckles in a way that comes off as kind of threatening, like he's about to throw punches or something. "And she's not."

"I didn't lie."

"You also didn't tell them the full truth," Adam says.

Hot offense rises in Cora's chest. Why does everyone always assume it's her fault? "I'm the one who got up and left. I'm the one who—"

"Guys! It doesn't matter." Grace swallows a bite of ice cream. "We read through Summer's scheduled posts. She had them all saved on Instagram, and the password she gave me a few months ago still works. The ones about Laney, Adam, and me prove that we all had motive to kill Summer. She knew our secrets and was planning to use them."

"What about me?" Cora asks. "What did the post about me say?" Grace shrugs. "There wasn't one about you, Cora."

"What? Nothing?" Cora should be happy that none of the posts give her motive for killing Summer. That, coupled with the fact that she went to the police first, should prevent her from going down for killing Summer. But nothing?

She shouldn't be surprised. It's the story of her life. No matter how hard she tries, people just don't notice her, they don't care about her. Her mom is so focused on Amanda, she didn't even notice that Cora went out. And Summer didn't give two craps about her, not enough to share credit on her book. Cora wasn't on Summer's radar enough for her to even write a post.

"Just look at this post, will you?" Laney asks.

Cora speed-reads the post Laney shows her. "Wait. Do you think Mr. Cartwright killed Summer? Because she knew he ripped off a writer?" Cora knows most people don't think she's the smartest in the world, but she's smart enough to know that motive is weak at best.

"It sounds like it was more than one," Adam says. "Summer's book could have ruined his career. Think about the headlines. 'Wealthy Studio Exec Screws Talented Young Black Writer Out of Her Own Story.' It would have been all over the news. The studio board never would have allowed him to stay in his position."

"People do love it when the Everyman takes down the Rich Guy," Laney says.

Cora wants it to be true. Wouldn't it be the most amazing ever if none of her new friends had to go to jail for killing Summer? There could be cookouts! Beach days! The only thing is, there's no way Mr. Cartwright could have done it.

She says so. "Remember? He was in Dubai the night of the party?"

But instead of looking dejected, Grace laces her fingers together and smiles a small smile. "The detectives told me they're pretty sure the nicotine was administered in Summer's green smoothie. She made them in advance and froze them. Mr. Cartwright could have easily poisoned one before he left. It's the perfect alibi."

"So what?" Cora says. "The detectives already told me about the scheduled posts, so that's nothing new. They know about them."

"If we can go to the police with documents to prove what Summer said is true, that Mr. Cartwright really had motive and would have lost everything if Summer's book came out." Grace shrugs. "It's better than nothing."

"But where would we get those documents?"

Grace, Adam, and Laney look at one another like they've already made a plan. Why is Cora the last one to know? Then it dawns on her what the others want to do.

"We can't just break into the Cartwrights' loft! What if someone's home?" Cora bites her nail and winces at the taste of nail polish. The polish was supposed to help her stop, but no luck yet.

"I texted Harrison earlier and asked him to meet me for dinner in Santa Monica." Grace checks her watch. "With traffic, he'll be gone for hours before he realizes I'm standing him up. And Mr. and Mrs. Cartwright won't be home either. They go to the country club every Tuesday for dinner."

"Even this week? After everything?" Laney asks.

"Especially this week. The Cartwrights need to keep up appearances that they're mourning the loss of their daughter. There's no better place to do that than in front of everyone they know."

"Sounds about right," Adam says. "Summer learned from the best."

"I can't get caught." Cora jumps to her feet, ready to leave. "If I do anything right now, my mom will totally panic and pull me out of school and make me homeschool with my sister, and I can't—"

"We won't get caught," Adam says. "In and out."

Laney raises an eyebrow. "Alarm system?"

"I have the code," Grace says. "I spent enough time at Summer's that she told me, and if anyone catches us, we'll just say Harrison invited us. He'll cover for me."

This is a really, really bad idea. Adam, Laney, and Grace look at Cora like she's the biggest coward ever if she says no. She could leave right now, just call an Uber home and forget about being friends with them. She could let the police think what they think. Grace might go to jail, but at least Cora's life would have some semblance of normal, right?

But . . . Cora makes eye contact with each of them, and she can't say no. For the first time ever, they need her. They want her.

She takes a deep breath. "Okay."

Wednesday, October 20, three weeks ago, 10:02 p.m.
Outside the Cartwrights' Loft

*Cora met Summer outside her building at the same bench where
Summer had found her months earlier. Cora's hands shook until she
clasped them behind her back.*

*"Literally what, Cora?" Summer wore her silk pajama shorts, slippers,
and a robe. She'd tied her hair back in a low ponytail, and somehow,
still looked perfect. A guy with a takeout bag of Chinese food almost
walked into a pole staring at her as he passed. Summer didn't even
notice.*

*Lately, she hadn't been her usual nice self, and a few times when Cora
said hello to her in the hallway at school, she'd breezed right past without
saying hi back. Then Cora found out about some of the stuff in Summer's
memoir.*

*Cora knew that to have any self-respect, she needed to confront
Summer. The deal they struck all those months ago was that if Cora
wrote Instagram posts for Summer whenever she needed them, Cora got
an all-access pass to Summer's life—pictures and the inside scoop for
her closet page with affiliate links so Cora could make some extra cash,
invites to beach bonfires and rides to away football games, a chance to be
a somebody. The book wasn't part of the deal.*

*The idea of confronting Summer was terrifying. She'd almost
chickened out when Amanda begged her to stay home. She did feel
bad leaving her alone, and the last time she'd snuck out, she'd gotten
grounded for two weeks. But grounding or no, this was worth it.*

"Is it true your book includes some of your Instagram posts?" Cora asked.

"Yeah. And?"

"You . . ." Cora took a deep breath. "You can't use the ones I wrote without giving me credit. It's not fair."

Summer laughed. "Please. You gave me a few ideas, but it's not like I'm plagiarizing you."

Panic rose in Cora's chest. This wasn't how she thought this would go. Initially, Summer had been so grateful for the help. She was just so busy with schoolwork and friends and Adam. Cora was thrilled to help. Yeah, Summer asked Cora not to tell anyone, but Cora thought for sure that now that Summer's book was coming out, it couldn't hurt to just . . . give credit where it was due. Cora wasn't even asking for money. "But . . . it kind of is plagiarism? If I wrote it and you use it."

"Tell if you want. No one will believe you."

"I can prove it. I have the drafts—"

"All that proves is that you're obsessed with me, and everyone knows that already."

Summer's words were a dagger to Cora's heart. She'd heard people call her a Summer knockoff, but Summer had never treated her that way before. She'd always made Cora feel special, like she had the potential to be more than she was. And that . . . that was why she needed Summer to give her just a tiny bit of credit. For the smallest fraction of time, Cora could be somebody, and part of her knew that this might be her only chance to live the life she had always wanted— fame, glamour, love, acceptance—before she morphed into a younger version of her mother.

Even though Cora tried to hold her tears back, one spilled onto her cheek. Her lip quivered. She wanted to defend herself, but maybe Summer was right about her. "I didn't think you felt that way."

A top floor window slammed open, and Mr. Cartwright stuck his head out. "Summer. It's late."

"I don't have time for this," Summer said. "Back off, Cora. Just leave it."

"Summer! Inside. Now."

"I did everything for you," Cora said. "I helped you cancel Avalon even though she didn't deserve that. I made you better."

"You're so pathetic. God."

Cora's heart cracked. "I thought we were friends."

"Don't you get it?" Summer balled her hands into fists. "I. Don't. Have. Friends."

"Summer—"

"Stay the hell away from me, Cora. I mean it. If you come near me again, I'll get a restraining order. Freak."

Summer stormed back into her building while her father watched from the penthouse window. Cora didn't have the willpower to follow her. A restraining order? Was that really what Summer thought of her, that she was a stalker? All these months, Cora had done everything Summer asked of her and for what?

She sank to the sidewalk and wrapped her arms around her knees until she could stop herself from shaking. She wasn't sure how much time passed, but her legs were cold, and the street was empty.

Cora had never felt lower or more worthless. Her parents cared more about family appearances than about her. She didn't have any real friends anymore. She'd been careful to only spend time with people who could boost her reputation. And in that moment, she realized—the only person who really loved her was Amanda, and she'd treated Amanda like trash.

She could still fix it, couldn't she? She'd buy some ice cream, go home, and watch Hallmark movies with her. Or listen to a true crime podcast, whatever Amanda wanted.

But when Cora got home, her mother, still in her black dress from Cora's dad's client dinner, stood by an ambulance in the driveway as paramedics loaded a stretcher inside. Amanda.

Cora rushed to her mother, who was much too still. "Mom?"

Cora's mother's eyes burned. "What were you thinking?"

"Is she okay?"

"She will be, no thanks to you. I thought I could trust you with this one thing. Time and time again, Cora, you disappoint me. You—"

"I'm sorry. I'm so sorry." Cora was sobbing now. She couldn't stop. It would be all her fault if Amanda died because she had a grand mal seizure without anyone home to help her, and Cora was worthless, so worthless.

"We're lucky I had a bad feeling and came home early," Cora's mom said. "Where were you?"

"I had to go to Summer's to—"

"I hope whatever you went for was worth as much as your sister's life."

"Mom—"

But the look of loathing her mother gave her then was too much. One more weight on Cora's back than she could carry without breaking. She shattered. In that moment, she wanted to die. It would be easier than living with the consequences of her actions.

As the ambulance drove away, though, its sirens blaring, Cora realized. It wasn't her fault.

It was Summer's.

PART 7

#MurderIsEasy

THIRTY FOUR

Elaine Miyamoto

Tuesday, November 10
8:34 p.m.

Laney parks her Civic in metered parking a block away from the Cartwrights' loft. It's dark outside, at least for LA, and every shadow seems like it could be hiding psychopathic murderers ready to pop out and shiv her. Even though she's doing her best to be chill about this break-in, as she shoulders her backpack, her heart is racing. If Julian Cartwright is Summer's killer, he's ruthless enough to murder his own child. What would stop him from killing a few random teenagers? It's also not lost on Laney that if Julian Cartwright is guilty, her recommendation letter to USC is less than worthless. It might even be a liability.

"Who's got quarters for the meter?" Laney asks.

Cora shakes her head. "Can't you just use the app?"

"Not for this one."

"I don't carry change," Adam says.

"Oh my god." Laney bangs her head against the steering wheel. "We can't even pull off parking for a heist."

"It'll be fine. And it's not a heist. More just . . . recon." When they're all out of the car, Grace takes a coin purse from her backpack and feeds the meter for an hour and a half. "Let's go."

Street lamps cast globes of light onto the sidewalk and elongate their four shadows as they wait on Summer's stoop.

Before typing in the unlock code, Grace logs onto the security app Summer loaded onto her phone and turns off the alarm. "Sometimes I'd come hang out here while Summer was finishing up her SAT prep class."

Laney rolls her eyes. "What, do they teach teens how to manufacture fake IDs?"

"Huh?" Light from the keypad catches on Cora's lip gloss. She's reapplied. Heaven forbid she not look her best for a break in. "Actually, never mind. Can we get this over with?"

The door buzzes quietly, and the four of them go inside, then up the elevator to the penthouse, where Grace scans something on her app so the elevator doors will open to let them inside. Summer must have disabled that security feature for the party. Despite herself, Laney is impressed with the level of paranoia. If someone wanted to break into Rebekah's house, all they'd have to do is jimmy the little window in the laundry room and it would pop right open.

In the Cartwrights' entryway, the giant ficus tree looms dark against the white walls. The air smells like vanilla and the sharp tang of Lysol and bleach. It's sterile, like a hospital.

"Did they bring cleaners in after . . . you know?" Laney whispers to Grace.

"They had already scheduled a full cleaning for after the party. The police made them wait a few days, but yeah. The whole place has been scoured at this point."

"Take off your shoes," Adam says. "Mrs. Cartwright will notice if you track dirt. She's that type."

Everything is quiet as they all slide their feet out of their shoes, but as Laney kicks off her flip-flops and tucks them inside her backpack, the memory of music, alive and vital, thrums in her chest. Summer's ghost flits down the hall, lemon hair swishing against her pineapple dress, completely unaware of what's about to hit her. Normal people don't worry about poison when they drink their smoothies.

Laney inhales and holds her breath. Releases it. "What now?"

"We need to find files that prove Julian Cartwright plagiarized Avalon's idea. So documentation, script drafts of *She Falls Hard* . . . something like that," Grace says.

"What about a contract showing he screwed her over?" Adam asks.

"That would work, too."

"So . . . his office?" Cora tangles her fingers in the front strands of her hair. If they don't hurry, Cora's going to lose her shit.

"If Summer found out about what he was doing, it's possible she has evidence in her room, too," Grace says.

The thought of seeing Summer's room again freaks Laney out. Death sucks the air from a space, and it never comes back. Laney would know. She lived in her Sacramento house without her mom for three years. "I say we start with the office."

"You head that way. I'll go through the bedrooms," Grace says.

Cora sidesteps so she's beside Grace. "Me too!"

"Classic horror movie mistake, guys," Laney says. "Never split up."

"There's only so much time before Harrison gets back," Grace says. "He texted me twenty minutes ago to ask me where I am. He got a table at the restaurant."

"Okay, fine. I'll go get murdered in Mr. Cartwright's office alone. Whatever. Camera pans out to show unimportant side character opening the door, behind which the killer lurks."

"No, I'll go with you." Adam's eyes don't leave Grace. "Unless—"

"We'll be good." Grace gestures for Cora to follow her down the hallway toward the bedrooms.

Laney and Adam turn left through the french doors into Julian Cartwright's office. Laney's bare feet sink into the Oriental rug. The office doesn't smell like the same cleaning supplies as the rest of the loft, so maybe Mr. Cartwright didn't let the cleaners inside? That has to bode well for their search.

When Adam turns on a brass lamp and yellow light floods the desk, Laney about has a heart attack. "Don't be stupid. What if there are cameras?"

"There's just the one pointed at that painting."

"It might register the change in light."

Adam turns the lamp back off. "Paranoid much?"

"Only when it comes to my entire future." Laney keeps her cell phone flashlight pointed toward the floor so it illuminates her black toenail polish against the rug. Unless Mr. Cartwright has reorganized since Laney went through his stuff at the party, contracts are in the filing cabinet at the back of the room. "I'll take the filing cabinet over here. You search the desk drawers."

When Adam sits in the leather desk chair and starts yanking open drawers, Laney swallows her dread. She can do this. And if what she finds might ruin everything for her . . . Well. She'll deal with that, too.

The filing cabinet drawer clangs loudly against the silence of the loft. Laney jumps. She's not usually this girl. She can sit through a horror movie and not cover her eyes once, but the real-life tension of possibly getting caught climbs her spine and digs its claws into her neck.

The top drawer contains meticulously organized tax documentation, both for the family and for the studio, numbers on numbers
enough to make Laney's head swim. The second one is almost empty.

"Anything?" Adam whispers.

"Not yet."

"Me neither."

"Maybe we should quit while we're ahead." But she knows Adam
won't because of Grace, and Grace can't because the police think she
murdered Summer. And Laney can't because she drove everyone, and
she might be mean sometimes, but she's not the girl who'd abandon
even pseudo-friends to their unsavory fates. Besides, they paid for
ninety minutes of parking.

Laney slides the wide bottom drawer of the filing cabinet open. It
contains a fat file labeled *Contracts: Classified*. Her heart beats faster.
There must be over a hundred. Inside, three deep, is the contract for
She Falls Hard by Avalon James with an NDA attached. Laney's no
lawyer, but if what Summer wrote is right, she'd be willing to bet this
contract is manipulative, heavily weighted in Julian Cartwright's favor,
and probably a disaster for his reputation if it got out. Shit.

Laney's future starts to fray. If the world finds out what Julian
Cartwright did—and by the looks of it has done more than once,
maybe throughout his whole career—there'll be no stellar recommendation from a respected studio head for film school. Probably she'll
end up at some state university studying accounting so she can work
with her father for the rest of her life keeping books and doing taxes.
The right thing to do would be to take the file, to help Avalon James
prove to the world that *She Falls Hard* is her story.

Then again, maybe Laney should just . . . leave it to the universe. If
she pretends like she never saw the contract, the police might still find
it, and she won't have played a role. Besides, there's no way to know

for sure at this point that Julian Cartwright is the killer. Why draw unnecessary attention?

But as Laney weighs her decision, she can't help but think of a conversation she had with Rebekah just this past weekend when Laney said no for the millionth time to getting brunch with her.

"I'm working on sound effects for a new short my film class is making."

"Can I hear it?"

Laney hesitated. She didn't want to share any part of it with Rebekah. "It's just—"

"I know. It's something you used to do with your mom," Rebekah said. "If it's hard to let me be a part of that, I get it."

"Sorry." Awkwardness washed over Laney. She didn't want to shut Rebekah out, not really. But how could she not?

"I didn't know your mom." Rebekah sat on the edge of Laney's bed. "But I'm a mom, too, so I know this. She wanted you to be happy."

"I know. She did everything for me."

Rebekah chewed her lip, deep in thought. "Listen . . . this is probably way off base, and if it is, yell at me, tell me to go away. Whatever. But you know that the car accident . . . it had nothing to do with you?"

Laney felt like the air was sucked out of her lungs.

"Your dad told me you and your mom had been up late studying before her shift, so she was overtired going into work," Rebekah continued. "But, Laney . . . that's not your fault."

Laney curled up in her desk chair with her head on her knees to hide the tears that sprung to her eyes, betraying her. "Are you sure?"

"I'm sure." She stood to leave.

When Rebekah's hand was on the doorknob, Laney blurted, "What if I don't know how to be happy anymore?"

"You'll find a way." Rebekah smiled. "I know it."

Laney had tried to find a way to be happy. She worked herself half to death to achieve everything her mom wanted for her to honor her memory, to make up for what happened. But maybe some things are out of her control. Maybe happiness isn't found in faking perfection or pretending like she doesn't need anyone. Maybe it's found in doing her best, taking each day one at a time, and doing the right thing when she knows what the right thing is.

Laney slides Avalon's contract into her backpack. She'll give it to Avalon and let her decide what to do. Film school isn't the only way for her to be happy, and it isn't the only way to honor her mother's memory.

Just as she's about to tell Adam she found the file, the silence shatters. At first Laney can't process the noise, because it's so piercing it hurts her brain, but when she and Adam make eye contact, his eyes are so wide, she can see the whites all the way around in the dim light cast by her phone. He mouths one word.

Alarm.

The alarm is going off. The police will be here in minutes.

Transcript: *Call to 911;*
November 10; 8:49 p.m.

Operator: 911, what is your emergency?

Caller: *[Alarm sounding in the background]* Oh
my god. I—

Operator: Are you all right?

Operator: Hello?

Caller: She's . . . she's trying to kill me.

Operator: What is your location?

Operator: We're tracing your call.

Operator: A unit was already dispatched in
response to your alarm. Stay on the
line if you can.

Caller: Hurry.

Interview conducted by Supervising Detective Jonah Mwanthi and Detective Nicole Lombardo, LAPD

Detective Jonah Mwanthi:
Amanda, you were telling our receptionist that you tracked your sister this evening?

Amanda Pruitt:
With Find My Friends. Yeah, I . . . Sorry.

JM: Tissue?

AP: I'll be fine. I don't know why I can't stop crying.

Nicole Lombardo:
I think it makes perfect sense. It takes a lot of courage to speak out against your own sister.

AP: What kind of sister am I even?

NL: A good one. One who's worried about Cora's welfare. That's why you're here, isn't it?

AP: Yeah.

JM: So you tracked Cora to the Cartwrights' loft?

AP:	Yes. I think . . . I think Cora killed Summer.
NL:	That's a serious accusation. Does your mother know you're here?
AP:	She's waiting in the car trying to get ahold of my dad. She signed the forms so I could talk to you alone. I told her I remembered some things about Grace. She doesn't know why . . . why I'm here.
JM:	What makes you think Cora could be guilty?
AP:	Is it true that the killer wrote all over Summer's face like the rumors say?
JM:	Yes.
AP:	Can I . . . see a picture?
JM:	Oh. I don't know if—
NL:	She's a big girl. Let her.
JM:	All right. Here.
AP:	Oh my god.
JM:	I knew this was a bad—
AP:	No. This . . . um. Wow. It proves it. I just . . .
NL:	Take that tissue, Amanda. And take your time.

AP: I don't know where to start.

NL: Start from the moment you began to suspect. We'll ask questions as we need.

AP: Okay. Um . . . So the other day, I went into Cora's room, and she had all this stuff on her bed that she was throwing away. All random stuff, and I didn't think anything of it until I saw her walk right past our garbage can to throw it away in our neighbor's trash.

NL: You got curious.

AP: Yeah. I dug the bag out and really looked at the stuff, and it hit me that there was this sweater? One I was pretty sure Summer was wearing in her profile pic on her Instagram. I went on her page, and yeah. I was right.

JM: You're saying Cora was collecting things that belonged to Summer?

AP: Right. So then, I started watching her a little more closely? And she's been weird . . . like . . . sneaking out and stuff. She only ever did that once before, and it had to do with Summer Cartwright. And tonight, she totally blew me off when she went out.

JM: Did that make you mad?

AP: Mostly just worried. So I went back in her room, and she'd left her diary sitting out. I know I shouldn't have, but I read it. And look what I found. The October twenty-first entry.

NL: Oh . . . oh wow. You were right to
         come to us, Amanda.

JM: "SHE'S TOXIC! TOXIC!! And no one sees
         it but me." Detective Lombardo, tell
         me . . . does this handwriting look—

NL: I'll get it to our analysts ASAP, but
         yes. To my eyes, it's identical to the
         writing on Summer's face.

AP: There's more.

JM: Oh?

AP: In that same entry . . . Look . . .
         Cora talks about how she . . . um
         . . . is the one who wrote most
         of Summer's Instagram posts. She
         volunteered to do it to free up time
         for Summer, who was really busy, I
         guess? When Summer sold her book, the
         biggest sell was obviously her account.
         But she didn't give Cora any credit at
         all. And when Cora asked her about it,
         she just, like, refused.

NL: That sounds like motive.

AP: I know.

NL: And you just found this out?

AP: Tonight, I swear. So then, I don't
         know, if you look at the next entries,
         it's like Cora kind of lost it? She
         started following Summer around,
         sending her DMs to freak her out.
         Stuff about stealing and being fake
         and stuff.

JM: Cora obviously had access to Summer's account if she was writing these posts. In your opinion, Amanda, did she also write the new posts on Summer's page?

AP: No, she didn't.

JM: You sound very certain. Why?

AP: Because . . . um. I wrote them? Not the first one, the one at the party. I didn't do that.

NL: What?

AP: I know. It's awful. I didn't mean anything by it . . . It's just . . . I'm really into true crime podcasts?

NL: And?

AP: Well . . . I found Summer's password on Cora's computer last week. It didn't seem like a big deal. I knew she helped her respond to her thousands of DMs in exchange for pics for her closet account. So after that super dramatic update right before her death, I thought . . . wow. Wouldn't a podcast about Summer's murder investigation be interesting? I was in the perfect position to do it, you know? Lots of insider info. But then there was this part of me that felt like it needed another . . . something. So I wrote the new posts on her account. I thought it would be helpful. I could get more information for you . . . It sounds dumb now.

NL: Have you started this podcast?

AP: I have a few episodes recorded. I haven't posted them anywhere yet.

NL: Amanda, you understand this is serious.

AP: I do. I see now how wrong it was, and—

NL: You've had us running in circles trying to connect the dots.

AP: I'm sorry. Oh my god. This is a nightmare . . .

JM: Thank you for telling us the truth.

AP: I didn't feel like I had another choice. I love my sister, but . . . if she killed Summer, she needs help.

THIRTY FIVE

Cora Pruitt

Tuesday, November 10
8:42 p.m.

After finding nothing strange in Mr. and Mrs. Cartwright's bedroom (other than a nose hair trimmer, a few bottles of prescription pills with names that sounded kind of familiar to Cora, and way more silky robes than any one person really needed to own), she and Grace move to Summer's room. Like Grace said earlier, it's possible Summer found proof of her dad ripping off Avalon's screenplay and hid it in a drawer.

The room feels stuffy, like . . . Cora knows this sounds weird . . . but like Summer's aura or something is pent up inside with them. She can't breathe. Quickly, she flings open the french doors that lead to Summer's balcony and lets the fresh night air flow into the room. The wicker chandelier creaks. The curtains ripple.

She takes a deep breath and feels a little better.

But as Cora goes through Summer's bra drawer (La Perla, La

Perla, La Perla, oh my god Saint Laurent?), her anger rises again.
Summer was gifted all this stuff because of her Instagram page and
book deal, and what did Cora get from it? Nothing but a few pics
for her closet account. It's not fair. Also, who was Summer to call
out her own father for plagiarism when she did the same exact thing
to Cora? Summer wrote that whole post about Adam being just like
her dad, but really, the apple didn't fall far from the tree, did it?
Did it?

"Anything?" Grace asks.

"Nope." Cora restrains herself from stealing the Saint Laurent bra.
Summer was a cup size bigger than her anyway. Of course.

"Only one place left to look."

Grace flattens herself beside the bed and reaches beneath it to pull
out a shoebox decoupaged with pictures of Summer with her friends.
Grace. Adam. A few Cora doesn't know. Her family. The box looks
shockingly lowbrow, like something Cora would have made in sixth
grade to keep her treasures in, not something that would ever be in
Summer Cartwright's bedroom.

"What's that?" Cora asks.

"Summer's memory box. Help me go through it?"

With fingers trembling half from awe that she has the chance to
get to know Summer in this new way and half with anger that after
everything, she's not in a single one of the decoupaged pictures, Cora
opens the box's lid.

Inside, there's a stack of Polaroids, a bag full of notebook paper
notes folded into tiny squares. A copy of her manuscript. A trophy
from a photography contest in middle school. A refrigerator magnet of
a skeleton saying *But it's a dry heat!* which Grace lifts out of the box
with a rueful shake of her head.

"I brought this back for her when my mom and I road-tripped to the Grand Canyon last year. Summer was way more sentimental than most people realized. Hey, look!" Grace reaches into the box again. "A note from you."

As Grace unfolds the floral stationary that Cora got for Christmas last year, Cora can't help but smile a small smile. Summer cared enough about her to save her note! Cora wrote it in March to thank her for helping her set up her closet account and get it off the ground.

Cora rummages through the box again. Movie ticket stubs. One of those key chain picture things that you can buy on the beach. When she holds up a beaded bracelet that says BFF to show Grace, Grace's expression is strange. Her eyes are narrowed, her forehead creased. The note from Cora is still in her hand.

"You know, we forgot about one thing earlier," Grace says.

"What?"

"Even if Mr. Cartwright could poison Summer's green smoothies in the freezer before he went on his trip . . . how did that writing get on her face?"

Cora freezes. Her handwriting. It's the same in the note as it was on Summer's cheeks. *#TOXIC #TOXIC #TOXIC.* The room spins around her as she tries to reconcile the development of Grace knowing that she, Cora Pruitt of the Boston Pruitts, wrote all over a dead girl's face with lipstick.

"It's not what you think," Cora says.

Grace stands. "Then what?"

"Okay, yes. I did write that stuff on Summer's face, but I thought she was passed out drunk. It wouldn't have been the first time, right? I wanted to get back at her a little. I wrote almost all of those Instagram posts that she's using in her book, and—"

Grace takes a step away from Cora toward the balcony and reaches into her pocket for her phone. She's going to leave and call the police or tell Laney and Adam.

Cora stands, too. "I didn't kill her, Grace! You have to believe me!"

When Cora reaches out both hands to put them on Grace's shoulders to beg her for belief, for a chance to explain, Grace's breathing hitches and she steps back out onto the balcony.

"Don't touch me."

Wind whips Grace's hair wildly around her face. When Cora steps outside, too, the wind catches the sides of her hoodie so it flaps behind her. "Do you believe me, Grace? Say you believe me."

"Okay, Cora. Fine. I believe you. Can we just . . ." Grace loses her ability to speak.

Cora narrows her eyes. She realizes what that look on Grace's face is: fear. But she hadn't meant to corner Grace—she's not dangerous—and Cora wouldn't hurt her. She wouldn't! But a part of her, usually compartmentalized and hidden away inside herself, savors the power she feels in this moment. Grace sees her, she's scared of her, she doesn't pity Cora anymore.

"Let's just go back inside to find Laney and Adam, okay?" Grace says.

But Cora isn't ready to go inside. She takes another step forward, and Grace takes a step back. Finally, finally, someone is listening. Grace has to listen to her, and it feels so good to say what she's always wanted to say. "You weren't even a good friend to Summer. I would have been better."

"What do you have against me? I don't know you."

"Maybe you should have tried a little harder to get to know me." And maybe for once, Cora should be the one who's happy.

"Go get your own life, Cora." Grace's eyes darken. "You're just jealous that Summer was a better version of you."

A pain inside Cora flares until it's unbearably sharp. She takes another step toward Grace so she's forced closer to the wrought-iron balcony. "You have no idea what it's like to be me. Everyone always ignores me. I'm always treated like second-best, even at home."

"Have you wondered if maybe the problem isn't other people? Maybe it's you." Grace's fear in her eyes is gone now, replaced with something else Cora can't quite identify.

"Summer saw my potential."

"And used it for herself, because she knew you weren't even close to good enough to succeed on your own."

Cora gasps. Her pain blossoms, bright and orange, a tiger lily in the nighttime. Instead of squashing it, she feeds it so it grows and grows and grows. She takes another step toward Grace and shoves her, hard. She shouldn't have to be alone in her pain. Someone else should feel it with her.

Grace's back touches the railing. Her eyes widen with fear.

If Grace can't see the real Cora, then she shouldn't be allowed to see at all. *That's* what's fair.

THIRTY SIX

Grace Godwin

Tuesday, November 10
8:48 p.m.

The railing bites into Grace's spine, and even though she's look-ing away from the street below, the five stories beneath her pull at her back. Maybe she shouldn't have antagonized Cora—she sees that now—but she's so sick of trying to please everyone, to be the one who has to do what's right. Summer should have seen that, Summer should have seen how much Grace did for her, but mostly Summer should have loved her. Why didn't she? Summer lied about Adam, she used Grace, and when she found out about the one secret that Grace kept close to her chest because she had to, Summer tried to use it to hurt her.

So Grace doesn't care anymore whether she does the right thing or not. As if being liked matters at all or makes any sort of difference? She and her mom have survived together on their own for years. Grace is a survivor.

She grips the railing with her left hand, her phone still clutched in her right hand behind her. "Get off me."

Cora's jaw is set, her cheeks are red, and her eyes, which reflect the balcony twinkle lights, are wild. "Give me your phone."

A terrible, disassociated calm descends over Grace as she faces Cora. She'll do what needs to be done. Cora can't hurt her. No one can. Grace feels invincible. Still, she's not stupid. Cora has the upper hand right now, and the only way to get it back is to calm her down.

"Your phone, Grace."

"Why are you doing this?" Behind her back, Grace fumbles with her phone. What buttons does she have to hit to make an emergency call without unlocking her phone?

"I needed a friend." Cora steps so close to Grace that saliva hits Grace's cheek when she speaks. "But you all pushed me away because you think I'm not good enough for you. I'm a human being, too!"

"You're a grade younger." Why is it so hard to dial without looking? "I thought you had your own friends."

"I sit alone at lunch every day. So are you stupid or just a bitch?"

"I'm sorry." Grace feigns a shiver. She moves her head slightly so she can just see her phone's screen. Using her peripheral vision, she taps the security app. "Can we talk inside? Where it's warmer?"

"I'm tired of talking. I'm tired of everything."

When Cora moves her arm off Grace's to swipe an angry tear from her cheek, Grace hits the button to activate the alarm. Inside the condo, the alarm wails. Maybe she does scream and just can't hear herself.

"What are you doing?" Cora lunges for the phone, but Grace has already dialed 911.

It connects. "Nine-one-one, what is your emergency?"

Cora lunges again, slamming Grace into the railing so hard it knocks her breath out. Sharp pain radiates through her wrist. It hangs limp. She can't breathe. "Oh my god. I—"

"Are you all right?" The 911 operator's voice sounds tinny with the phone away from her ear. Or maybe it's because her ears are ringing.

"You're going to get us thrown in jail." Cora reaches again, this time raking her nails across Grace's arm so hard it draws blood. "Give me the phone."

Grace gasps for air, but Cora shoves her again, harder this time so Grace's back bends over the railing far enough that she sees the cloud-blurred moon above her. The time for de-escalation is over, but with only one uninjured arm, how can she fight back? "She's . . . she's trying to kill me."

"What is your location?"

"You." Cora's voice rasps. Grace can feel her breath on her face. "You're just as toxic as she was."

"We're tracing your call." The 911 operator is still on the line.

"Shut up, Grace, shut up!" Cora slaps Grace hard across the cheek. "Shut up!"

"A unit was already dispatched in response to your alarm. Stay on the line if you can."

"Hurry!"

When Cora tries to rip the phone out of her good hand, all the rage Grace has compressed and made smaller so other people would be more comfortable explodes. She hurls her phone over the balcony so both her hands are free, and when Cora is distracted watching it fall, Grace elbows her in the nose so she buckles over, holding her face as blood pours between her fingers. It's the most blood Grace has ever seen. Funny, considering.

"The police are on their way," Grace says. "Tell them the truth, or I will."

"I told you, I only wrote on Summer's face. But now we're all going to jail. We broke in here." Cora holds her hand to her face. "You broke my nose."

"You pushed me first." Grace steps to the side as subtly as she can to position herself so Cora is between her and the balcony edge.

Cora's lips part in fear. The anger washes away, and she looks young, innocent. The girl she maybe was before Summer. Time pauses for an instant, and it's just Cora and Grace, two human beings who made mistakes and loved and lost and were hurt and broken. They both masked their pain instead of sharing the burden with someone else. Maybe they aren't that different at all. Maybe that's the problem.

Then Cora's eyes harden again. "I hate you. I hate you more than I hated her. You think I'm a knockoff? At least I know who I am. You're just . . . nobody."

Cora shoves her again, gripping Grace's good wrist with both of her hands so Grace is helpless. She struggles for solid footing, for leverage to shove Cora back, but she slips on the tiled balcony. When her back hits the railing again, pain throbs in her wrist until she could throw up. She's going to fall.

Then something inside her snaps. She is Gina's daughter. She is a survivor, and she'll do what has to be done.

Gripping her bare feet to the tile, Grace wrenches her body to the side and shoves Cora into the railing with her throbbing arm. There's a popping noise. Her shoulder?

Grace leans against her so Cora bends almost double. "You don't hate me, Cora. You hate yourself."

Cora's eyes are wide with fear. "Please."

"It's self-defense. No one can prove otherwise." And Grace shoves Cora over the railing.

When Grace's mom pulls up in front of the Cartwrights' loft an hour later, Grace and Adam are waiting on the stoop beside the decaying jack-o'-lanterns. Grace's left arm is balanced in a makeshift sling until she can get it X-rayed and casted. At some point—she's not sure when—Adam took her uninjured hand in his and wove their fingers together so tightly she doesn't think she could let go even if she wanted to. Which she doesn't. It's cold outside, but the side of her squished next to him is warm.

Grace's rage subsided the moment Cora fell onto the downstairs neighbor's balcony. When the police and paramedics arrived, Cora was still unconscious while Grace told them how Cora had been the one to write on Summer's face, how she pushed Grace and broke her wrist. Between Grace's story and Amanda's testimony at the police station, Detectives Mwanthi and Lombardo felt confident enough to officially charge Cora with Summer's murder. Aside from a concussion and some bruises to her ribs, Cora will be fine. Physically, anyway.

Mr. Miyamoto picked up Laney about twenty minutes after that. Before she left, Laney gave Grace a half smile and said, "Maybe now we can move on from Summer. Do you think we can?"

Laney has no idea how far Grace will be moving. Gina idles at the curb with the backseat of her car stuffed to the brim with suitcases and their quilts folded on top of the passenger seat. Grace doesn't have to ask her mom what's happening. They're leaving LA. Not at the end of the school year. Now. When her mom catches her eye, she waves frantically for Grace to get in the car. By morning, they'll be hundreds of miles away. It won't be the first time, because Grace and Gina do what they need to do to survive.

When Grace pulls her hand away from Adam's, physical pain slices through her chest. What do you do when you lose your best friend, when you know you might never see or talk to him again? There's no protocol for it, only hurt. Grace's life has been marked by loss, but this one . . . this one is the worst.

Adam doesn't know that tonight is their end, but he still lets Grace hug him longer than usual.

"I'll text you tomorrow?" he says when she finally pulls away.

"My phone shattered, remember?"

"Right. I'll come by your apartment, then. We can grab some lunch or coffee at the Beanery or whatever."

She doesn't have the heart to tell him that her apartment will be empty. She wants to make plans with him, because even though she knows they're delusional, they make her feel more solid, like the suitcases are nothing. "Okay."

"Look." Adam glances at Gina, who drums her steering wheel with her fingers, impatient to leave. "I know my timing is all wrong. I know that."

Grace has waited years to hear what she thinks he's about to say, but he has no idea the extent of how wrong his timing is. "Adam—"

"Please. Let me say this." He rocks back on his heels, then, as though he's finally gathered the courage, he looks her in the eyes. "I love you, Grace."

She holds her breath and counts to five. Would it be wrong for her to say it back when she's leaving? Maybe it would be better for her to be horrible to him, to make letting go easier. But she's tired of pretending, of acting like everything is fine when it isn't, of filtering what she shares because she's scared of getting hurt.

Life is painful and hard—Grace knows this as well as anyone—but what if her fear prevents her from sifting through hardships until she finds something beautiful?

So she gathers her courage and smiles. "I love you, too."

The relief and happiness that wash over Adam's face as she gives him one last hug and slides into the car make her even sadder. But love is the sweetest sort of sadness. She's leaving LA with regrets. Everyone has them. But she doesn't regret telling Adam the truth.

Her mom tries to smile at her but only manages a grimace. She knows the weight this moment has for Grace, because she feels it, too.

As Gina shifts the car from park to drive, Adam knocks on Grace's window.

Gina sighs. "Make it quick."

Grace rolls down her window. "What's up?"

"You guys going on a trip or something?" He gestures to the bags in the back.

"Impromptu road trip," Gina interjects.

"Oh." Adam makes a face at Grace. "Then I won't see you tomorrow, huh?"

"Guess not."

"I'd better do this now, then." Adam smiles. And even with her mom sitting right there, he slides one hand into Grace's hair and kisses her, not desperate this time like it was on the playground that day. This kiss is long and sweet, the type that hints at many more to come. This kiss breaks Grace's heart.

Adam pulls away first. Of course he does, because Grace can't bring herself to let him go. "See you when you get back?"

"Sure." Grace tries to smile, to memorize him. His dark eyes, his curls, the way his mouth pulls to the side when he smiles. She tries to memorize the way she feels with him when he turns back over his shoulder to smile at her. Eventually this feeling will fade from her memory and that will be easier than remembering. Adam is a good person, but Grace isn't sure what type of person she is. Maybe she doesn't deserve him anyway. Maybe when she turns eighteen, she'll find him. Who knows?

Her mom reaches across the center console to squeeze her knee, and they drive away from the Cartwrights' loft. From LA. From this life that Grace worked so hard to build. They have to.

Transcript: *Police Interview with Nicholas Orsini. Summer Cartwright Murder Investigation* November 11; 4:18 p.m.

Interview conducted by Supervising Detective Jonah Mwanthi, LAPD

Detective Jonah Mwanthi:
What can I do for you, Mr. . . . Orsini?

Nicholas Orsini:
I was watching the news last night and saw a girl's face. Said she lived out here. Pretty sure she's my daughter.

JM: Who do you mean?

NO: My daughter, Gracie. From what I saw, she's going as Grace Godwin right now, but her real last name is Orsini.

JM: I'm sorry, but I can't give out information about a minor.

NO: I'm her legal guardian. Here.

JM: *[sounds of rustling papers]*

NO: Paperwork in order?

JM: It . . . does appear so. Birth certificate . . . Wow, school photos. Definitely the same girl, though she must be what . . . nine here?

NO: Eight.

JM: Mr. Orsini, to my knowledge Grace lives
        with her mother. They seem very close.
        Are you claiming that Gina is not—

NO: No, that's not what I'm saying. Gina's
        my ex. But we went to court after the
        divorce, and I got full custody. Gina
        didn't like that, so she took Gracie
        and bolted.

JM: How long ago was this?

NO: Eight years.

JM: I had no idea.

NO: I don't hold it against you.

JM: Give me a few hours here to confirm
        this data with the Providence Police
        Department, then I'll send officers to
        Gina and Grace's apartment.

NO: Thank you, Detective. I look forward
        to bringing my Gracie home.

PROVIDENCE JOURNAL

Missing Third Grader Causes Fireworks at Independence Day Celebration

by Jamison Tuttweiler
July 5

Celebrations were dampened last night at India Point Park when an AMBER Alert was issued for eight-year-old Gracie Orsini of nearby Warwick, RI. Gracie was attending the fireworks display with friends when she disappeared. Sources close to the family claim that Gracie's mother, thirty-five-year-old Gina Orsini, née Ellison, likely kidnapped her from the event. Police have found no trace of Gracie or Ms. Orsini.

After a fraught legal battle between Gracie's parents, her father, thirty-seven-year-old Nicholas Orsini, was granted full custody. According to an insider source, Mr. Orsini was represented by a team of lawyers from Gunther, Anderson, and Oglethorpe. Ms. Orsini represented herself.

LA TIMES

Murder Victim's Memoir Locked in Legal Battle

by Lucy MacGuff
Nov. 26
UPDATED 12:34 PM PT

Sixteen-year-old Summer Cartwright's memoir, *All Your Likes Can't Buy Me Love,* which was set to debut in a few short weeks, is locked in a nasty battle of wills between Julian Cartwright, (Summer's father and studio head of Golden Gate) and Swift Eagle Press. According to Cartwright, parts of the memoir are libelous, written through the filter of a teenaged girl, and likely embellished by her editors. Sources close to the legal team claim the lawsuit could drag on for months, potentially years, complicated by evidence-based allegations made by Avalon James, an influencer who has accused Cartwright of plagiarizing her work for his new movie *She Falls Hard.*

Last month, Summer was murdered in her loft at her Halloween party. The LAPD's fifteen-year-old suspect awaits trial.

EPILOGUE

Grace Godwin

Thursday, November 26
2:15 p.m.

Grace scrolls through the *LA Times* article on her new phone. Massive plates of greasy Thanksgiving food cover the diner table in front of her, a poor substitute for a home-cooked meal, but whatever. Her mom's never been a good cook anyway, and at least they're safe and together. That's reason enough for thanksgiving. Grace has to admit, though, that Artesia, New Mexico, wouldn't have been her first choice for finishing high school. After LA, Artesia is a blip on the horizon, desert and suburban. She starts back to school after Christmas with a forged set of records her mom got from who knows where with the name Grace Martin on the cover page.

She used to doodle *Grace Orsini* on her notebooks, in the dirt, in the sand at the beach as a way of remembering, but now that she's Grace Martin, she misses the last name Godwin way more. It's been her identity for five years.

Grace takes a bite of stuffing and swipes out of the article. As much as she despises Julian Cartwright, his total self-absorption works to her benefit. By the time Summer's book comes out, if it ever does, Grace will be eighteen, and no one will be able to force her to live with her father. She'll never go back there and neither will her mom.

What's less certain is the statute of limitations on kidnapping. Because even though Gina is her mother, she did technically kidnap Grace all those years ago. Grace will never forget that night—the blackness of the sky over Providence, the explosion of colors during the fireworks finale. The feel of her mom's hand in hers as she led her to her car, as they drove away and never looked back. Grace will fight tooth and nail to keep her mom out of prison. She'll do anything. She already has.

Gina slides into the booth opposite Grace, back from the bathroom. "Told you, it's basically the law. Get up and go to the bathroom, and your food appears. Magic!"

"I promise there was a waitress involved." Grace nods across the diner to a middle-aged woman in an apron. "Bethany."

"I'm skeptical." Gina takes a bite of turkey and makes a face. "Bland."

"It's not that bad. It's kind of festive."

"Festive Thanksgiving food should not include anything this jiggly. What I'd give for a good street taco right now, huh?" It's the closest Gina's come to acknowledging their old life in LA since they left.

"Me too." Grace sniffs. "Did you go outside to smoke?"

"It was just one! One tiny cigarette!"

"Mom!"

"What? I tried the whole e-cigarette thing. It didn't work for me."

"How about the patch?"

"Fine." Gina smiles and salts her turkey. "Everything will be okay, you know that?"

"It already is."

"Another thing." Gina glances behind her to see if Bethany-the-waitress is close, but they're alone. "You can tell your mama anything, you know that? I'll love you no matter what?"

Grace is certain what Gina wants to hear, what she instinctively already knows about Grace. When you only have one person in your life whom you can be honest with, keeping secrets from them is hard. Almost impossible.

All it took was a few e-cigarette cartridges and a green smoothie. Murder is easy, really, because humans are shockingly frail. The real miracle is that most people live to be old at all. Murder is easy, but living with yourself afterward is hard.

Grace has followed every piece of news about the Cartwright murder investigation and Cora's arrest. She hopes Oscar is right, that the evidence leaves room for doubt. But it does make Grace feel better that because Cora is only fifteen and because she's not stable, she'll likely be admitted to a psychiatric facility for treatment rather than juvie. That's good. She'll be out by the time she's eighteen and able to live a life. Hopefully a good one.

It doesn't take away the guilt, but it helps. Still, Grace will have to learn to live with what she did. Maybe it will take her a lifetime. Maybe Summer will haunt her forever.

"Grace?" Gina asks. "You know you can tell me anything?"

"Of course." Grace takes a big bite of turkey. She'll never tell her mother what she did on Halloween to protect her. "I vote pumpkin pie for dessert. Thoughts?"

Monday, October 26, five days before Summer's death
5:18 p.m.
Summer's Balcony

Grace found Summer, still in her school uniform, curled up in the yellow Adirondack chair on her balcony. She'd kicked off her shoes so she could tuck her feet beneath herself. On the table beside Summer, her phone lit up with a million notifications. Grace knew what they'd be—comments about how Adam dumped her in the courtyard at school two hours ago. Some people would be supportive, some would be thrilled that Summer got "what she deserved." Why were people like that? Why did they assume that if you shared your life online, you were fair game to be treated like trash?

Everyone said Summer had it all, but what was it exactly? Money? Fame? Beauty? What did any of that do when you felt alone? Summer might put on the armor of perfect imperfection, but she was a real girl. She was sometimes vulnerable, often insecure. Always a little bit alone.

Grace had to tell Summer the truth about Adam kissing her last month. It was the right thing to do, but how do you tell your best friend that you screwed up that bad? For days, her brain wouldn't even accept that Adam had kissed her, and by the time she had processed it, a week had gone by. Maybe normal people didn't need time like that. Maybe Summer wouldn't understand why she'd waited.

"Hey, Sum?" Grace sat beside Summer in the purple Adirondack chair. "You okay?"

"Do I look okay?"

"*I know you've been through a lot today, and the last thing I want to do is add to your plate. But I . . .*" Grace took a deep breath and steeled herself. "*There's something I need to tell you. About Adam and me.*"

Summer snorted. "*Please. You think I don't know? I saw you, Grace.*"

"*What?*" Grace stared at her in disbelief.

"*You and Adam on the swings? I came over because something happened, and I needed you.*"

"*Oh my god. Sum, I'm so—*"

"*Well, I don't need you anymore. Screw you and Adam both.*" Her voice was measured, but Grace knew Summer well enough to know that she was close to tears. "*I trusted you.*"

"*But you knew I had feelings for Adam, and you—*"

"*Too bad! He didn't want you, and he still doesn't. He's using you to get back at me. Congratulations.*"

Her words cut straight to Grace's heart, because deep down, she wondered if Summer was right. "*I'm sorry, Sum. You're my best friend. I made a mistake, a horrible one, but—*"

"*Sorry isn't enough. How could you do that to me? There was no one in my entire life I loved more than you, and you screwed me over. The good news is, my book comes out in a few months, and I'll have enough money to leave my family and my so-called friends and do whatever the hell I want. And, Grace . . .*" Summer locked eyes with her. "*I won't lie in my book.*"

A wave of dizziness crashed into Grace. Was it possible that Summer planned to include the information she'd found in the filing cabinet? That Grace's real name was Gracie Orsini? Was it possible that after doing some googling, Summer knew all about Grace's past, knew that Gina had a warrant out for her arrest, knew that if she put this in her book, Gina would go to jail, and Grace would be sent back to Rhode Island to live with her father?

"*What do you mean?*" *Grace whispered.*

"*You know what I mean.*"

"*Sum . . . please. My father . . . he—*"

"*I don't care. My book is a tell-all, Gracie Grace. Not a tell-some.*"

"*Look, I'm not asking you to lie.*" *Grace's breath lodged in her throat. There was a sharp pain in her chest. She clenched and unclenched her fists, counted to five, blinked hard against the blackness that washed across her vision like spilled paint.* "*Just . . . please. Keep this one thing out. Say whatever you want about me. But not that.*"

"*Our actions have consequences. We have to pay for them.*" *Summer smiled, a nasty expression that made her look just like her father. The heat, the anger of moments ago was gone, replaced by a cold calm.* "*Should I tell my mom you're staying for dinner, or . . .*"

"*No.*" *Grace felt like she was dying. The pain of it was too much. Her brain couldn't handle it.*

"*Good,*" *Summer said.* "*Because the sight of you makes me sick. See you at school tomorrow.*" *Summer turned back around in her chair to look out over her balcony at the darkening city. With one sentence, Summer had ended Grace's life. Was that it? Was it over?*

As Grace walked away, she vaguely heard Harrison calling her name, but she couldn't talk to him right now.

Grace's mom might not have been her entire world, but she held her entire world up by a thread. If Gina went to jail, Grace's life disintegrated, and she couldn't let her mom pay for protecting her all those years ago when she took Grace away from her father. And Grace wouldn't go back there.

She thought of that day in Griffith Park when she and the others had talked about nicotine poisoning. It sounded so simple. Dump a cartridge from an e-cigarette into a green smoothie, hit blend, and wait. The only hiccup was Cora's writing all over Summer's face. It made Summer's death look like murder instead of an accident, so when Grace went to Summer's room after she saw her leave the kitchen with Adam and saw Summer sprawled in her bathroom, #TOXIC all over her face, Grace had to improvise. She wrote a post that threw suspicion on everyone in Summer's life. And that was it.

Grace had always prided herself on being a good person. She followed every rule, was a good daughter and friend. Until she wasn't. She didn't want to hurt Summer. But maybe to be the hero in her own story, she had to become the villain in someone else's.

The_Summer_Cartwright
Hello, world!! ✨ 🍪 😎 😊 🌞 ✨

.

New account, new me!

.

A few fun facts about me!
*My favorite singer is Justin Bieber. I 🤍 him, okay? No
judging allowed.
*I'm almost done with eighth grade, and then I'll be a high
schooolllllllerrrrrr! 💃 💃 💃
*I could eat pasta every single day. 🍜 🍜
*I'm the girl who dances like no one's watching . . . but I like it
when everyone's watching. So sue me. I'm cute!
*Whenever I get stressed out, I like to color. Like kids'
coloring books with princesses or the more adult-y ones that
are like Screw You, I'm Coloring! with a bunch of complex
lines within flowers and birds and stuff. 😍
*My best friend's name is Grace. 👯 She's literally nothing
like me, but I think that works, you know? I'm all fashion, and
she's all function, and we're kind of great together. I have this
dream where we're little old ladies in a ritzy retirement home
bc we're obvs going to get really rich, and Grace and I play
bingo and talk about how hott we used to be. But we don't
worry about our saggy boobs, bc there's so much more to life
like knitting hats for orphan children or taking walks around
the lake. If I become a famous influencer, I'll buy Grace and
me a house in Malibu!! And don't worry, Gracieeeee. Even if I
get famous, you'll still come first. #lolz

*My biggest fear is not having a life well-lived. 😔 Like . . . just existing to make 💵 to keep existing and missing out on all the good stuff like chocolate and traveling and skinny dipping and riding in a hot air balloon and falling in real 🤍 and getting my heart broken 💔 and . . . all of it.

.

I want to feel all of it. Doesn't everyone?

Your new bestie!!!
SumSum 🤍

₪ ❤ ▶

⏱ MAY 14, 3 YEARS AGO

ACKNOWLEDGMENTS

Whenen I first decided to write a book, it seemed like such a long shot. Me? Write a book? How . . . ? In large part, it's because of the following people:

My agent, Richard Abate—thank you for seeing my potential and championing my writing.

My incredible team at Hyperion: Melissa de la Cruz, thank you for taking a chance on a newbie. It means the world to me. Cassidy Leyendecker—my editor extraordinaire—your notes and thoughtful feedback not only made this book better, but also made me a better writer forever. A huge thank-you to Sara Liebling, Guy Cunningham, and Kelsey Sullivan. Hyperion really has a rock-star editorial team. Crystal McCoy, Dina Sherman, Holly Nagel, and Matt Schweitzer, thank you for all that you've done to get my book out into the world and into the hands of readers. Marci Senders and Michael Heath, the design and cover you created for this book blow me away. Thank you!

My writing buddies, what would I do without you? Tracey Lange, from the beginning, you have always been the person willing to hash out plot holes and "throw spaghetti" with me. I'm eternally grateful. Jacquie Franzoni, thank you for always being excited with me and for sharing my manuscript with Richard early on. Kim Young and Bob

Murney, our writing group kept me going during the (many) times I felt like it would be easier to quit. Ashley Cannon, thank you for reading early drafts and responding logically to my panic texts. I'd be lost without you. Malena Watrous, my mentor in the Stanford OWC program, thank you for cheering for me and guiding me to become a better writer.

My early readers, thank goodness for you. You were my cheering section, my feedback friends, my sounding boards. Big shout-out to my former middle and high school students who read my first (unpublishable) books and said things like, "Hmmmm . . . I like it . . . but it's kind of boring, don't you think?" Your humor and honesty will always be a part of whatever I write.

Brittney Scherrer, Claudia Bucher, and Janna Madsen, my Colorado found family and no-matter-what friends, you encouraged me and prayed for me when I was at my best and my worst. Thank you for being the most incredible support system.

Thank you to my family, Bells and Weavers, for your support and for buying way more copies than you'll ever need, specifically my mom, who read eight thousand drafts of multiple books and was excited about all of them.

Thank you to my sweet and silly daughters, Averie and Ellea, for being the most adorable writing companions, and to my husband, Ben, for the countless cups of tea, brainstorming date nights, and most of all, understanding. I wouldn't be an author if you hadn't told me, "I think you should write a book." You love me like no one else could.

And thank you to Jesus for giving me the ability to write. All glory to God.